The Yellow Crayon

The Yellow Crayon
E. Phillips Oppenheim

MINT EDITIONS

The Yellow Crayon was first published in 1903.

This edition published by Mint Editions 2021.

ISBN 9781513281254 | E-ISBN 9781513286273

Published by Mint Editions®

 MINT
EDITIONS

minteditionbooks.com

Publishing Director: Jennifer Newens
Design & Production: Rachel Lopez Metzger
Project Manager: Micaela Clark
Typesetting: Westchester Publishing Services

Contents

I

I t was late summer-time, and the perfume of flowers stole into the darkened room through the half-opened window. The sunlight forced its way through a chink in the blind, and stretched across the floor in strange zigzag fashion. From without came the pleasant murmur of bees and many lazier insects floating over the gorgeous flower beds, resting for a while on the clematis which had made the piazza a blaze of purple splendour. And inside, in a high-backed chair, there sat a man, his arms folded, his eyes fixed steadily upon vacancy. As he sat then, so had he sat for a whole day and a whole night. The faint sweet chorus of glad living things, which alone broke the deep silence of the house, seemed neither to disturb nor interest him. He sat there like a man turned to stone, his forehead riven by one deep line, his straight firm mouth set close and hard. His servant, the only living being who had approached him, had set food by his side, which now and then he had mechanically taken. Changeless as a sphinx, he had sat there in darkness and in light, whilst sunlight had changed to moonlight, and the songs of the birds had given place to the low murmuring of frogs from a lake below the lawns.

At last it seemed that his unnatural fit had passed away. He stretched out his hand and struck a silver gong which had been left within his reach. Almost immediately a man, pale-faced, with full dark eyes and olive complexion, dressed in the sombre garb of an indoor servant, stood at his elbow.

"Duson."

"Your Grace!"

"Bring wine—Burgundy."

It was before him, served with almost incredible despatch—a small cobwebbed bottle and a glass of quaint shape, on which were beautifully emblazoned a coronet and fleur-de-lis. He drank slowly and deliberately. When he set the glass down it was empty.

"Duson!"

"Your Grace!"

"You will pack my things and your own. We shall leave for New York this evening. Telegraph to the Holland House for rooms."

"For how many days, your Grace?"

"We shall not return here. Pay off all the servants save two of the most trustworthy, who will remain as caretakers."

The man's face was as immovable as his master's.

"And Madame?"

"Madame will not be returning. She will have no further use for her maid. See, however, that her clothes and all her personal belongings remain absolutely undisturbed."

"Has your Grace any further orders?"

"Take pencil and paper. Send this cablegram. Are you ready?"

The man's head moved in respectful assent.

> To Felix,
> No 27, Rue de St. Pierre,
> Avenue de L'Opera, Paris.
>
> Meet me at Sherry's Restaurant, New York, one month to-day, eleven P.M.
>
> V. S.

"It shall be sent immediately, your Grace. The train for New York leaves at seven-ten. A carriage will be here in one hour and five minutes."

The man moved towards the door. His master looked up.

"Duson!"

"Your Grace!"

"The Duc de Souspennier remains here—or at the bottom of the lake—what matters! It is Mr. Sabin who travels to New York, and for whom you engage rooms at the Holland House. Mr. Sabin is a cosmopolitan of English proclivities."

"Very good, sir!"

"Lock this door. Bring my coat and hat five minutes before the carriage starts. Let the servants be well paid. Let none of them attempt to see me."

The man bowed and disappeared. Left to himself, Mr. Sabin rose from his chair, and pushing open the windows, stood upon the verandah. He leaned heavily upon his stick with both hands, holding it before him. Slowly his eyes traveled over the landscape.

It was a very beautiful home which he was leaving. Before him stretched the gardens—Italian in design, brilliant with flowers, with here and there a dark cedar-tree drooping low upon the lawn. A yew hedge bordered the rose-garden, a fountain was playing in the middle of a lake. A wooden fence encircled the grounds, and beyond was a smooth rolling park, with little belts of pine plantations and a few larger trees here and there. In the far distance the red flag was waving on one of the putting greens. Archie Green was strolling up the hillside,—his pipe in his mouth, and his driver under his arm. Mr. Sabin watched, and the lines in his face grew deeper and deeper.

"I am an old man," he said softly, "but I will live to see them suffer who have done this evil thing."

He turned slowly back into the room, and limping rather more than was usual with him, he pushed aside a portiere and passed into a charmingly furnished country drawing-room. Only the flowers hung dead in their vases; everything else was fresh and sweet and dainty. Slowly he threaded his way amongst the elegant Louis Quinze furniture, examining as though for the first time the beautiful old tapestry, the Sevres china, the Chippendale table, which was priceless, the exquisite portraits painted by Greuze, and the mysterious green twilights and grey dawns of Corot. Everywhere treasures of art, yet everywhere the restraining hand of the artist. The faint smell of dead rose leaves hung about the room. Already one seemed conscious of a certain emptiness as though the genius of the place had gone. Mr. Sabin leaned heavily upon his stick, and his head drooped lower and lower. A soft, respectful voice came to him from the other room.

"In five minutes, sir, the carriage will be at the door. I have your coat and hat here."

Mr. Sabin looked up.

"I am quite ready, Duson!" he said.

THE SERVANTS IN THE HALL stood respectfully aside to let him pass. On the way to the depot he saw nothing of those who saluted him. In the car he sat with folded arms in the most retired seat, looking steadfastly out of the window at the dying day. There were mountains away westwards, touched with golden light; sometimes for long minutes together the train was rushing through forests whose darkness was like that of a tunnel. Mr. Sabin seemed indifferent to these changes. The coming of night did not disturb him. His brain was at work, and the things which he saw were hidden from other men.

Duson, with a murmur of apology, broke in upon his meditations.

"You will pardon me, sir, but the second dinner is now being served. The restaurant car will be detached at the next stop."

"What of it?" Mr. Sabin asked calmly.

"I have taken the liberty of ordering dinner for you, sir. It is thirty hours since you ate anything save biscuits."

Mr. Sabin rose to his feet.

"You are quite right, Duson," he said. "I will dine."

In half-an-hour he was back again. Duson placed before him silently a box of cigarettes and matches. Mr. Sabin smoked.

Soon the lights of the great city flared in the sky, the train stopped more frequently, the express men and newspaper boys came into evidence. Mr. Sabin awoke from his long spell of thought. He bought a newspaper, and glanced through the list of steamers which had sailed during the week. When the train glided into the depot he was on his feet and ready to leave it.

"You will reserve our rooms, Duson, for one month," he said on the way to the hotel. "We shall probably leave for Europe a month to-morrow."

"Very good, sir."

"You were Mrs. Peterson's servant, Duson, before you were mine!"

"Yes, sir."

"You have been with her, I believe, for many years. You are doubtless much attached to her!"

"Indeed I am, sir!"

"You may have surmised, Duson, that she has left me. I desire to ensure your absolute fidelity, so I take you into my confidence to this extent. Your mistress is in the hands of those who have some power over her. Her absence is involuntary so far as she is concerned. It has been a great blow to me. I am prepared to run all risks to discover her whereabouts. It is late in my life for adventures, but it is very certain that adventures and dangers are before us. In accompanying me you will associate yourself with many risks. Therefore—"

Duson held up his hand.

"I beg, sir," he exclaimed, "that you will not suggest for a moment my leaving your service on that account. I beg most humbly, sir, that you will not do me that injustice."

Mr. Sabin paused. His eyes, like lightning, read the other's face.

"It is settled then, Duson," he said. "Kindly pay this cabman, and follow me as quickly as possible."

Mr. Sabin passed across the marble hall, leaning heavily upon his stick. Yet for all his slow movements there was a new alertness in his eyes and bearing. He was once more taking keen note of everybody and everything about him. Only a few days ago she had been here.

He claimed his rooms at the office, and handed the keys to Duson, who by this time had rejoined him. At the moment of turning away he addressed an inquiry to the clerk behind the counter.

"Can you tell me if the Duchess of Souspennier is staying here?" he inquired.

The young man glanced up.

"Been here, I guess. Left on Tuesday."

Mr. Sabin turned away. He did not speak again until Duson and he were alone in the sitting-room. Then he drew out a five dollar bill.

"Duson," he said, "take this to the head luggage porter. Tell him to bring his departure book up here at once, and there is another waiting for him. You understand?"

"Certainly, sir!"

Mr. Sabin turned to enter his bed-chamber. His attention was attracted, however, by a letter lying flat upon the table. He took it up. It was addressed to Mr. Sabin.

"This is very clever," he mused, hesitating for a moment before opening it. "I wired for rooms only a few hours ago—and I find a letter. It is the commencement."

He tore open the envelope, and drew out a single half-sheet of note-paper. Across it was scrawled a single sentence only.

"Go back to Lenox."

There was no signature, nor any date. The only noticeable thing about this brief communication was that it was written in yellow pencil of a peculiar shade. Mr. Sabin's eyes glittered as he read.

"The yellow crayon!" he muttered.

Duson knocked softly at the door. Mr. Sabin thrust the letter and envelope into his breast coat pocket.

II

This is the luggage porter, sir," Duson announced. "He is prepared to answer any questions."

The man took out his book. Mr. Sabin, who was sitting in an easy-chair, turned sideways towards him.

"The Duchess of Souspennier was staying here last week," he said. "She left, I believe, on Thursday or Friday. Can you tell me whether her baggage went through your hands?"

The man set down his hat upon a vacant chair, and turned over the leaves of his book.

"Guess I can fix that for you," he remarked, running his forefinger down one of the pages. "Here we are. The Duchess left on Friday, and we checked her baggage through to Lenox by the New York, New Haven & Hartford."

Mr. Sabin nodded.

"Thank you," he said. "She would probably take a carriage to the station. It will be worth another ten dollars to you if you can find me the man who drove her."

"Well, we ought to manage that for you," the man remarked encouragingly. "It was one of Steve Hassell's carriages, I guess, unless the lady took a hansom."

"Very good," Mr. Sabin said. "See if you can find him. Keep my inquiries entirely to yourself. It will pay you."

"That's all right," the man remarked. "Don't you go to bed for half-an-hour, and I guess you'll hear from me again."

Duson busied himself in the bed-chamber, Mr. Sabin sat motionless in his easy chair. Soon there came a tap at the door. The porter reappeared ushering in a smart-looking young man, who carried a shiny coachman's hat in his hand.

"Struck it right fust time," the porter remarked cheerfully. "This is the man, sir."

Mr. Sabin turned his head.

"You drove a lady from here to the New York, New Haven & Hartford Depot last Friday?" he asked.

"Well, not exactly, sir," the man answered. "The Duchess took my cab, and the first address she gave was the New York, New Haven & Hartford Depot, but before we'd driven a hundred yards she pulled the

E. PHILLIPS OPPENHEIM

check-string and ordered me to go to the Waldorf. She paid me there, and went into the hotel."

"You have not seen her since?"

"No, sir!"

"You knew her by sight, you say. Was there anything special about her appearance?"

The man hesitated.

"She'd a pretty thick veil on, sir, but she raised it to pay me, and I should say she'd been crying. She was much paler, too, than last time I drove her."

"When was that?" Mr. Sabin asked.

"In the spring, sir,—with you, begging your pardon. You were at the Netherlands, and I drove you out several times."

"You seem," Mr. Sabin said, "to be a person with some powers of observation. It would pay you very well indeed if you would ascertain from any of your mates at the Waldorf when and with whom the lady in question left that hotel."

"I'll have a try, sir," the man answered. "The Duchess was better known here, but some of them may have recognised her."

"She had no luggage, I presume?" Mr. Sabin asked.

"Her dressing-case and jewel-case only, sir."

"So you see," Mr. Sabin continued, "it is probable that she did not remain at the Waldorf for the night. Base your inquiries on that supposition."

"Very good, sir."

"From your manners and speech," Mr. Sabin said, raising his head, "I should take you to be an Englishman."

"Quite correct, sir," the man answered. "I drove a hansom in London for eight years."

"You will understand me then," Mr. Sabin continued, "when I say that I have no great confidence in the police of this country. I do not wish to be blackmailed or bullied. I would ask you, therefore, to make your inquiries with discretion."

"I'll be careful, sir," the man answered.

Mr. Sabin handed to each of them a roll of notes. The cabdriver lingered upon the threshold. Mr. Sabin looked up.

"Well?"

"Could I speak a word to you—in private, sir?"

Mr. Sabin motioned Duson to leave the room. The baggage porter had already departed.

"When I cleaned out my cab at night, sir, I found this. I didn't reckon it was of any consequence at first, but from the questions you have been asking it may be useful to you."

Mr. Sabin took the half-sheet of note-paper in silence. It was the ordinary stationery of the Waldorf Astoria Hotel, and the following words were written upon it in a faint delicate handwriting, but in yellow pencil:—

Sept. 10th

To LUCILLE, Duchesse de SOUSPENNIER.

You will be at the Waldorf Astoria Hotel in the main corridor at four o'clock this afternoon."

The thin paper shook in Mr. Sabin's fingers. There was no signature, but he fancied that the handwriting was not wholly unfamiliar to him. He looked slowly up towards the cabman.

"I am much obliged to you," he said. "This is of interest to me."

He stretched out his hand to the little wad of notes which Duson had left upon the table, but the cabdriver backed away.

"Beg pardon, sir," he said. "You've given me plenty. The letter's of no value to me. I came very near tearing it up, but for the peculiar colour pencil it's written with. Kinder took my fancy, sir."

"The letter is of value," Mr. Sabin said. "It tells me much more than I hoped to discover. It is our good fortune."

The man accepted the little roll of bills and departed. Mr. Sabin touched the bell.

"Duson, what time is it?"

"Nearly midnight, sir!"

"I will go to bed!"

"Very good, sir!"

"Mix me a sleeping draught, Duson. I need rest. See that I am not disturbed until ten o'clock to-morrow morning."

III

A t precisely ten o'clock on the following morning Duson brought chocolate, which he had prepared himself, and some dry toast to his master's bedside. Upon the tray was a single letter. Mr. Sabin sat up in bed and tore open the envelope. The following words were written upon a sheet of the Holland House notepaper in the same peculiar coloured crayon.

"The first warning addressed to you yesterday was a friendly one. Profit by it. Go back to Lenox. You are only exposing yourself to danger and the person you seek to discomfort. Wait there, and some one shall come to you shortly who will explain what has happened, and the necessity for it."

Mr. Sabin smiled, a slow contemplative smile. He sipped his chocolate and lit a cigarette.

"Our friends, then," he said softly, "do not care about pursuit and inquiries. It is ridiculous to suppose that their warning is given out of any consideration to me. Duson!"

"Yes, sir!"

"My bath. I shall rise now."

Mr. Sabin made his toilet with something of the same deliberation which characterised all his movements. Then he descended into the hall, bought a newspaper, and from a convenient easy-chair kept a close observation upon every one who passed to and fro for about an hour. Later on he ordered a carriage, and made several calls down town.

At a few minutes past twelve he entered the bar of the Fifth Avenue Hotel, and ordering a drink sat down at one of the small tables. The room was full, but Mr. Sabin's attention was directed solely to one group of men who stood a short distance away before the counter drinking champagne. The central person of the group was a big man, with an unusually large neck, a fat pale face, a brown moustache tinged with grey, and a voice and laugh like a fog-horn. It was he apparently who was paying for the champagne, and he was clearly on intimate terms with all the party. Mr. Sabin watched for his opportunity, and then rising from his seat touched him on the shoulder.

"Mr. Skinner, I believe?" he said quietly.

The big man looked down upon Mr. Sabin with the sullen offensiveness of the professional bully.

"You've hit it first time," he admitted. "Who are you, anyway?"

Mr. Sabin produced a card.

"I called this morning," he said, "upon the gentleman whose name you will see there. He directed me to you, and told me to come here."

The man tore the card into small pieces.

"So long, boys," he said, addressing his late companions. "See you to-night."

They accepted his departure in silence, and one and all favoured Mr. Sabin with a stare of blatant curiosity.

"I should be glad to speak with you," Mr. Sabin said, "in a place where we are likely to be neither disturbed nor overheard."

"You come right across to my office," was the prompt reply. "I guess we can fix it up there."

Mr. Sabin motioned to his coachman, and they crossed Broadway. His companion led him into a tall building, talking noisily all the time about the pals whom he had just left. An elevator transported them to the twelfth floor in little more than as many seconds, and Mr. Skinner ushered his visitor into a somewhat bare-looking office, smelling strongly of stale tobacco smoke. Mr. Skinner at once lit a cigar, and seating himself before his desk, folded his arms and leaned over towards Mr. Sabin.

"Smoke one?" he asked, pointing to the open box.

Mr. Sabin declined.

"Get right ahead then."

"I am an Englishman," Mr. Sabin said slowly, "and consequently am not altogether at home with your ways over here. I have always understood, however, that if you are in need of any special information such as we should in England apply to the police for, over here there is a quicker and more satisfactory method of procedure."

"You've come a long way round," Mr. Skinner remarked, spitting upon the floor, "but you're dead right."

"I am in need of some information," Mr. Sabin continued, "and accordingly I called this morning on Mr.—"

Mr. Skinner held up his hand.

"All right," he said. "We don't mention names more than we can help. Call him the boss."

"He assured me that the information I was in need of was easily to be obtained, and gave me a card to you."

"Go right on," Mr. Skinner said. "What is it?"

"On Friday last," Mr. Sabin said, "at four o'clock, the Duchess of Souspennier, whose picture I will presently show you, left the Holland House Hotel for the New York, New Haven & Hartford Depot, presumably for her home at Lenox, to which place her baggage had already been checked. On the way she ordered the cabman to set her down at the Waldorf-Astoria Hotel, which he did at a few minutes past four. The Duchess has not returned home or been directly heard from since. I wish to ascertain her movements since she arrived at the Waldorf."

"Sounds dead easy," Mr. Skinner remarked reassuringly. "Got the picture?"

Mr. Sabin touched the spring of a small gold locket which he drew from an inside waistcoat pocket, and disclosed a beautifully painted miniature. Mr. Skinner's thick lips were pursed into a whistle. He was on the point of making a remark when he chanced to glance into Mr. Sabin's face. The remark remained unspoken.

He drew a sheet of note-paper towards him and made a few notes upon it.

"The Duchess many friends in New York?"

"At present none. The few people whom she knows here are at Newport or in Europe just now."

"Any idea whom she went to the Waldorf to see? More we know the better."

Mr. Sabin handed him the letter which had been picked up in the cab. Mr. Skinner read it through, and spat once more upon the floor.

"What the h—'s this funny coloured pencil mean?"

"I do not know," Mr. Sabin answered. "You will see that the two anonymous communications which I have received since arriving in New York yesterday are written in the same manner."

Mr. Sabin handed him the other two letters, which Mr. Skinner carefully perused.

"I guess you'd better tell me who you are," he suggested.

"I am the husband of the Duchess of Souspennier," Mr. Sabin answered.

"The Duchess send any word home at all?" Mr. Skinner asked.

Mr. Sabin produced a worn telegraph form. It was handed in at Fifth Avenue, New York, at six o'clock on Friday. It contained the single word 'Good-bye.'

"H'm," Mr. Skinner remarked. "We'll find all you want to know by to-morrow sure."

"What do you make of the two letters which I received?" Mr. Sabin asked.

"Bunkum!" Mr. Skinner replied confidently.

Mr. Sabin nodded his head.

"You have no secret societies over here, I suppose?" he said.

Mr. Skinner laughed loudly and derisively.

"I guess not," he answered. "They keep that sort of rubbish on the other side of the pond."

"Ah!"

Mr. Sabin was thoughtful for a moment. "You expect to find, then," he remarked, "some other cause for my wife's disappearance?"

"There don't seem much room for doubt concerning that, sir," Mr. Skinner said; "but I never speculate. I will bring you the facts to-night between eight and eleven. Now as to the business side of it."

Mr. Sabin was for a moment puzzled.

"What's the job worth to you?" Mr. Skinner asked. "I am willing to pay," Mr. Sabin answered, "according to your demands."

"It's a simple case," Mr. Skinner admitted, "but our man at the Waldorf is expensive. If you get all your facts, I guess five hundred dollars will about see you through."

"I will pay that," Mr. Sabin answered.

"I will bring you the letters back to-night," Mr. Skinner said. "I guess I'll borrow that locket of yours, too."

Mr. Sabin shook his head.

"That," he said firmly, "I do not part with." Mr. Skinner scratched his ear with his penholder. "It's the only scrap of identifying matter we've got," he remarked. "Of course it's a dead simple case, and we can probably manage without it. But I guess it's as well to fix the thing right down."

"If you will give me a piece of paper," Mr. Sabin said, "I will make you a sketch of the Duchess. The larger the better. I can give you an idea of the sort of clothes she would probably be wearing."

Mr. Skinner furnished him with a double sheet of paper, and Mr. Sabin, with set face and unflinching figures, reproduced in a few simple strokes a wonderful likeness of the woman he loved. He pushed it away from him when he had finished without remark. Mr. Skinner was loud in its praises.

"I guess you're an artist, sir, for sure," he remarked. "This'll fix the thing. Shall I come to your hotel?"

"If you please," Mr. Sabin answered. "I shall be there for the rest of the day."

Mr. Skinner took up his hat.

"Guess I'll take my dinner and get right to work," he remarked. "Say, you come along, Mr. Sabin. I'll take you where they'll fix you such a beefsteak as you never tasted in your life."

"I thank you very much," Mr. Sabin said, "but I must beg to be excused. I am expecting some despatches at my hotel. If you are successful this afternoon you will perhaps do me the honour of dining with me to-night. I will wait until eight-thirty."

The two men parted upon the pavement. Mr. Skinner, with his small bowler hat on the back of his head, a fresh cigar in the corner of his mouth, and his thumbs in the armholes of his waistcoat, strolled along Broadway with something akin to a smile parting his lips, and showing his yellow teeth.

"Darned old fool," he muttered. "To marry a slap-up handsome woman like that, and then pretend not to know what it means when she bolts. Guess I'll spoil his supper to-night."

Mr. Sabin, however, was recovering his spirits. He, too, was leaning back in the corner of his carriage with a faint smile brightening his hard, stern face. But, unlike Mr. Skinner, he did not talk to himself.

IV

R. Sabin, who was never, for its own sake, fond of solitude, had ordered dinner for two at eight-thirty in the general dining-room. At a few minutes previous to that hour Mr. Skinner presented himself.

Mr. Skinner was not in the garb usually affected by men of the world who are invited to dine out. The long day's exertion, too, had had its effect upon his linen. His front, indeed, through a broad gap, confessed to a foundation of blue, and one of his cuffs showed a marked inclination to escape from his wrist over his knuckles. His face was flushed, and he exhaled a strong odour of cigars and cocktails. Nevertheless, Mr. Sabin was very glad to see him, and to receive the folded sheet of paper which he at once produced.

"I have taken the liberty," Mr. Sabin remarked, on his part, "of adding a trifle to the amount we first spoke of, which I beg you will accept from me as a mark of my gratitude for your promptness."

"Sure!" Mr. Skinner answered tersely, receiving the little roll of bills without hesitation, and retreating into a quiet corner, where he carefully counted and examined every one. "That's all right!" he announced at the conclusion of his task. "Come and have one with me now before you read your little billet-doux, eh?"

"I shall not read your report until after dinner," Mr. Sabin said, "and I think if you are ready that we might as well go in. At the head-waiter's suggestion I have ordered a cocktail with the oysters, and if we are much later he seemed to fear that it might affect the condition of the—I think it was terrapin, he said."

Mr. Skinner stopped short. His tone betrayed emotion.

"Did you say terrapin, sir?"

Mr. Sabin nodded. Mr. Skinner at once took his arm.

"Guess we'll go right in," he declared. "I hate to have a good meal spoiled."

They were an old-looking couple. Mr. Sabin quietly but faultlessly attired in the usual evening dinner garb, Mr. Skinner ill-dressed, untidy, unwashed and frowsy. But here at least Mr. Sabin's incognito had been unavailing, for he had stayed at the hotel several times—as he remembered with an odd little pang—with Lucille, and the head-waiter, with a low bow, ushered them to their table. Mr. Skinner saw the preparations for their repast, the oysters, the cocktails in tall glasses, the magnum of champagne in ice, and chuckled. To take supper with a duke was a novelty to him, but he was not shy. He sat down and tucked his serviette into his waistcoat, raised his glass, and suddenly set it down again.

"The boss!" he exclaimed in amazement.

Mr. Sabin turned his head in the direction which his companion had indicated. Coming hastily across the room towards them, already out of breath as though with much hurrying, was a thick-set, powerful man, with the brutal face and coarse lips of a prizefighter; a beard cropped so short as to seem the growth of a few days only covered his chin, and his moustache, treated in the same way, was not thick enough to conceal a cruel mouth. He was carefully enough dressed, and a great diamond flashed from his tie. There was a red mark round his forehead where his hat had been, and the perspiration was streaming from his forehead. He strode without hesitation to the table where Mr. Sabin and his guest were sitting, and without even a glance at the former turned upon his myrmidon.

"Where's that report?" he cried roughly. "Where is it?"

Mr. Skinner seemed to have shrunk into a smaller man. He pointed across the table.

"I've given it to him," he said. "What's wrong, boss?"

The newcomer raised his hand as though to strike Skinner. He gnashed his teeth with the effort to control himself.

"You damned blithering idiot," he said hoarsely, gripping the side of the table. "Why wasn't it presented to me first?"

"Guess it didn't seem worth while," Skinner answered. "There's nothing in the darned thing."

"You ignorant fool, hold your tongue," was the fierce reply.

The newcomer sank into a chair and wiped the perspiration from his streaming forehead. Mr. Sabin signaled to a waiter.

"You seem upset, Mr. Horser," he remarked politely. "Allow me to offer you a glass of wine."

Mr. Horser did not immediately reply, but he accepted the glass which the waiter brought him, and after a moment's hesitation drained its contents. Then he turned to Mr. Sabin.

"You said nothing about those letters you had had when you came to see me this morning!"

"It was you yourself," Mr. Sabin reminded him, "who begged me not to enter into particulars. You sent me on to Mr. Skinner. I told him everything."

Mr. Horser leaned over the table. His eyes were bloodshot, his tone was fierce and threatening. Mr. Sabin was coldly courteous. The difference between the demeanour of the two men was remarkable.

"You knew what those letters meant! This is a plot! Where is Skinner's report?"

Mr. Sabin raised his eyebrows. He signaled to the head-waiter.

"Be so good as to continue the service of my dinner," he ordered. "The champagne is a trifle too chilled. You can take it out of the cooler."

The man bowed, with a curious side glance at Horser.

"Certainly, your Grace!"

Horser was almost speechless with anger.

"Are you going to answer my questions?" he demanded thickly.

"I have no particular objection to doing so," Mr. Sabin answered, "but until you can sit up and compose yourself like an ordinary individual, I decline to enter into any conversation with you at all."

Again Mr. Horser raised his voice, and the glare in his eyes was like the glare of a wild beast.

"Do you know who I am?" he asked. "Do you know who you're talking to?"

Mr. Sabin looked at him coolly, and fingered his wineglass.

"Well," he said, "I've a shocking memory for names, but yours is— Mr. Horser, isn't it? I heard it for the first time this morning, and my memory will generally carry me through four-and-twenty hours."

There was a moment's silence. Horser was no fool. He accepted his defeat and dropped the bully.

"You're a stranger in this city, Mr. Sabin, and I guess you aren't altogether acquainted with our ways yet," he said. "But I want you to understand this. The report which is in your pocket has got to be returned to me. If I'd known what I was meddling with I wouldn't have touched your business for a hundred thousand dollars. It's got to be returned to me, I say!" he repeated in a more threatening tone.

Mr. Sabin helped himself to fish, and made a careful examination of the sauce.

"After all," he said meditatively, "I am not sure that I was wise in insisting upon a sauce piquante. I beg your pardon, Mr. Horser. Please do not think me inattentive, but I am very hungry. So, I believe, is my friend, Mr. Skinner. Will you not join us—or perhaps you have already dined?"

There was an ugly flush in Mr. Horser's cheeks, but he struggled to keep his composure.

E. PHILLIPS OPPENHEIM

"Will you give me back that report?"

"When I have read it, with pleasure," Mr. Sabin answered. "Before, no."

Mr. Horser swallowed an exceedingly vicious oath. He struck the table lightly with his forefinger.

"Look here," he said. "If you'd lived in New York a couple of years, even a couple of months, you wouldn't talk like that. I tell you that I hold the government of this city in my right hand. I don't want to be unpleasant, but if that paper is not in my hands by the time you leave this table I shall have you arrested as you leave this room, and the papers taken from you."

"Dear me," Mr. Sabin said, "this is serious. On what charge may I ask should I be exposed to this inconvenience?"

"Charge be damned!" Mr. Horser answered. "The police don't want particulars from me. When I say do a thing they do it. They know that if they declined it would be their last day on the force."

Mr. Sabin filled his glass and leaned back in his chair.

"This," he remarked, "is interesting. I am always glad to have the opportunity of gaining an insight into the customs of different countries. I had an idea that America was a country remarkable for the amount of liberty enjoyed by its inhabitants. Your proposed course of action seems scarcely in keeping with this."

"What are you going to do? Come, I've got to have an answer."

"I don't quite understand," Mr. Sabin remarked, with a puzzled look, "what your official position is in connection with the police."

Mr. Horser's face was a very ugly sight. "Oh, curse my official position," he exclaimed thickly. "If you want proof of what I say you shall have it in less than five minutes. Skinner, be off and fetch a couple of constables."

"I really must protest," Mr. Sabin said. "Mr. Skinner is my guest, and I will not have him treated in this fashion, just as the terrapin is coming in, too. Sit down, Mr. Skinner, sit down. I will settle this matter with you in my room, Mr. Horser, after I have dined. I will not even discuss it before."

Mr. Horser opened his mouth twice, and closed it again. He knew that his opponent was simply playing to gain time, but, after all, he held the trump card. He could afford to wait. He turned to a waiter and ordered a cigar. Mr. Sabin and Mr. Skinner continued their dinner.

Conversation was a little difficult, though Mr. Sabin showed no signs of an impaired appetite. Skinner was white with fear, and glanced every now and then nervously at his chief. Mr. Horser smoked without ceasing, and maintained an ominous silence. Mr. Sabin at last, with a sigh, rose, and lighting a cigarette, took his stick from the waiter and prepared to leave.

"I fear, Mr. Horser," he remarked, "that your presence has scarcely contributed to the cheerfulness of our repast. Mr. Skinner, am I to be favoured with your company also upstairs?"

Horser clutched that gentleman's arm and whispered a few words in his ear.

"Mr. Skinner," he said, "will join us presently. What is your number?"

"336," Mr. Sabin answered. "You will excuse my somewhat slow progress."

They crossed the hall and entered the elevator. Mr. Horser's face began to clear. In a moment or two they would be in Mr. Sabin's sitting-room-alone. He regarded with satisfaction the other's slim, delicate figure and the limp with which he moved. He felt that the danger was already over.

V

B ut, after all, things did not exactly turn out as Mr. Horser had imagined. The sight of the empty room and the closed door were satisfactory enough, and he did not hesitate for a moment.

"Look here, sir," he said, "you and I are going to settle this matter quick. Whatever you paid Skinner you can have back again. But I'm going to have that report."

He took a quick step forward with uplifted hand—and looked into the shining muzzle of a tiny revolver. Behind it Mr. Sabin's face, no longer pleasant and courteous, had taken to itself some very grim lines.

"I am a weak man, Mr. Horser, but I am never without the means of self-defence," Mr. Sabin said in a still, cold tone. "Be so good as to sit down in that easy-chair."

Mr. Horser hesitated. For one moment he stood as though about to carry out his first intention. He stood glaring at his opponent, his face contracted into a snarl, his whole appearance hideous, almost bestial. Mr. Sabin smiled upon him contemptuously—the maddening, compelling smile of the born aristocrat.

"Sit down!"

Mr. Horser sat down, whereupon Mr. Sabin followed suit.

"Now what have you to say to me?" Mr. Sabin asked quietly.

"I want that report," was the dogged answer.

"You will not have it," Mr. Sabin answered. "You can take that for granted. You shall not take it from me by force, and I will see that you do not charm it out of my pocket by other means. The information which it contains is of the utmost possible importance to me. I have bought it and paid for it, and I shall use it."

Mr. Horser moistened his dry lips.

"I will give you," he said, "twenty thousand dollars for its return."

Mr. Sabin laughed softly.

"You bid high," he said. "I begin to suspect that our friends on the other side of the water have been more than ordinarily kind to you."

"I will give you—forty thousand dollars."

Mr. Sabin raised his eyebrows.

"So much? After all, that sounds more like fear than anything. You cannot hope to make a profitable deal out of that. Dear me! It seems only a few minutes ago that I heard your interesting friend,

Mr. Skinner, shake with laughter at the mention of such a thing as a secret society."

"Skinner is a blasted fool," Horser exclaimed fiercely. "Listen here, Mr. Sabin. You can read that report if you must, but, as I'm a living man you'll not stir from New York if you do. I'll make your life a hell for you. Don't you understand that no one but a born fool would dare to quarrel with me in this city? I hold the prison keys, the police are mine. I shall make my own charge, whatever I choose, and they shall prove it for me."

Mr. Sabin shook his head.

"This sounds very shocking," he remarked. "I had no idea that the largest city of the most enlightened country in the world was in such a sorry plight."

"Oh, curse your sarcasm," Mr. Horser said. "I'm talking facts, and you've got to know them. Will you give up that report? You can find out all there is in it for yourself. But I'm going to give it you straight. If I don't have that report back unread, you'll never leave New York."

Mr. Sabin was genuinely amused.

"My good fellow," he said, "you have made yourself a notorious person in this country by dint of incessant bullying and bribing and corruption of every sort. You may possess all the powers you claim. Your only mistake seems to be that you are too thick-headed to know when you are overmatched. I have been a diplomatist all my life," Mr. Sabin said, rising slowly to his feet, and with a sudden intent look upon his face, "and if I were to be outwitted by such a novice as you I should deserve to end my days—in New York."

Mr. Horser rose also to his feet. A smile of triumph was on his lips.

"Well," he said, "we—Come in! Come in!" The door was thrown open. Skinner and two policemen entered. Mr. Sabin leaned towards the wall, and in a second the room was plunged in darkness.

"Turn on the lights!" Skinner shouted. "Seize him! He's in that corner. Use your clubs!" Horser bawled. "Stand by the door one of you. Damnation, where is that switch?"

He found it with a shout of triumph. Lights flared out in the room. They stared around into every corner. Mr. Sabin was not there. Then Horser saw the door leading into the bed-chamber, and flung himself against it with a hoarse cry of rage.

"Break it open!" he cried to the policemen.

They hammered upon it with their clubs. Mr. Sabin's quiet voice came to them from the other side.

"Pray do not disturb me, gentlemen," he said. "I am reading."

"Break it open, you damned fools!" Horser cried. They battered at it sturdily, but the door was a solid one. Suddenly they heard the key turn in the lock. Mr. Sabin stood upon the threshold.

"Gentlemen!" he exclaimed. "These are my private apartments. Why this violence?"

He held out the paper.

"This is mine," he said. "The information which it contains is bought and paid for. But if the giving it up will procure me the privilege of your departure, pray take it."

Horser was purple with rage. He pointed with shaking fist to the still, calm figure.

"Arrest him," he ordered. "Take him to the cells."

Mr. Sabin shrugged his shoulders.

"I am ready," he said, "but it is only fair to give you this warning. I am the Duke of Souspennier, and I am well known in England and France. The paper which you saw me hand to the porter in the hall as we stepped into the elevator was a despatch in cipher to the English Ambassador at Washington, claiming his protection. If you take me to prison to-night you will have him to deal with to-morrow."

Mr. Horser bore himself in defeat better than at any time during the encounter. He turned to the constables.

"Go down stairs and wait for me in the hall," he ordered. "You too, Skinner."

They left the room. Horser turned to Mr. Sabin, and the veins on his forehead stood out like whipcord.

"I know when I'm beaten," he said. "Keep your report, and be damned to you. But remember that you and I have a score to settle, and you can ask those who know me how often Dick Horser comes out underneath in the long run."

He followed the others. Mr. Sabin sat down in his easy-chair with a quiet smile upon his lips. Once more he glanced through the brief report. Then his eyes half closed, and he sat quite still—a tired, weary-looking man, almost unnaturally pale.

"They have kept their word," he said softly to himself, "after many years. After many years!"

DUSON CAME IN TO UNDRESS him shortly afterwards. He saw signs of the struggle, but made no comment. Mr. Sabin, after a moment's hesitation, took a phial from his pocket and poured a few drops into a wineglassful of water.

"Duson," he said, "bring me some despatch forms and a pencil."

"Yes, sir."

Mr. Sabin wrote for several moments. Then he placed the forms in an envelope, sealed it, and handed it to Duson.

"Duson," he said, "that fellow Horser is annoyed with me. If I should be arrested on any charge, or should fail to return to the hotel within reasonable time, break that seal and send off the telegrams."

"Yes, sir."

Mr. Sabin yawned.

"I need sleep," he said. "Do not call me to-morrow morning until I ring. And, Duson!"

"Yes, sir."

"The Campania will sail from New York somewhere about the tenth of October. I wish to secure the whole of stateroom number twenty-eight. Go round to the office as soon as they open, secure that room if possible, and pay a deposit. No other will do. Also one for yourself."

"Very good, sir."

VI

Here's a lady inquiring for you, sir—just gone up to your room in the elevator," the hotel clerk remarked to Mr. Sabin as he paused on his way to the door to hand in his key. "Shall I send a boy up?"

Mr. Sabin hesitated.

"A lady?" he remarked tentatively.

The hotel clerk nodded.

"Yes. I didn't notice the name, but she was an Englishwoman. I'll send up."

"Thank you, I will return," Mr. Sabin said. "If I should miss her on the way perhaps you will kindly redirect her to my rooms."

He rang for the elevator, and was swiftly transported to his own floor. The door of his sitting-room was open. Duson was talking to a tall fair woman, who turned swiftly round at the sound of his approach.

"Ah, they found you, then!" she exclaimed, coming towards him with outstretched hands. "Isn't this a strange place and a strange country for us to meet once more in?"

He greeted her gallantly, but with a certain reserve, of which she was at once aware.

"Are there any countries in the world left which are strange to so great a traveler as Lady Muriel Carey?" he said. "The papers here have been full of your wonderful adventures in South Africa."

She laughed.

"Everything shockingly exaggerated, of course," she declared. "I have really been plagued to death since I got here with interviewers, and that sort of person. I wonder if you know how glad I am to see you again?"

"You are very kind, indeed," he said. "Certainly there was no one whom I expected less to see over here. You have come for the yacht races, I suppose?"

She looked at him with a faint smile and raised eyebrows.

"Come," she said, "shall we lie to one another? Is it worth while? Candour is so much more original."

"Candour by all means then, I beg," he answered.

"I have come over with the Dalkeiths, ostensibly to see the yacht races. Really I have come to see you."

Mr. Sabin bowed.

"I am delightfully flattered," he murmured.

"I don't exactly mean for the pleasure of gazing into your face once more," she continued. "I have a mission!"

Mr. Sabin looked up quickly.

"Great heavens! You, too!" he exclaimed.

She nodded.

"Why not?" she asked coolly. "I have been in it for years, you know, and when I got back from South Africa everything seemed so terribly slow that I begged for some work to do."

"And they sent you here—to me?"

"Yes," she answered, "and I was here also a few weeks ago, but you must not ask me anything about that."

Mr. Sabin's eyebrows contracted, his face darkened. She shrank a little away from him.

"So it is you who have robbed me of her, then," he said slowly. "Yes, the description fits you well enough. I ask you, Lady Carey, to remember the last time when chance brought you and me together. Have I deserved this from you?"

She made a little gesture of impotence.

"Do be reasonable!" she begged. "What choice had I?"

He looked at her steadfastly.

"The folly of women—of clever women such as you," he said, "is absolutely amazing. You have deliberately made a slave of yourself—"

"One must have distraction," she murmured.

"Distraction! And so you play at this sort of thing. Is it worth while?"

Her eyes for a moment clouded over with weariness.

"When one has filled the cup of life to the brim for many years," she said, "what remains that is worth while?"

He bowed.

"You are a young woman," he said. "You should not yet have learned to speak with such bitterness. As for me—well, I am old indeed. In youth and age the affections claim us. I am approaching my second childhood."

She laughed derisively, yet not unkindly. "What folly!" she exclaimed.

"You are right," he admitted. "I suppose it is the fault of old associations."

"In a few minutes," she said, smiling at him, "we should have become sentimental."

"I," he admitted, "was floundering already."

She shrugged her shoulders.

"You talk as though sentiment were a bog."

"There have been worse similes," he declared.

"How horrid! And do you know, sir, for all your indignation you have not yet even inquired after your wife's health."

"I trust," he said, "that she is well."

"She is in excellent health."

"Your second visit to this country," he remarked, "follows very swiftly upon your first."

She nodded.

"I am here," she said, "on your account."

"You excite my interest," he declared. "May I know your mission?"

"I have to remind you of your pledge," she said, "to assure you of Lucille's welfare, and to prevent your leaving the country."

"Marvelous!" he exclaimed, with a slight mocking smile. "And may I ask what means you intend to employ to keep me here?"

"Well," she said, "I have large discretionary powers. We have a very strong branch over on this side, but I would very much rather induce you to stay here without applying to them."

"And the inducements?" he asked.

She took a cigarette from a box which stood on the table and lit one.

"Well," she said, "I might appeal to your hospitality, might I not? I am in a strange country which you have made your home. I want to be shown round. Do you remember dining with me one night at the Ambassador's? It was very hot, even for Paris, and we drove afterwards in the Bois. Ask me to dine with you here, won't you? I have never quite forgotten the last time."

Mr. Sabin laughed softly, but with undisguised mirth.

"Come," he said, "this is an excellent start. You are to play the Circe up to date, and I am to be beguiled. How ought I to answer you? I do remember the Ambassador's, and I do remember driving down the Bois in your victoria, and holding—I believe I am right—your hand. You have no right to disturb those charming memories by attempting to turn them into bathos."

She blew out a little cloud of tobacco smoke, and watched it thoughtfully.

"Ah!" she remarked. "I wonder who is better at that, you or I? I may not be exactly a sentimental person, but you—you are a flint."

"On the contrary," Mr. Sabin assured her earnestly, "I am very much in love with my wife."

"Dear me!" she exclaimed. "You carry originality to quixoticism. I have met several men before in my life whom I have suspected of such a thing, but I never heard any one confess it. This little domestic contretemps is then, I presume, disagreeable to you!"

"To the last degree," Mr. Sabin asserted. "So much so that I leave for England by the Campania."

She shook her head slowly.

"I wouldn't if I were you."

"Why not?"

Lady Carey threw away the end of her cigarette, and looked for a moment thoughtfully at her long white fingers glittering with rings. Then she began to draw on her gloves.

"Well, in the first place," she said, "Lucille will have no time to spare for you. You will be de trop in decidedly an uncomfortable position. You wouldn't find London at all a good place to live in just now, even if you ever got there—which I am inclined to doubt. And secondly, here am I—"

"Circe!" he murmured.

"Waiting to be entertained, in a strange country, almost friendless. I want to be shown everything, taken everywhere. And I am dying to see your home at Lenox. I do not think your attitude towards me in the least hospitable."

"Come, you are judging me very quickly," he declared. "What opportunities have I had?"

"What opportunities can there be if you sail by the Campania?"

"You might dine with me to-night at least."

"Impossible! The Dalkeiths have a party to meet me. Come too, won't you? They love dukes—even French ones."

He shook his head.

"There is no attraction for me in a large party," he answered. "I am getting to an age when to make conversation in return for a dinner seems scarcely a fair exchange."

"From your host's point of view, or yours?"

"From both! Besides, one's digestion suffers."

"You are certainly getting old," she declared. "Come, I must go. You haven't been a bit nice to me. When shall I see you again?"

"It is," he answered, "for you to say."

She looked at him for a moment thoughtfully.

"Supposing," she said, "that I cried off the yacht race to-day. Would you take me out to lunch?"

He smiled.

"My dear lady," he said, "it is for Circe to command—and for me to obey."

"And you'll come and have tea with me afterwards at the Waldorf?"

"That," Mr. Sabin declared, "will add still further to my happiness."

"Will you call for me, then—and where shall we have lunch, and at what time? I must go and develop a headache at once, or that tiresome Dalkeith boy will be pounding at my door."

"I will call for you at the Waldorf at half-past one," Mr. Sabin said. "Unless you have any choice, I will take you to a little place downtown where we can imagine ourselves back on the Continent, and where we shall be spared the horror of green corn."

"Delightful," she murmured, buttoning her glove. "Then you shall take me for a drive to Fifth Avenue, or to see somebody's tomb, and my woman shall make some real Russian tea for us in my sitting-room. Really, I think I'm doing very well for the first day. Is the spell beginning to work?"

"Hideously," he assured her. "I feel already that the only thing I dread in life are these two hours before luncheon."

She nodded.

"That is quite as it should be. Don't trouble to come down with me. I believe that Dalkeith pere is hanging round somewhere, and in view of my headache perhaps you had better remain in the background for the moment. At one-thirty, then!"

Mr. Sabin smiled as she passed out of the room, and lit a cigarette.

"I think," he said to himself, "that the arrival of Felix is opportune."

VII

They sat together at a small table, looking upon a scene which was probably unique in the history of the great restaurant. The younger man was both frankly interested and undoubtedly curious. Mr. Sabin, though his eyes seemed everywhere, retained to the full extent that nonchalance of manner which all his life he had so assiduously cultivated.

"It is wonderful, my dear Felix," he said, leisurely drawing his cigarette-case from his pocket, "wonderful what good fellowship can be evolved by a kindred interest in sport, and a bottle or so of good champagne. But, after all, this is not to be taken seriously."

"Shamrock the fourth! Shamrock the fourth!"

A tall young American, his thick head of hair, which had once been carefully parted in the middle, a little disheveled, his hard, clean-cut face flushed with enthusiasm, had risen to his feet and stood with a brimming glass of champagne high over his head. Almost every one in the room rose to their feet. A college boy sprang upon a table with extended arms. The Yale shout split the room. The very glasses on the table rattled.

"Columbia! Columbia!"

It was an Englishman now who had leaped upon a vacant table with upraised glass. There was an answering roar of enthusiasm. Every one drank, and every one sat down again with a pleasant thrill of excitement at this unique scene. Felix leaned back in his chair and marveled.

"One would have imagined," he murmured, "that America and England together were at war with the rest of the world and had won a great victory. To think that this is all the result of a yacht race. It is incredible!"

"All your life, my dear Felix," Mr. Sabin remarked, "you have underrated the sporting instinct. It has a great place amongst the impulses of the world. See how it has brought these people together."

"But they are already of the same kin," Felix remarked. "Their interests and aims are alike. Their destinies are surely identical."

Mr. Sabin, who had lit his cigarette, watched the blue smoke curl upwards, and was thoughtful for a moment.

"My dear Felix!" he said. "You are very, very young. The interests of two great nations such as America and England can never be alike. It is the language of diplomacy, but it is also the language of fools."

Their conversation was for the moment interrupted by a fresh murmur of applause, rising above the loved hum of conversation, the laughter of women, and the popping of corks. A little troop of waiters had just wheeled into the room two magnificent models of yachts hewn out of blocks of solid ice and crowned with flowers. On the one were the Stars and Stripes, on the other the Shamrock and Thistle. There was much clapping of hands and cheering. Lady Carey, who was sitting at the next table with her back to them, joined in the applause so heartily that a tiny gold pencil attached to her bracelet became detached and rolled unobserved to Mr. Sabin's side. Felix half rose to pick it up, but was suddenly checked by a quick gesture from his companion.

"Leave it," Mr. Sabin whispered. "I wish to return it myself."

He stooped and picked it up, a certain stealthiness apparent in his movement. Felix watched him in amazement.

"It is Lady Carey's, is it not?" he asked.

"Yes. Be silent. I will give it back to her presently."

A waiter served them with coffee. Mr. Sabin was idly sketching something on the back of his menu card. Felix broke into a little laugh as the man retired.

"Mysterious as ever," he remarked.

Mr. Sabin smiled quietly. He went on with his sketch.

"I do not want," Felix said, "to seem impatient, but you must remember that I have come all the way from Europe in response to a very urgent message. As yet I have done nothing except form a very uncomfortable third at a luncheon and tea party, and listen to a good deal of enigmatic conversation between you and the charming Lady Carey. This evening I made sure that I should be enlightened. But no! You have given me a wonderful dinner—from you I expected it. We have eaten terrapin, canvas-back duck, and many other things the names of which alone were known to me. But of the reason for which you have summoned me here—I know nothing. Not one word have you spoken. I am beginning to fear from your avoidance of the subject that there is some trouble between you and Lucille. I beg that you will set my anxiety at rest."

Mr. Sabin nodded.

"It is reasonable," he said. "Look here!"

He turned the menu card round. On the back he had sketched some sort of a device with the pencil which he had picked up, and which instead of black-lead contained a peculiar shade of yellow crayon. Felix sat as though turned to stone.

"Try," Mr. Sabin said smoothly, "and avoid that air of tragedy. Some of these good people might be curious."

Felix leaned across the table. He pointed to the menu card.

"What does that mean?" he muttered.

Mr. Sabin contemplated it himself thoughtfully. "Well," he said, "I rather thought that you might be able to explain that to me. I have an idea that there is a society in Europe—sort of aristocratic odd-fellows, you know—who had adopted it for their crest. Am I not right?"

Felix looked at him steadfastly.

"Tell me two things," he said. "First, why you sent for me, and secondly, what do you mean—by that?"

"Lucille," Mr. Sabin said, "has been taken away from me."

"Lucille! Great God!"

"She has been taken away from me," Mr. Sabin said, "without a single word of warning."

Felix pointed to the menu card.

"By them?" he asked.

"By them. It was a month ago. Two days before my cable."

Felix was silent for several moments. He had not the self-command of his companion, and he feared to trust himself to speech.

"She has been taken to Europe," Mr. Sabin continued. "I do not know, I cannot even guess at the reason. She left no word. I have been warned not to follow her."

"You obey?"

"I sail to-morrow."

"And I?" Felix asked.

Mr. Sabin looked for, a moment at the drawing on the back of the menu card, and up at Felix. Felix shook his head.

"You must know," he said, "that I am powerless."

"You may be able to help me," Mr. Sabin said, "without compromising yourself."

"Impossible!" Felix declared. "But what did they want with Lucille?"

"That," Mr. Sabin said, "is what I am desirous of knowing. It is what I trust that you, my dear Felix, may assist me to discover."

"You are determined, then, to follow her?"

Mr. Sabin helped himself to a liqueur from the bottle by his side.

"My dear Felix," he said reproachfully, "you should know me better than to ask me such a question."

Felix moved uneasily in his chair.

"Of course," he said, "it depends upon how much they want to keep you apart. But you know that you are running great risks?"

"Why, no," Mr. Sabin said. "I scarcely thought that. I have understood that the society was by no means in its former flourishing condition."

Felix laughed scornfully.

"They have never been," he answered, "richer or more powerful. During the last twelve months they have been active in every part of Europe."

Mr. Sabin's face hardened.

"Very well!" he said. "We will try their strength."

"We!" Felix laughed shortly. "You forget that my hands are tied. I cannot help you or Lucille. You must know that."

"You cannot interfere directly," Mr. Sabin admitted. "Yet you are Lucille's brother, and I am forced to appeal to you. If you will be my companion for a little while I think I can show you how you can help Lucille at any rate, and yet run no risk."

The little party at the next table were breaking up at last. Lady Carey, pale and bored, with tired, swollen eyes—they were always a little prominent—rose languidly and began to gather together her belongings. As she did so she looked over the back of her chair and met Mr. Sabin's eyes. He rose at once and bowed. She cast a quick sidelong glance at her companions, which he at once understood.

"I have the honour, Lady Carey," he said, "of recalling myself to your recollection. We met in Paris and London not so very many years ago. You perhaps remember the cardinal's dinner?"

A slight smile flickered upon her lips. The man's adroitness always excited her admiration.

"I remember it perfectly, and you, Duke," she answered. "Have you made your home on this side of the water?"

Mr. Sabin shook his head slowly.

"Home!" he repeated. "Ah, I was always a bird of passage, you remember. Yet I have spent three very delightful years in this country."

"And I," she said, lowering her tone and leaning towards him, "one very stupid, idiotic day."

Mr. Sabin assumed the look of a man who denies any personal responsibility in an unfortunate happening.

"It was regrettable," he murmured, "but I assure you that it was unavoidable. Lucille's brother must have a certain claim upon me, and it was his first day in America."

She was silent for a moment. Then she turned abruptly towards the door. Her friends were already on the way.

"Come with me," she said. "I want to speak to you."

He followed her out into the lobby. Felix came a few paces behind. The restaurant was still full of people, the hum of conversation almost drowning the music. Every one glanced curiously at Lady Carey, who was a famous woman. She carried herself with a certain insolent indifference, the national deportment of her sex and rank. The women whispered together that she was "very English."

In the lobby she turned suddenly upon Mr. Sabin.

"Will you take me back to my hotel?" she asked pointedly.

"I regret that I cannot," he answered. "I have promised to show Felix some of the wonders of New York by night."

"You can take him to-morrow."

"To-morrow," Mr. Sabin said, "he leaves for the West."

She looked closely into his impassive face.

"I suppose that you are lying," she said shortly.

"Your candour," he answered coldly, "sometimes approaches brutality."

She leaned towards him, her face suddenly softened.

"We are playing a foolish game with one another," she murmured. "I offer you an alliance, my friendship, perhaps my help."

"What can I do," he answered gravely, "save be grateful—and accept?"

"Then—"

She stopped short. It was Mr. Sabin's luck which had intervened. Herbert Daikeith stood at her elbow.

"Lady Carey," he said, "they're all gone but the mater and I. Forgive my interrupting you," he added hastily.

"You can go on, Herbert," she added. "The Duc de Souspennier will bring me."

Mr. Sabin, who had no intention of doing anything of the sort, turned towards the young man with a smile.

"Lady Carey has not introduced us," he said, "but I have seen you at Ranelagh quite often. If you are still keen on polo you should have a try over here. I fancy you would find that these American youngsters can hold their own. All right, Felix, I am ready now. Lady Carey, I shall do myself the honour of waiting upon you early to-morrow morning, as I have a little excursion to propose. Good-night."

She shrugged her shoulders ever so slightly as she turned away. Mr. Sabin smiled—faintly amused. He turned to Felix.

"Come," he said, "we have no time to lose."

VIII

I regret," Mr. Sabin said to Felix as they sat side by side in the small coupe, "that your stay in this country will be so brief."

"Indeed," Felix answered. "May I ask what you call brief?"

Mr. Sabin looked out of the carriage window.

"We are already," he said, "on the way to England."

Felix laughed.

"This," he said, "is like old times."

Mr. Sabin smiled.

"The system of espionage here," he remarked, "is painfully primitive. It lacks finesse and judgment. The fact that I have taken expensive rooms on the Campania, and that I have sent many packages there, that my own belongings are still in my rooms untouched, seems to our friends conclusive evidence that I am going to attempt to leave America by that boat. They have, I believe, a warrant for my arrest on some ridiculous charge which they intend to present at the last moment. They will not have the opportunity."

"But there is no other steamer sailing to-morrow, is there?" Felix asked.

"Not from New York," Mr. Sabin answered, "but it was never my intention to sail from New York. We are on our way to Boston now, and we sail in the Saxonia at six o'clock to-morrow morning."

"We appear to be stopping at the Waldorf," Felix remarked.

"It is quite correct," Mr. Sabin answered. "Follow me through the hall as quickly as possible. There is another carriage waiting at the other entrance, and I expect to find in it Duson and my dressing-case."

They alighted and made their way though the crowded vestibules. At the Thirty-fourth Street entrance a carriage was drawn up. Duson was standing upon the pavement, his pale, nervous face whiter than ever under the electric light. Mr. Sabin stopped short.

"Felix," he said, "one word. If by any chance things have gone wrong they will not have made any arrangements to detain you. Catch the midnight train to Boston and embark on the Saxonia. There will be a cable for you at Liverpool. But the moment you leave me send this despatch."

Felix nodded and put the crumpled-up piece of paper in his pocket. The two men passed on. Duson took off his hat, but his fingers were trembling. The carriage door was opened and a tall, spare man descended.

"This is Mr. Sabin?" he remarked.

Mr. Sabin bowed.

"That is my name," he admitted, "by which I have been generally called in this democratic country. What is your business with me?"

"I rather guess that you're my prisoner," the man answered. "If you'll step right in here we can get away quietly."

"The suggestion," Mr. Sabin remarked, "sounds inviting, but I am somewhat pressed for time. Might I inquire the nature of the charge you have against me?"

"They'll tell you that at the office," the man answered. "Get in, please."

Mr. Sabin looked around for Felix, but he had disappeared. He took out his cigarette-case.

"You will permit me first to light a cigarette," he remarked.

"All right! Only look sharp."

Mr. Sabin kept silence in the carriage. The drive was a long one. When they descended he looked up at Duson, who sat upon the box.

"Duson," he said, and his voice, though low, was terrible, "I see that I can be mistaken in men. You are a villain."

The man sprung to his feet, hat in hand. His face was wrung with emotion.

"Your Grace," he said, "it is true that I betrayed you. But I did it without reward. I am a ruined man. I did it because the orders which came to me were such as I dare not disobey. Here are your keys, your Grace, and money."

Mr. Sabin looked at him steadily.

"You, too, Duson?"

"I too, alas, your Grace!"

Mr. Sabin considered for a moment.

"Duson," he said, "I retain you in my service. Take my luggage on board the Campania to-morrow afternoon, and pay the bill at the hotel. I shall join you on the boat."

Duson was amazed. The man who was standing by laughed.

"If you take my advice, sir," he remarked, "you'll order your clothes to be sent here. I've a kind of fancy the Campania will sail without you to-morrow."

"You have my orders, Duson," Mr. Sabin said. "You can rely upon seeing me."

The detective led the way into the building, and opened the door leading into a large, barely furnished office.

"Chief's gone home for the night, I guess," he remarked. "We can fix up a shakedown for you in one of the rooms behind."

"I thank you," Mr. Sabin said, sitting down in a high-backed wooden chair; "I decline to move until the charge against me is properly explained."

"There is no one here to do it just now," the man answered. "Better make yourself comfortable for a bit."

"You detain me here, then," Mr. Sabin said, "without even a sight of your warrant or any intimation as to the charge against me?"

"Oh, the chief'll fix all that," the man answered. "Don't you worry."

Mr. Sabin smiled.

In a magnificently furnished apartment somewhere in the neighbourhood of Fifth Avenue a small party of men were seated round a card table piled with chips and rolls of bills. On the sideboard there was a great collection of empty bottles, spirit decanters and Vichy syphons. Mr. Horser was helping himself to brandy and water with one hand and holding himself up with the other. There was a knock at the door.

A man who was still playing looked up. He was about fifty years of age, clean shaven, with vacuous eyes and a weak mouth. He was the host of the party.

"Come in!" he shouted.

A young man entered in a long black overcoat and soft hat. He looked about him without surprise, but he seemed to note Mr. Horser's presence with some concern. The man at the table threw down his cards.

"What the devil do you want, Smith?"

"An important despatch from Washington has just arrived, sir. I have brought it up with the codebook."

"From Washington at this time of the night," he exclaimed thickly. "Come in here, Smith."

He raised the curtains leading into a small anteroom, and turned up the electric light. His clerk laid the message down on the table before him.

"Here is the despatch, Mr. Mace," he said, "and here is the translation."

"English Ambassador demands immediate explanation of arrest of Duke Souspennier at Waldorf to-night. Reply immediately what charge and evidence. Souspennier naturalised Englishman."

Mr. Mace sprang to his feet with an oath. He threw aside the curtain which shielded the room from the larger apartment.

"Horser, come here, you damned fool!"

Horser, with a stream of magnificent invectives, obeyed the summons. His host pointed to the message.

"Read that!"

Mr. Horser read and his face grew even more repulsive. A dull purple flush suffused his cheeks, his eyes were bloodshot, and the veins on his forehead stood out like cords. He leaned for several moments against the table and steadily cursed Mr. Sabin, the government at Washington, and something under his breath which he did not dare to name openly.

"Oh, shut up!" his host said at last. "How the devil are we going to get out of this?"

Mr. Horser left the room and returned with a tumbler full of brandy and a very little water.

"Take a drink yourself," he said. "It'll steady you."

"Oh, I'm steady enough," Mr. Mace replied impatiently. "I want to know how you're going to get us out of this. What was the charge, anyhow?"

"Passing forged bills," Horser answered. "Parsons fixed it up."

Mr. Mace turned a shade paler.

"Where the devil's the sense in a charge like that?" he answered fiercely. "The man's a millionaire. He'll turn the tables on us nicely."

"We've got to keep him till after the Campania sails, anyhow," Horser said doggedly.

"We're not going to keep him ten minutes," Mace replied. "I'm going to sign the order for his release."

Horser's speech was thick with drunken fury. "By—I'll see that you don't!" he exclaimed.

Mace turned upon him angrily.

"You selfish fool!" he muttered. "You're not in the thing, anyhow. If you think I'm going to risk my position for the sake of one little job you're wrong. I shall go down myself and release him, with an apology."

"He'll have his revenge all the same," Horser answered. "It's too late now to funk the thing. They can't budge you. We'll see to that. We hold New York in our hands. Be a man, Mace, and run a little risk. It's fifty thousand."

Mace looked up at him curiously.

"What do you get out of it, Horser?"

Horser's face hardened.

"Not one cent!" he declared fiercely. "Only if I fail it might be unpleasant for me next time I crossed."

"I don't know!" Mace declared weakly. "I don't know what to do. It's twelve hours, Horser, and the charge is ridiculous."

"You have me behind you."

"I can't tell them that at Washington," Mace said.

"It's a fact, all the same. Don't be so damned nervous."

Mace dismissed his clerk, and found his other guests, too, on the point of departure. But the last had scarcely left before a servant entered with another despatch.

"Release Souspennier."

Mace handed it to his companion.

"This settles it," he declared. "I shall go round and try and make my peace with the fellow."

Horser stood in the way, burly, half-drunk and vicious. He struck his host in the face with clenched fist. Mace went down with scarcely a groan. A servant, hearing the fall, came hurrying back.

"Your master is drunk and he has fallen down," Horser said. "Put him to bed—give him a sleeping draught if you've got one."

The servant bent over the unconscious man.

"Hadn't I better fetch a doctor, sir?" he asked. "I'm afraid he's hurt."

"Not he!" Horser answered contemptuously. "He's cut his cheek a little, that's all. Put him to bed. Say I shall be round again by nine o'clock."

Horser put on his coat and left the house. The morning sunlight was flooding the streets. Away down town Mr. Sabin was dozing in his high-backed chair.

IX

Felix, after an uneventful voyage, landed duly at Liverpool. To his amazement the first person he saw upon the quay was Mr. Sabin, leaning upon his stick and smoking a cigarette.

"Come, come, Felix!" he exclaimed. "Don't look at me as though I were a ghost. You have very little confidence in me, after all, I see."

"But—how did you get here?"

"The Campania, of course. I had plenty of time. It was easy enough for those fellows to arrest me, but they never had a chance of holding me."

"But how did you get away in time?"

Mr. Sabin sighed.

"It was very simple," he said. "One day, while one of those wonderful spies was sleeping on my doormat I slipped away and went over to Washington, saw the English Ambassador, convinced him of my bonafides, told him very nearly the whole truth. He promised if I wired him that I was arrested to take my case up at once. You sent the despatch, and he kept his word. I breakfasted on Saturday morning at the Waldorf, and though a great dray was driven into my carriage on the way to the boat, I escaped, as I always do—and here I am."

"Unhurt!" Felix remarked with a smile, "as usual!"

Mr. Sabin nodded.

"The driver of my carriage was killed, and Duson had his arm broken," he said. "I stepped out of the debris without a scratch. Come into the Customs House now and get your baggage through. I have taken a coupe on the special train and ordered lunch."

Before long they were on the way to London. Mr. Sabin, whilst luncheon was being served, talked only of the lightest matters. But afterwards, when coffee was served and he had lit a cigarette, he leaned over towards Felix.

"Felix," he said, "your sister is dear to you?"

"She is the only creature on earth," Felix said, "whom I care for. She is very dear to me, indeed."

"Am I right," Mr. Sabin asked, "in assuming that the old enmity between us is dead, that the last few years has wiped away the old soreness.

"Yes," Felix answered. "I know that she was happy with you. That is enough for me."

"You and I," Mr. Sabin continued, "must work out her salvation. Do not be afraid that I am going to ask you impossibilities. I know that our ways must lie apart. You can go to her at once. It may be many, many months before I can catch even a glimpse of her. Never mind. Let me feel that she has you within the circle, and I without, with our lives devoted to her."

"You may rely upon that," Felix answered. "Wherever she is I am going. I shall be there. I will watch over her."

Mr. Sabin sighed.

"The more difficult task is mine," he said, "but I have no fear of failure. I shall find her surrounded by spies, by those who are now my enemies. Still, they will find it hard to shake me off. It may be that they took her from me only out of revenge. If that be so my task will be easier. If there are other dangers which she is called upon to face, it is still possible that they might accept my service instead."

"You would give it?" Felix exclaimed.

"To the last drop of blood in my body," Mr. Sabin answered. "Save for my love for her I am a dead man upon the earth. I have no longer politics or ambition. So the past can easily be expunged. Those who must be her guiding influence shall be mine."

"You will win her back," Felix said. "I am sure of it."

"I am willing to pay any price on earth," Mr. Sabin answered. "If they can forget the past I can. I want you to remember this. I want her to know it. I want them to know it. That is all, Felix."

Mr. Sabin leaned back in his seat. He had left this country last a stricken and defeated man, left it with the echoes of his ruined schemes crashing in his ears. He came back to it a man with one purpose only, and that such a purpose as never before had guided him—the love of a woman. Was it a sign of age, he wondered, this return to the humanities? His life had been full of great schemes, he had wielded often a gigantic influence, more than once he had made history. And now the love of these things had gone from him. Their fascination was powerless to quicken by a single beat his steady pulse. Monarchy or republic—what did he care? It was Lucille he wanted, the woman who had shown him how sweet even defeat might be, who had made these three years of his life so happy that they seemed to have passed in one delightful dream. Were they dead, annihilated, these old ambitions, the old love of great doings, or did they only slumber? He moved in his seat uneasily.

At Euston the two men separated with a silent handshake. Mr. Sabin

E. PHILLIPS OPPENHEIM

drove to one of the largest and newest of the modern hotels de luxe. He entered his name as Mr. Sabin—the old exile's hatred of using his title in a foreign country had become a confirmed habit with him—and mingled freely with the crowds who thronged into the restaurant at night. There were many faces which he remembered, there were a few who remembered him. He neither courted nor shunned observation. He sat at dinner-time at a retired table, and found himself watching the people with a stir of pleasure. Afterwards he went round to a famous club, of which he had once been made a life member, but towards midnight he was wearied of the dull decorum of his surroundings, and returning to the hotel, sought the restaurant once more. The stream of people coming in to supper was greater even than at dinner-time. He found a small table, and ordered some oysters. The sight of this bevy of pleasure-seekers, all apparently with multitudes of friends, might have engendered a sense of loneliness in a man of different disposition. To Mr. Sabin his isolation was a luxury. He had an uninterrupted opportunity of pursuing his favourite study.

There entered a party towards midnight, to meet whom the head-waiter himself came hurrying from the further end of the room, and whose arrival created a little buzz of interest. The woman who formed the central figure of the little group had for two years known no rival either at Court or in Society. She was the most beautiful woman in England, beautiful too with all the subtle grace of her royal descent. There were women upon the stage whose faces might have borne comparison with hers, but there was not one who in a room would not have sunk into insignificance by her side. Her movements, her carriage were incomparable—the inherited gifts of a race of women born in palaces.

Mr. Sabin, who neither shunned nor courted observation, watched her with a grim smile which was not devoid of bitterness. Suddenly she saw him. With a little cry of wonder she came towards him with outstretched hands.

"It is marvelous," she exclaimed. "You? Really you?"

He bowed low over her hands.

"It is I, dear Helene," he answered. "A moment ago I was dreaming. I thought that I was back once more at Versailles, and in the presence of my Queen."

She laughed softly.

"There may be no Versailles," she murmured, "but you will be a courtier to the end of your days."

"At least," he said, "believe me that my congratulations come from my heart. Your happiness is written in your face, and your husband must be the proudest man in England."

He was standing now by her side, and he held out his hand to Mr. Sabin.

"I hope, sir," he said pleasantly, "that you bear me no ill-will."

"It would be madness," Mr. Sabin answered. "To be the most beautiful peeress in England is perhaps for Helene a happier fate than to be the first queen of a new dynasty."

"And you, uncle?" Helene said. "You are back from your exile then. How often I have felt disposed to smile when I thought of you, of all men, in America."

"I went into exile," Mr. Sabin answered, "and I found paradise. The three years which have passed since I saw you last have been the happiest of my life."

"Lucille!" Helene exclaimed.

"Is my wife," Mr. Sabin answered.

"Delightful!" Helene murmured. "She is with you then, I hope. Indeed, I felt sure that I saw her the other night at the opera."

"At the opera!" Mr. Sabin for a moment was silent. He would have been ashamed to confess that his heart was beating strongly, that a crowd of eager questions trembled upon his lips. He recovered himself after a moment.

"Lucille is not with me for the moment," he said in measured tones. "I am detaining you from your guests, Helene. If you will permit me I will call upon you."

"Won't you join us?" Lord Camperdown asked courteously. "We are only a small party—the Portuguese Ambassador and his wife, the Duke of Medchester, and Stanley Phillipson."

Mr. Sabin rose at once.

"I shall be delighted," he said.

Lord Camperdown hesitated for a moment.

"I present Monsieur le Due de Souspennier, I presume?" he remarked, smiling.

Mr. Sabin bowed.

"I am Mr. Sabin," he said, "at the hotels and places where one travels. To my friends I have no longer an incognito. It is not necessary."

It was a brilliant little supper party, and Mr. Sabin contributed at least his share to the general entertainment. Before they dispersed he

E. PHILLIPS OPPENHEIM

had to bring out his tablets to make notes of his engagements. He stood on the top of the steps above the palm-court to wish them good-bye, leaning on his stick. Helene turned back and waved her hand.

"He is unchanged," she murmured, "yet I fear that there must be trouble."

"Why? He seemed cheerful enough," her husband remarked.

She dropped her voice a little.

"Lucille is in London. She is staying at Dorset House."

X

M r. Sabin was deep in thought. He sat in an easy-chair with his back to the window, his hands crossed upon his stick, his eyes fixed upon the fire. Duson was moving noiselessly about the room, cutting the morning's supply of newspapers and setting them out upon the table. His master was in a mood which he had been taught to respect. It was Mr. Sabin who broke the silence.

"Duson!"

"Your Grace!"

"I have always, as you know, ignored your somewhat anomalous position as the servant of one man and the slave of a society. The questions which I am about to ask you you can answer or not, according to your own apprehensions of what is due to each."

"I thank your Grace!"

"My departure from America seemed to incite the most violent opposition on the part of your friends. As you know, it was with a certain amount of difficulty that I reached this country. Now, however, I am left altogether alone. I have not received a single warning letter. My comings and goings, although purposely devoid of the slightest secrecy, are absolutely undisturbed. Yet I have some reason to believe that your mistress is in London."

"Your Grace will pardon me," Duson said, "but there is outside a gentleman waiting to see you to whom you might address the same questions with better results, for compared with him I know nothing. It is Monsieur Felix."

"Why have you kept him waiting?" Mr. Sabin asked.

"Your Grace was much absorbed," Duson answered.

Felix was smoking a cigarette, and Mr. Sabin greeted him with a certain grim cordiality.

"Is this permitted—this visit?" he asked, himself selecting a cigarette and motioning his guest to a chair.

"It is even encouraged," Felix answered.

"You have perhaps some message?"

"None."

"I am glad to see you," Mr. Sabin said. "Just now I am a little puzzled. I will put the matter to you. You shall answer or not, at your own discretion."

"I am ready," Felix declared.

"You know the difficulty with which I escaped from America," Mr. Sabin continued. "Every means which ingenuity could suggest seemed brought to bear against me. And every movement was directed, if not from here, from some place in Europe. Well, I arrived here four days ago. I live quite openly, I have even abjured to some extent my incognito. Yet I have not received even a warning letter. I am left absolutely undisturbed."

Felix looked at him thoughtfully.

"And what do you deduce from this?" he asked.

"I do not like it," Mr. Sabin answered drily.

"After all," Felix remarked, "it is to some extent natural. The very openness of your life here makes interference with you more difficult, and as to warning letters—well, you have proved the uselessness of them."

"Perhaps," Mr. Sabin answered. "At the same time, if I were a superstitious person I should consider this inaction ominous."

"You must take account also," Felix said, "of the difference in the countries. In England the police system, if not the most infallible in the world, is certainly the most incorruptible. There was never a country in which security of person and life was so keenly watched over as here. In America, up to a certain point, a man is expected to look after himself. The same feeling does not prevail here."

Mr. Sabin assented.

"And therefore," he remarked, "for the purposes of your friends I should consider this a difficult and unpromising country in which to work."

"Other countries, other methods!" Felix remarked laconically.

"Exactly! It is the new methods which I am anxious to discover," Mr. Sabin said. "No glimmering of them as yet has been vouchsafed to me. Yet I believe that I am right in assuming that for the moment London is the headquarters of your friends, and that Lucille is here?"

"If that is meant for a question," Felix said, "I may not answer it."

Mr. Sabin nodded.

"Yet," he suggested, "your visit has an object. To discover my plans perhaps! You are welcome to them."

Felix thoughtfully knocked the ashes off his cigarette.

"My visit had an object," he admitted, "but it was a personal one. I am not actually concerned in the doings of those whom you have called my friends."

"We are alone," Mr. Sabin reminded him. "My time is yours."

"You and I," Felix said, "have had our periods of bitter enmity. With your marriage to Lucille these, so far as I am concerned, ended for ever. I will even admit that in my younger days I was prejudiced against you. That has passed away. You have been all your days a bold and unscrupulous schemer, but ends have at any rate been worthy ones. To-day I am able to regard you with feelings of friendliness. You are the husband of my dear sister, and for years I know that you made her very happy. I ask you, will you believe in this statement of my attitude towards you?"

"I do not for a single moment doubt it," Mr. Sabin answered.

"You will regard the advice which I am going to offer as disinterested?"

"Certainly!"

"Then I offer it to you earnestly, and with my whole heart. Take the next steamer and go back to America."

"And leave Lucille? Go without making any effort to see her?"

"Yes."

Mr. Sabin was for a moment very serious indeed. The advice given in such a manner was full of forebodings to him. The lines from the corners of his mouth seemed graven into his face.

"Felix," he said slowly, "I am sometimes conscious of the fact that I am passing into that period of life which we call old age. My ambitions are dead, my energies are weakened. For many years I have toiled—the time has come for rest. Of all the great passions which I have felt there remains but one—Lucille. Life without her is worth nothing to me. I am weary of solitude, I am weary of everything except Lucille. How then can I listen to such advice? For me it must be Lucille, or that little journey into the mists, from which one does not return."

Felix was silent. The pathos of this thing touched him.

"I will not dispute the right of those who have taken her from me," Mr. Sabin continued, "but I want her back. She is necessary to me. My purse, my life, my brains are there to be thrown into the scales. I will buy her, or fight for her, or rejoin their ranks myself. But I want her back."

Still Felix was silent. He was looking steadfastly into the fire.

"You have heard me," Mr. Sabin said.

"I have heard you," Felix answered. "My advice stands."

"I know now," Mr. Sabin said, "that I have a hard task before me. They shall have me for a friend or an enemy. I can still make myself felt as either. You have nothing more to say?"

"Nothing!"

"Then let us part company," Mr. Sabin said, "or talk of something more cheerful. You depress me, Felix. Let Duson bring us wine. You look like a death's head."

Felix roused himself.

"You will go your own way," he said. "Now that you have chosen I will tell you this. I am glad. Yes, let Duson bring wine. I will drink to your health and to your success. There have been times when men have performed miracles. I shall drink to that miracle."

Duson brought also a letter, which Mr. Sabin, with a nod towards Felix, opened. It was from Helene.

> 15 Park Lane, London,
> Thursday Morning
>
> My Dear Uncle,
>
>   "I want you to come to luncheon to-day. The Princess de Catelan is here, and I am expecting also Mr. Brott, the Home Secretary—our one great politician, you know. Many people say that he is the most interesting man in England, and must be our next Prime Minister. Such people interest you, I know. Do come.
>
> Yours sincerely,
> Helene

Mr. Sabin repeated the name to himself as he stood for a moment with the letter in his hand.

"Brott! What a name for a statesman! Well, here is your health, Felix. I do not often drink wine in the morning, but—"

He broke off in the middle of his sentence. The glass which Felix had been in the act of raising to his lips lay shattered upon the floor, and a little stream of wine trickled across the carpet. Felix himself seemed scarcely conscious of the disaster. His cheeks were white, and he leaned across the table towards Mr. Sabin.

"What name did you say—what name?"

Mr. Sabin referred again to the letter which he held in his hand.

"Brott!" he repeated. "He is Home Secretary, I believe."

"What do you know about him?"

"Nothing," Mr. Sabin answered. "My niece, the Countess of Camperdown, asks me to meet him to-day at luncheon. Explain yourself, my young friend. There is a fresh glass by your side."

Felix poured himself out a glass and drank it off. But he remained silent.

"Well?"

Felix picked up his gloves and stick.

"You are asked to meet Mr. Brott at luncheon to-day?"

"Yes."

"Are you going?"

"Certainly!"

Felix nodded.

"Very good," he said. "I should advise you to cultivate his acquaintance. He is a very extraordinary man."

"Come, Felix," Mr. Sabin said. "You owe me something more lucid in the way of explanations. Who is he?"

"A statesman—successful, ambitious. He expects to be Prime Minister."

"And what have I to do with him, or he with me?" Mr. Sabin asked quietly.

Felix shook his head.

"I cannot tell you," he said. "Yet I fancy that you and he may some time be drawn together."

Mr. Sabin asked no more questions, but he promptly sat down and accepted his niece's invitation. When he looked round Felix had gone. He rang the bell for Duson and handed him the note.

"My town clothes, Duson," he ordered. "I am lunching out."

The man bowed and withdrew. Mr. Sabin remained for a few moments in deep thought.

"Brott!" he repeated. "Brott! It is a singular name."

XI

S o this was the man! Mr. Sabin did not neglect his luncheon, nor was he ever for a moment unmindful of the grey-headed princess who chatted away by his side with all the vivacity of her race and sex. But he watched Mr. Brott.

A man this! Mr. Sabin was a judge, and he appraised him rightly. He saw through that courteous geniality of tone and gesture; the ready-made smile, although it seemed natural enough, did not deceive him. Underneath was a man of iron, square-jawed, nervous, forceful. Mr. Brott was probably at that time the ablest politician of either party in the country. Mr. Sabin knew it. He found himself wondering exactly at what point of their lives this man and he would come into contact.

After luncheon Helene brought them together.

"I believe," she said to Mr. Brott, "that you have never met my UNCLE. May I make you formally acquainted? UNCLE, this is Mr. Brott, whom you must know a great deal about even though you have been away for so long—the Duc de Souspennier."

The two men bowed and Helene passed on. Mr. Sabin leaned upon his stick and watched keenly for any sign in the other's face. If he expected to find it he was disappointed. Either this man had no knowledge of who he was, or those things which were to come between them were as yet unborn.

They strolled together after the other guests into the winter gardens, which were the envy of every hostess in London. Mr. Sabin lit a cigarette, Mr. Brott regretfully declined. He neither smoked nor drank wine. Yet he was disposed to be friendly, and selected a seat where they were a little apart from the other guests.

"You at least," he remarked, in answer to an observation of Mr. Sabin's, "are free from the tyranny of politics. I am assuming, of course, that your country under its present form of government has lost its hold upon you."

Mr. Sabin smiled.

"It is a doubtful boon," he said. "It is true that I am practically an exile. Republican France has no need of me. Had I been a soldier I could still have remained a patriot. But for one whose leanings were towards politics, neither my father before me nor I could be of service to our country. You should be thankful," he continued with a slight smile, "that you are an Englishman. No constitution in the world can offer so much to the politician who is strong enough and fearless enough."

Mr. Brott glanced towards his twinkling eyes.

"Do you happen to know what my politics are?" he asked.

Mr. Sabin hesitated.

"Your views, I know, are advanced," he said. "For the rest I have been abroad for years. I have lost touch a little with affairs in this country."

"I am afraid," Mr. Brott said, "that I shall shock you. You are an aristocrat of the aristocrats, I a democrat of the democrats. The people are the only masters whom I own. They first sent me to Parliament."

"Yet," Mr. Sabin remarked, "you are, I understand, in the Cabinet."

Mr. Brott glanced for a moment around. The Prime Minister was somewhere in the winter gardens.

"That," he declared, "is an accident. I happened to be the only man available who could do the work when Lord Kilbrooke died. I am telling you only what is an open secret. But I am afraid I am boring you. Shall we join the others?"

"Not unless you yourself are anxious to," Mr. Sabin begged. "It is scarcely fair to detain you talking to an old man when there are so many charming women here. But I should be sorry for you to think me hidebound in my prejudices. You must remember that the Revolution decimated my family. It was a long time ago, but the horror of it is still a live thing."

"Yet it was the natural outcome," Mr. Brott said, "of the things which went before. Such hideous misgovernment as generations of your countrymen had suffered was logically bound to bring its own reprisal."

"There is truth in what you say," Mr. Sabin admitted. He did not want to talk about the French Revolution.

"You are a stranger in London, are you not?" Mr. Brott asked.

"I feel myself one," Mr. Sabin answered. "I have been away for a few years, and I do not think that there is a city in the world where social changes are so rapid. I should perhaps except the cities of the country from which I have come. But then America is a universe of itself."

For an instant Mr. Brott gave signs of the man underneath. The air of polite interest had left his face. He glanced swiftly and keenly at his companion. Mr. Sabin's expression was immutable. It was he who scored, for he marked the change, whilst Mr. Brott could not be sure whether he had noticed it or not.

"You have been living in America, then?"

"For several years—yes."

"It is a country," Mr. Brott said, "which I am particularly anxious to visit. I see my chances, however, grow fewer and fewer as the years go by."

"For one like yourself," Mr. Sabin said, "whose instincts and sympathies are wholly with the democracy, a few months in America would be very well spent."

"And you," Mr. Brott remarked, "how did you get on with the people?"

Mr. Sabin traced a pattern with his stick upon the marble floor.

"I lived in the country," he said, "I played golf and read and rested."

"Were you anywhere near New York?" Mr. Brott asked.

"A few hours' journey only," Mr. Sabin answered. "My home was in a very picturesque part, near Lenox."

Mr. Brott leaned a little forward.

"You perhaps know then a lady who spent some time in that neighbourhood—a Mrs. James Peterson. Her husband was, I believe, the American consul in Vienna."

Mr. Sabin smiled very faintly. His face betrayed no more than a natural and polite interest. There was nothing to indicate the fact that his heart was beating like the heart of a young man, that the blood was rushing hot through his veins.

"Yes," he said, "I know her very well. Is she in London?"

Mr. Brott hesitated. He seemed a little uncertain how to continue.

"To tell you the truth," he said, "I believe that she has reasons for desiring her present whereabouts to remain unknown. I should perhaps not have mentioned her name at all. It was, I fancy, indiscreet of me. The coincidence of hearing you mention the name of the place where I believe she resided surprised my question. With your permission we will abandon the subject."

"You disappoint me," Mr. Sabin said quietly. "It would have given me much pleasure to have resumed my acquaintance with the lady in question."

"You will, without doubt, have an opportunity," Mr. Brott said, glancing at his watch and suddenly rising. "Dear me, how the time goes."

He rose to his feet. Mr. Sabin also rose.

"Must I understand," he said in a low tone, "that you are not at liberty to give me Mrs. Peterson's address?"

"I am not at liberty even," Mr. Brott answered, with a frown, "to mention her name. It will give me great pleasure, Duke, to better my acquaintance with you. Will you dine with me at the House of Commons one night next week?"

"I shall be charmed," Mr. Sabin answered. "My address for the next few days is at the Carlton. I am staying there under my family name of Sabin—Mr. Sabin. It is a fancy of mine—it has been ever since I became an alien—to use my title as little as possible."

Mr. Brott looked for a moment puzzled.

"Your pseudonym," he remarked thoughtfully, "seems very familiar to me."

Mr. Sabin shrugged his shoulders.

"It is a family name," he remarked, "but I flattered myself that it was at least uncommon."

"Fancy, no doubt," Mr. Brott remarked, turning to make his adieux to his hostess.

Mr. Sabin joined a fresh group of idlers under the palms. Mr. Brott lingered over his farewells.

"Your Uncle, Lady Camperdown," he said, "is delightful. I enjoy meeting new types, and he represents to me most perfectly the old order of French aristocracy."

"I am glad," Helene said, "that you found him interesting. I felt sure you would. In fact, I asked him especially to meet you."

"You are the most thoughtful of hostesses," he assured her. "By the bye, your Uncle has just told me the name by which he is known at the hotel. Mr. Sabin! Sabin! It recalls something to my mind. I cannot exactly remember what."

She smiled upon him. People generally forgot things when Helene smiled.

"It is an odd fancy of his to like his title so little," she remarked. "At heart no one is prouder of their family and antecedents. I have heard him say, though, that an exile had better leave behind him even his name."

"Sabin!" Mr. Brott repeated. "Sabin!"

"It is an old family name," she murmured.

His face suddenly cleared. She knew that he had remembered. But he took his leave with no further reference to it.

"Sabin!" he repeated to himself when alone in his carriage. "That was the name of the man who was supposed to be selling plans to the German Government. Poor Renshaw was in a terrible stew about it. Sabin! An uncommon name."

He had ordered the coachman to drive to the House of Commons. Suddenly he pulled the check-string.

"Call at Dorset House," he directed.

MR. SABIN LINGERED TILL NEARLY THE last of the guests had gone. Then he led Helene once more into the winter gardens.

"May I detain you for one moment's gossip?" he asked. "I see your carriage at the door."

She laughed.

"It is nothing," she declared. "I must drive in the Park for an hour. One sees one's friends, and it is cool and refreshing after these heated rooms. But at any time. Talk to me as long as you will, and then I will drop you at the Carlton."

"It is of Brott!" he remarked. "Ah, I thank you, I will smoke. Your husband's taste in cigarettes is excellent."

"Perhaps mine!" she laughed.

Mr. Sabin shrugged his shoulders.

"In either case I congratulate you. This man Brott. He interests me."

"He interests every one. Why not? He is a great personality."

"Politically," Mr. Sabin said, "the gauge of his success is of course the measure of the man. But he himself—what manner of a man is he?"

She tapped with her fingers upon the little table by their side.

"He is rich," she said, "and an uncommon mixture of the student and the man of society. He refuses many more invitations than he accepts, he entertains very seldom but very magnificently. He has never been known to pay marked attentions to any woman, even the scandal of the clubs has passed him by. What else can I say about him, I wonder?" she continued reflectively. "Nothing, I think, except this. He is a strong man. You know that that counts for much."

Mr. Sabin was silent. Perhaps he was measuring his strength in some imagined encounter with this man. Something in his face alarmed Helene. She suddenly leaned forward and looked at him more closely.

"UNCLE," she exclaimed in a low voice, "there is something on your mind. Do not tell me that once more you are in the maze, that again you have schemes against this country."

He smiled at her sadly enough, but she was reassured.

"You need have no fear," he told her. "With politics—I have finished. Why I am here, what I am here for I will tell you very soon. It is to find one whom I have lost—and who is dear to me. Forgive me if for to-day I say no more. Come, if you will you shall drive me to my hotel."

He offered his arm with the courtly grace which he knew so well how to assume. Together they passed out to her carriage.

XII

A fter all," Lady Carey sighed, throwing down a racing calendar
and lighting a cigarette, "London is the only thoroughly civilized
Anglo-Saxon capital in the world. Please don't look at me like that,
Duchess. I know—this is your holy of holies, but the Duke smokes
here—I've seen him. My cigarettes are very tiny and very harmless."

The Duchess, who wore gold-rimmed spectacles, and was a person
of weight in the councils of the Primrose League, went calmly on with
her knitting.

"My dear Muriel," she said, "if my approval or disapproval was of the
slightest moment to you, it is not your smoking of which I should first
complain. I know, however, that you consider yourself a privileged person.
Pray do exactly as you like, but don't drop the ashes upon the carpet."

Lady Carey laughed softly.

"I suppose I am rather a thorn in your side as a relative," she remarked.
"You must put it down to the roving blood of my ancestors. I could no
more live the life of you other women than I could fly. I must have
excitement, movement, all the time."

A tall, heavily built man, who had been reading some letters at the
other end of the room, came sauntering up to them.

"Well," he said, "you assuredly live up to your principles, for you
travel all over the world as though it were one vast playground."

"And sometimes," she remarked, "my journeys are not exactly
successful. I know that that is what you are dying to say."

"On the contrary," he said, "I do not blame you at all for this last affair.
You brought Lucille here, which was excellent. Your failure as regards
Mr. Sabin is scarcely to be fastened upon you. It is Horser whom we
hold responsible for that."

She laughed.

"Poor Horser! It was rather rough to pit a creature like that against
Souspennier."

The man shrugged his shoulders.

"Horser," he said, "may not be brilliant, but he had a great organisation
at his back. Souspennier was without friends or influence. The contest
should scarcely have been so one-sided. To tell you the truth, my dear
Muriel, I am more surprised that you yourself should have found the
task beyond you."

Lady Carey's face darkened.

"It was too soon after the loss of Lucille," she said, "and besides, there was his vanity to be reckoned with. It was like a challenge to him, and he had taken up the glove before I returned to New York."

The Duchess looked up from her work.

"Have you had any conversation with my husband, Prince?" she asked.

The Prince of Saxe Leinitzer twirled his heavy moustache and sank into a chair between the two women.

"I have had a long talk with him," he announced. "And the result?" the Duchess asked.

"The result I fear you would scarcely consider satisfactory," the Prince declared. "The moment that I hinted at the existence of—er—conditions of which you, Duchess, are aware, he showed alarm, and I had all that I could do to reassure him. I find it everywhere amongst your aristocracy—this stubborn confidence in the existence of the reigning order of things, this absolute detestation of anything approaching intrigue."

"My dear man, I hope you don't include me," Lady Carey exclaimed.

"You, Lady Muriel," he answered, with a slow smile, "are an exception to all rules. No, you are a rule by yourself."

"To revert to the subject then for a moment," the Duchess said stiffly. "You have made no progress with the Duke?"

"None whatever," Saxe Leinitzer admitted. "He was sufficiently emphatic to inspire me with every caution. Even now I have doubts as to whether I have altogether reassured him. I really believe, dear Duchess, that we should be better off if you could persuade him to go and live upon his estates."

The Duchess smiled grimly.

"Whilst the House of Lords exists," she remarked, "you will never succeed in keeping Algernon away from London. He is always on the point of making a speech, although he never does it."

"I have heard of that speech," Lady Carey drawled, from her low seat. "It is to be a thoroughly enlightening affair. All the great social questions are to be permanently disposed of. The Prime Minister will come on his knees and beg Algernon to take his place."

The Duchess looked up over her knitting.

"Algernon is at least in earnest," she remarked drily. "And he has the good conscience of a clean living and honest man."

E. PHILLIPS OPPENHEIM

"What an unpleasant possession it must be," Lady Carey remarked sweetly. "I disposed of my conscience finally many years ago. I am not sure, but I believe that it was the Prince to whom I entrusted the burying of it. By the bye, Lucille will be here directly, I suppose. Is she to be told of Souspennier's arrival in London?"

"I imagine," the Prince said, with knitted brows, "that it will not be wise to keep it from her. It is impossible to conceal her whereabouts, and the papers will very shortly acquaint her with his."

"And," Lady Carey asked, "how does the little affair progress?"

"Admirably," the Prince answered. "Already some of the Society papers are beginning to chatter about the friendship existing between a Cabinet Minister and a beautiful Hungarian lady of title, etc., etc. The fact of it is that Brott is in deadly earnest. He gives himself away every time. If Lucille has not lost old cleverness she will be able to twist him presently around her little finger."

"If only some one would twist him on the rack," the Duchess murmured vindictively. "I tried to read one of his speeches the other day. It was nothing more nor less than blasphemy. I do not think that I am naturally a cruel woman, but I would hand such men over to the public executioner with joy."

Lucille came in, as beautiful as ever, but with tired lines under her full dark eyes. She sank into a low chair with listless grace.

"Reginald Brott again, I suppose," she remarked curtly. "I wish the man had never existed."

"That is a very cruel speech, Lucille," the Prince said, with a languishing glance towards her, "for if it had not been for Brott we should never have dared to call you out from your seclusion."

"Then more heartily than ever," Lucille declared, "I wish the man had never been born. You cannot possibly flatter yourself, Prince, that your summons was a welcome one."

He shrugged his shoulders.

"I shall never, be able to believe," he said, "that the Countess Radantz was able to do more than support existence in a small American town—without society, with no scope for her ambitions, detached altogether from the whole civilized world."

"Which only goes to prove, Prince," Lucille remarked contemptuously, "that you do not understand me in the least. As a place of residence Lenox would compare very favourably with—say Homburg, and for companionship you forget my husband. I never met the woman yet who did not prefer the company of one man, if only it were the right one, to the cosmopolitan throng we call society."

"It sounds idyllic, but very gauche," Lady Carey remarked drily. "In effect it is rather a blow on the cheek for you, Prince. Of course you know that the Prince is in love with you, Lucille?"

"I wish he were," she answered, looking lazily out of the window.

He bent over her.

"Why?"

"I would persuade him to send me home again," she answered coldly.

The Duchess looked up from her knitting. "Your husband has saved you the journey," she remarked, "even if you were able to work upon the Prince's good nature to such an extent."

Lucille started round eagerly.

"What do you mean?" she cried.

"Your husband is in London," the Duchess answered.

Lucille laughed with the gaiety of a child. Like magic the lines from beneath her eyes seemed to have vanished. Lady Carey watched her with pale cheeks and malevolent expression.

"Come, Prince," she cried mockingly, "it was only a week ago that you assured me that my husband could not leave America. Already he is in London. I must go to see him. Oh, I insist upon it."

Saxe Leinitzer glanced towards the Duchess. She laid down her knitting.

"My dear Countess," she said firmly, "I beg that you will listen to me carefully. I speak to you for your own good, and I believe I may add, Prince, that I speak with authority."

"With authority!" the Prince echoed.

"We all," the Duchess continued, "look upon your husband's arrival as inopportune and unfortunate. We are all agreed that you must be kept apart. Certain obligations have been laid upon you. You could not possibly fulfil them with a husband at your elbow. The matter will be put plainly before your husband, as I am now putting it before you. He will be warned not to attempt to see or communicate with you as your husband. If he or you disobey the consequences will be serious."

Lucille shrugged her shoulders.

"It is easy to talk," she said, "but you will not find it easy to keep Victor away when he has found out where I am."

The Prince intervened.

"We have no objection to your meeting," he said, "but it must be as acquaintances. There must be no intermission or slackening in your task, and that can only be properly carried out by the Countess Radantz and from Dorset House."

Lucille smothered her disappointment.

"Dear me," she said. "You will find Victor a little hard to persuade."

There was a moment's silence. Then the Prince spoke slowly, and watching carefully the effect of his words upon Lucille.

"Countess," he said, "it has been our pleasure to make of your task so far as possible a holiday. Yet perhaps it is wiser to remind you that underneath the glove is an iron hand. We do not often threaten, but we brook no interference. We have the means to thwart it. I bear no ill-will to your husband, but to you I say this. If he should be so mad as to defy us, to incite you to disobedience, he must pay the penalty."

A servant entered.

"Mr. Reginald Brott is in the small drawing-room, your Grace," he announced. "He enquired for the Countess Radantz."

Lucille rose. When the servant had disappeared she turned round for a moment, and faced the Prince. A spot of colour burned in her cheeks, her eyes were bright with anger.

"I shall remember your words, Prince," she said. "So far from mine being, however, a holiday task, it is one of the most wearisome and unpleasant I ever undertook. And in return for your warnings let me tell you this. If you should bring any harm upon my husband you shall answer for it all your days to me. I will do my duty. Be careful that you do not exceed yours."

She swept out of the room. Lady Carey laughed mockingly at the Prince.

"Poor Ferdinand!" she exclaimed.

XIII

He had been kept waiting longer than usual, and he had somehow the feeling that his visit was ill-timed, when at last she came to him. He looked up eagerly as she entered the little reception room which he had grown to know so well during the last few weeks, and it struck him for the first time that her welcome was a little forced, her eyes a little weary.

"I haven't," he said apologetically, "the least right to be here."

"At least," she murmured, "I may be permitted to remind you that you are here without an invitation."

"The worse luck," he said, "that one should be necessary."

"This is the one hour of the day," she remarked, sinking into a large easy-chair, "which I devote to repose. How shall I preserve my fleeting youth if you break in upon it in this ruthless manner?"

"If I could only truthfully say that I was sorry," he answered, "but I can't. I am here—and I would rather be here than anywhere else in the world."

She looked at him with curving lips; and even he, who had watched her often, could not tell whether that curve was of scorn or mirth.

"They told me," she said impressively, "that you were different—a woman-hater, honest, gruff, a little cynical. Yet those are the speeches of your salad days. What a disenchantment!"

"The things which one invents when one is young," he said, "come perhaps fresh from the heart in later life. The words may sound the same, but there is a difference."

"Come," she said, "you are improving. That at any rate is ingenious. Suppose you tell me now what has brought you here before four o'clock, when I am not fit to be seen?"

He smiled. She shrugged her shoulders.

"I mean it. I haven't either my clothes or my manners on yet. Come, explain."

"I met a man who interested me," he answered. "He comes from America, from Lenox!"

He saw her whiten. He saw her fingers clutch the sides of her chair.

"From Lenox? And his name?"

"The Duke of Souspennier! He takes himself so seriously that he even travels incognito. At the hotel he calls himself Mr. Sabin."

"Indeed!"

"I wondered whether you might not know him?"

"Yes, I know him."

"And in connection with this man," Brott continued, "I have something in the nature of a confession to make. I forgot for a moment your request. I even mentioned your name."

The pallor had spread to her cheeks, even to her lips. Yet her eyes were soft and brilliant, so brilliant that they fascinated him.

"What did he say? What did he ask?"

"He asked for your address. Don't be afraid. I made some excuse. I did not give it."

For the life of him he could not tell whether she was pleased or disappointed. She had turned her shoulder to him. She was looking steadily out of the window, and he could not see her face.

"Why are you curious about him?" she asked.

"I wish I knew. I think only because he came from Lenox."

She turned her face slowly round towards him. He was astonished to see the dark rings under her eyes, the weariness of her smile.

"The Duke of Souspennier," she said slowly, "is an old and a dear friend of mine. When you tell me that he is in London I am anxious because there are many here who are not his friends—who have no cause to love him."

"I was wrong then," he said, "not to give him your address."

"You were right," she answered. "I am anxious that he should not know it. You will remember this?" He rose and bowed over her hand.

"This has been a selfish interlude," he said. "I have destroyed your rest, and I almost fear that I have also disturbed your peace of mind. Let me take my leave and pray that you may recover both."

She shook her head.

"Do not leave me," she said. "I am low-spirited. You shall stay and cheer me."

There was a light in his eyes which few people would have recognised. She rose with a little laugh and stood leaning towards the fire, her elbow upon the broad mantel, tall, graceful, alluring. Her soft crimson gown, with its wealth of old lace, fell around her in lines and curves full of grace. The pallor of her face was gone now—the warmth of the fire burned her cheeks. Her voice became softer.

"Sit down and talk to me," she murmured. "Do you remember the old days, when you were a very timid young secretary of Sir George

Nomsom, and I was a maid-of-honour at the Viennese Court? Dear me, how you have changed!"

"Time," he said, "will not stand still for all of us. Yet my memory tells me how possible it would be—for indeed those days seem but as yesterday."

He looked up at her with a sudden jealousy. His tone shook with passion. No one would have recognised Brott now. In his fiercest hour of debate, his hour of greatest trial, he had worn his mask, always master of himself and his speech. And now he had cast it off. His eyes were hungry, his lips twitched.

"As yesterday! Lucille, I could kill you when I think of those days. For twenty years your kiss has lain upon my lips—and you—with you—it has been different."

She laughed softly upon him, laughed more with her eyes than with her lips. She watched him curiously.

"Dear me!" she murmured, "what would you have? I am a woman—I have been a woman all my days, and the memory of one kiss grows cold. So I will admit that with me—it has been different. Come! What then?"

He groaned.

"I wonder," he said, "what miserable fate, what cursed stroke of fortune brought you once more into my life?"

She threw her head back and laughed at him, this time heartily, unaffectedly.

"What adorable candour!" she exclaimed. "My dear friend, how amiable you are."

He looked at her steadfastly, and somehow the laugh died away from her lips.

"Lucille, will you marry me?"

"Marry you? I? Certainly not."

"And why not?"

"For a score of reasons, if you want them," she answered. "First, because I think it is delightful to have you for a friend. I can never quite tell what you are going to do or say. As a husband I am almost sure that you would be monotonous. But then, how could you avoid it? It is madness to think of destroying a pleasant friendship in such a manner."

"You are mocking me," he said sadly.

"Well," she said, "why not? Your own proposal is a mockery."

"A mockery! My proposal!"

"Yes," she answered steadily. "You know quite well that the very thought of such a thing between you and me is an absurdity. I abhor your politics, I detest your party. You are ambitious, I know. You intend to be Prime Minister, a people's Prime Minister. Well, for my part, I hate the people. I am an aristocrat. As your wife I should be in a perfectly ridiculous position. How foolish! You have led me into talking of this thing seriously. Let us forget all this rubbish."

He stood before her—waiting patiently, his mouth close set, his manner dogged with purpose.

"It is not rubbish," he said. "It is true that I shall be Prime Minister. It is true also that you will be my wife."

She shrank back from him—uneasily. The fire in his eyes, the ring in his tone distressed her.

"As for my politics, you do not understand them. But you shall! I will convert you to my way of thinking. Yes, I will do that. The cause of the people, of freedom, is the one great impulse which beats through all the world. You too shall hear it."

"Thank you," she said. "I have no wish to hear it. I do not believe in what you call freedom for the people. I have discovered in America how uncomfortable a people's country can be."

"Yet you married an American. You call yourself still the Countess Radantz. . . but you married Mr. James B. Peterson!"

"It is true, my friend," she answered. "But the American in question was a person of culture and intelligence, and at heart he was no more a democrat than I am. Further, I am an extravagant woman, and he was a millionaire."

"And you, after his death, without necessity—went to bury yourself in his country."

"Why not?"

"I am jealous of every year of your life which lies hidden from me," he said slowly.

"Dear me—how uncomfortable!"

"Before you—reappeared," he said, "I had learnt, yes I had learnt to do without you. I had sealed up the one chapter of my life which had in it anything to do with sentiment. Your coming has altered all that. You have disturbed the focus of my ambitions. Lucille! I have loved you for more than half a lifetime. Isn't it time I had my reward?"

He took a quick step towards her. In his tone was the ring of mastery, the light in his eyes was compelling. She shrank back, but he seized one of her hands. It lay between his, a cold dead thing.

"What have my politics to do with it?" he asked fiercely. "You are not an Englishwoman. Be content that I shall set you far above these gods of my later life. There is my work to be done, and I shall do it. Let me be judge of these things. Believe me that it is a great work. If you are ambitious—give your ambitions into my keeping, and I will gratify them. Only I cannot bear this suspense-these changing moods. Marry me-now at once, or send me back to the old life."

She drew her fingers away, and sank down into her easy-chair. Her head was buried in her hands. Was she thinking or weeping? He could not decide. While he hesitated she looked up, and he saw that there was no trace of tears upon her face.

"You are too masterful," she said gently. "I will not marry you. I will not give myself body and soul to any man. Yet that is what you ask. I am not a girl. My opinions are as dear to me in their way as yours are to you. You want me to close my eyes while you drop sugar plums into my mouth. That is not my idea of life. I think that you had better go away. Let us forget these things."

"Very well," he answered. "It shall be as you say." He did not wait for her to ring, nor did he attempt any sort of farewell. He simply took up his hat, and before she could realise his intention he had left the room. Lucille sat quite still, looking into the fire.

"If only," she murmured, "if only this were the end."

XIV .

D uson entered the sitting-room, noiseless as ever, with pale, passionless face, the absolute prototype of the perfect French servant, to whom any expression of vigorous life seems to savour of presumption. He carried a small silver salver, on which reposed a card.

"The gentleman is in the ante-room, sir," he announced.

Mr. Sabin took up the card and studied it.

"Lord Robert Foulkes."

"Do I know this gentleman, Duson?" Mr. Sabin asked.

"Not to my knowledge, sir," the man answered.

"You must show him in," Mr. Sabin said, with a sigh. "In this country one must never be rude to a lord."

Duson obeyed. Lord Robert Foulkes was a small young man, very carefully groomed, nondescript in appearance. He smiled pleasantly at Mr. Sabin and drew off his gloves.

"How do you do, Mr. Sabin?" he said. "Don't remember me, I daresay. Met you once or twice last time you were in London. I wish I could say that I was glad to see you here again."

Mr. Sabin's forehead lost its wrinkle. He knew where he was now.

"Sit down, Lord Robert," he begged. "I do not remember you, it is true, but I am getting an old man. My memory sometimes plays me strange tricks."

The young man looked at Mr. Sabin and laughed softly. Indeed, Mr. Sabin had very little the appearance of an old man. He was leaning with both hands clasped upon his stick, his face alert, his eyes bright and searching.

"You carry your years well, Mr. Sabin. Yet while we are on the subject, do you know that London is the unhealthiest city in the world?"

"I am always remarkably well here," Mr. Sabin said drily.

"London has changed since your last visit," Lord Robert said, with a gentle smile. "Believe me if I say—as your sincere well-wisher—that there is something in the air at present positively unwholesome to you. I am not sure that unwholesome is not too weak a word."

"Is this official?" Mr. Sabin asked quietly.

The young man fingered the gold chain which disappeared in his trousers pocket.

"Need I introduce myself?" he asked.

"Quite unnecessary," Mr. Sabin assured him. "Permit me to reflect for a few minutes. Your visit comes upon me as a surprise. Will you smoke? There are cigarettes at your elbow."

"I am entirely at your service," Lord Robert answered. "Thanks, I will try one of your cigarettes. You were always famous for your tobacco."

There was a short silence. Mr. Sabin had seldom found it more difficult to see the way before him.

"I imagined," he said at last, "from several little incidents which occurred previous to my leaving New York that my presence here was regarded as superfluous. Do you know, I believe that I could convince you to the contrary."

Lord Robert raised his eyebrows.

"Mr. dear Mr. Sabin," he said, "pray reflect. I am a messenger. No more! A hired commissionaire!"

Mr. Sabin bowed.

"You are an ambassador!" he said.

The young man shook his head.

"You magnify my position," he declared. "My errand is done when I remind you that it is many years since you visited Paris, that Vienna is as fascinating a city as ever, and Pesth a few hours journey beyond. But London—no, London is not possible for you. After the seventh day from this London would be worse than impossible."

Mr. Sabin smoked thoughtfully for a few moments.

"Lord Robert," he said, "I have, I believe, the right of a personal appeal. I desire to make it."

Lord Robert looked positively distressed.

"My dear sir," he said, "the right of appeal, any right of any sort, belongs only to those within the circle."

"Exactly," Mr. Sabin agreed. "I claim to belong there."

Lord Roberts shrugged his shoulders.

"You force me to remind you," he said, "of a certain decree—a decree of expulsion passed five years ago, and of which I presume due notification was given to you."

Mr. Sabin shook his head very slowly.

"I deny the legality of that decree," he said. "There can be no such thing as expulsion."

"There was Lefanu," Lord Robert murmured.

"He died," Mr. Sabin answered. "That was reasonable enough."

"Your services had been great," Lord Robert said, "and your fault was but venial."

"Nevertheless," Mr. Sabin said, "the one was logical, the other is not."

"You claim, then," the young man said, "to be still within the circle?"

"Certainly!"

"You are aware that this is a very dangerous claim?"

Mr. Sabin smiled, but he said nothing. Lord Robert hastened to excuse himself.

"I beg your pardon," he said. "I should have known better than to have used such a word to you. Permit me to take my leave."

Mr. Sabin rose.

"I thank you, sir," he said, "for the courteous manner in which you have discharged your mission."

Lord Robert bowed.

"My good wishes," he said, "are yours."

Mr. Sabin when alone called Duson to him.

"Have you any report to make, Duson?" he asked.

"None, sir!"

Mr. Sabin dismissed him impatiently.

"After all, I am getting old. He is young and he is strong—a worthy antagonist. Come, let us see what this little volume has to say about him."

He turned over the pages rapidly and read aloud.

"Reginald Cyril Brott, born 18—, son of John Reginald Brott, Esq., of Manchester. Educated at Harrow and Merton College, Cambridge, M.A., LL.D., and winner of the Rudlock History Prize. Also tenth wrangler. Entered the diplomatic service on leaving college, and served as junior attache at Vienna."

Mr. Sabin laid down the volume, and made a little calculation. At the end of it he had made a discovery. His face was very white and set.

"I was at Petersburg," he muttered. "Now I think of it, I heard something of a young English attache. But—"

He touched the bell.

"Duson, a carriage!"

At Camperdown House he learned that Helene was out—shopping, the hall porter believed. Mr. Sabin drove slowly down Bond Street, and was rewarded by seeing her brougham outside a famous milliner's. He waited for her upon the pavement. Presently she came out and smiled her greetings upon him.

"You were waiting for me?" she asked.

"I saw your carriage."

"How delightful of you. Let me take you back to luncheon."

He shook his head.

"I am afraid," he said, "that I should be poor company. May I drive home with you, at any rate, when you have finished?"

"Of course you may, and for luncheon we shall be quite alone, unless somebody drops in."

He took his seat beside her in the carriage. "Helene," he said, "I am interested in Mr. Brott. No, don't look at me like that. You need have no fear. My interest is in him as a man, and not as a politician. The other days are over and done with now. I am on the defensive and hard pressed."

Her face was bright with sympathy. She forgot everything except her old admiration for him. In the clashing of their wills the victory had remained with her. And as for those things which he had done, the cause at least had been a great one. Her happiness had come to her through him. She bore him no grudge for that fierce opposition which, after all, had been fruitless.

"I believe you, Uncle," she said affectionately. "If I can help you in any way I will."

"This Mr. Brott! He goes very little into society, I believe."

"Scarcely ever," she answered. "He came to us because my husband is one of the few Radical peers."

"You have not heard of any recent change in him—in this respect?"

"Well, I did hear Wolfendon chaffing him the other day about somebody," she said. "Oh, I know. He has been going often to the Duchess of Dorset's. He is such an ultra Radical, you know, and the Dorsets are fierce Tories. Wolfendon says it is a most unwise thing for a good Radical who wants to retain the confidence of the people to be seen about with a Duchess."

"The Duchess of Dorset," Mr. Sabin remarked, "must be, well—a middle-aged woman."

Helene laughed.

"She is sixty if she is a day. But I daresay she herself is not the attraction. There is a very beautiful woman staying with her—the Countess Radantz. A Hungarian, I believe."

Mr. Sabin sat quite still. His face was turned away from Helene. She herself was smiling out of the window at some acquaintances.

"I wonder if there is anything more that I can tell you?" she asked presently.

He turned towards her with a faint smile.

"You have told me," he said, "all that I want to know."

She was struck by the change in his face, the quietness of his tone was ominous.

"Am I meant to understand?" she said dubiously "because I don't in the least. It seems to me that have told you nothing. I cannot imagine what Mr. Brott and you have in common."

"If your invitation to lunch still holds good," he said, "may I accept it? Afterwards, if you can spare me a few minutes I will make things quite clear to you."

She laughed.

"You will find," she declared, "that I shall leave you little peace for luncheon. I am consumed with curiosity."

XV

Nevertheless, Mr. Sabin lunched with discretion, as usual, but with no lack of appetite. It chanced that they were alone. Lord Camperdown was down in the Midlands for a day's hunting, and Helene had ensured their seclusion from any one who might drop in by a whispered word to the hall porter as they passed into the house. It seemed to her that she had never found Mr. Sabin more entertaining, had never more appreciated his rare gift of effortless and anecdotal conversation. What a marvelous memory! He knew something of every country from the inside. He had been brought at various times during his long diplomatic career into contact with most of the interesting people in the world. He knew well how to separate the grain from the chaff according to the tastes of his listener. The pathos of his present position appealed to her irresistibly. The possibilities of his life had been so great, fortune had treated him always so strangely. The greatest of his schemes had come so near to success, the luck had turned against him only at the very moment of fruition. Helene felt very kindly towards her Uncle as she led him, after luncheon, to a quiet corner of the winter garden, where a servant had already arranged a table with coffee and liqueurs and cigarettes. Unscrupulous all his life, there had been an element of greatness in all his schemes. Even his failures had been magnificent, for his successes he himself had seldom reaped the reward. And now in the autumn of his days she felt dimly that he was threatened with some evil thing against which he stood at bay single-handed, likely perhaps to be overpowered. For there was something in his face just now which was strange to her.

"Helene," he said quietly, "I suppose that you, who knew nothing of me till you left school, have looked upon me always as a selfish, passionless creature—a weaver of plots, perhaps sometimes a dreamer of dreams, but a person wholly self-centred, always self-engrossed?"

She shook her head.

"Not selfish!" she objected. "No, I never thought that. It is the wrong word."

"At least," he said, "you will be surprised to hear that I have loved one woman all my life."

She looked at him half doubtfully.

"Yes," she said, "I am surprised to hear that."

"I will surprise you still more. I was married to her in America within a month of my arrival there. We have lived together ever since. And I have been very happy. I speak, of course, of Lucille!"

"It is amazing," she murmured. "You must tell me all about it."

"Not all," he answered sadly. "Only this. I met her first at Vienna when I was thirty-five, and she was eighteen. I treated her shamefully. Marriage seemed to me, with all my dreams of great achievements, an act of madness. I believed in myself and my career. I believed that it was my destiny to restore the monarchy to our beloved country. And I wanted to be free. I think that I saw myself a second Napoleon. So I won her love, took all that she had to give, and returned nothing.

"In the course of years she married the son of the American Consul at Vienna. I was obliged, by the bye, to fight her brother, and he carried his enmity to me through life. I saw her sometimes in the course of years. She was always beautiful, always surrounded by a host of admirers, always cold. When the end of my great plans here came, and I myself was a fugitive, her brother found me out. He gave me a letter to deliver in America. I delivered it—to his sister.

"She was as beautiful as ever, and alone in the world. It seemed to me that I realised then how great my folly had been. For always I had loved her, always there had been that jealously locked little chamber in my life. Helene, she pointed no finger of scorn to my broken life. She uttered no reproaches. She took me as I was, and for three years our life together has been to me one long unbroken harmony. Our tastes were very similar. She was well read, receptive, a charming companion. Ennui was a word of which I have forgotten the meaning. And it seemed so with her, too, for she grew younger and more beautiful."

"And why is she not with you?" Helene cried. "I must go and see her. How delightful it sounds!"

"One day, about three months ago," Mr. Sabin continued, "she left me to go to New York for two days. Her milliner in Paris had sent over, and twice a year Lucille used to buy clothes. I had sometimes accompanied her, but she knew how I detested New York, and this time she did not press me to go. She left me in the highest spirits, as tender and gracefully affectionate as ever. She never returned."

Helene started in her chair.

"Oh, UNCLE!" she cried.

"I have never seen her since," he repeated.

"Have you no clue? She could not have left you willingly. Have you no idea where she is?"

He bowed his head slowly.

"Yes," he said, "I know where she is. She came to Europe with Lady Carey. She is staying with the Duchess of Dorset."

"The Countess Radantz?" Helene cried.

"It was her maiden name," he answered.

There was a moment's silence. Helene was bewildered.

"Then you have seen her?"

He shook his head slowly.

"No. I did not even know where she was until you told me."

"But why do you wait a single moment?" she asked. "There must be some explanation. Let me order a carriage now. I will drive round to Dorset House with you."

She half rose. He held out his hand and checked her.

"There are other things to be explained," he said quickly. "Sit down, Helene."

She obeyed him, mystified.

"For your own sake," he continued, "there are certain facts in connection with this matter which I must withhold. All I can tell you is this. There are people who have acquired a hold upon Lucille so great that she is forced to obey their bidding. Lady Carey is one, the Duchess of Dorset is another. They are no friends of mine, and apparently Lucille has been taken away from me by them."

"A—a hold upon her?" Helene repeated vaguely.

"It is all I can tell you. You must suppose an extreme case. You may take my word for it that under certain circumstances Lucille would have no power to deny them anything."

"But—without a word of farewell. They could not insist upon her leaving you like that! It is incredible!"

"It is quite possible," Mr. Sabin said.

Helene caught herself looking at him stealthily. Was it possible that this wonderful brain had given way at last? There were no signs of it in his face or expression. But the Duchess of Dorset! Lady Carey! These were women of her own circle—Londoners, and the Duchess, at any rate, a woman of the very highest social position and unimpeached conventionality.

"This sounds—very extraordinary, Uncle!" she remarked a little lamely.

"It is extraordinary," he answered drily. "I do not wonder that you find it hard to believe me. I—"

"Not to believe—to understand!"

He smiled.

"We will not distinguish! After all, what does it matter? Assume, if you cannot believe, that Lucille's leaving me may have been at the instigation of these people, and therefore involuntary. If this be so I have hard battle to fight to win her back, but in the end I shall do it."

She nodded sympathetically.

"I am sure," she said, "that you will not find it difficult. Tell me, cannot I help you in any way? I know the Duchess very well indeed— well enough to take you to call quite informally if you please. She is a great supporter of what they call the Primrose League here. I do not understand what it is all about, but it seems that I may not join because my husband is a Radical."

Mr. Sabin looked for a moment over his clasped hands through the faint blue cloud of cigarette smoke, and sundry possibilities flashed through his mind to be at once rejected. He shook his head.

"No!" he said firmly. "I do not wish for your help at present, directly or indirectly. If you meet the Countess I would rather that you did not mention my name. There is only one person whom, if you met at Dorset House or anywhere where Lucille is, I would ask you to watch. That is Mr. Brott!"

It was to be a conversation full of surprises for Helene. Mr. Brott! Her hand went up to her forehead for a moment, and a little gesture of bewilderment escaped her.

"Will you tell me," she asked almost plaintively, "what on earth Mr. Brott can have to do with this business—with Lucille—with you— with any one connected with it?"

Mr. Sabin shrugged his shoulders.

"Mr. Brott," he remarked, "a Cabinet Minister of marked Radical proclivities, has lately been a frequent visitor at Dorset House, which is the very home of the old aristocratic Toryism. Mr. Brott was acquainted with Lucille many years ago—in Vienna. At that time he was, I believe, deeply interested in her. I must confess that Mr. Brott causes me some uneasiness."

"I think—that men always know," Helene said, "if they care to. Was Lucille happy with you?"

"Absolutely. I am sure of it."

"Then your first assumption must be correct," she declared. "You cannot explain things to me, so I cannot help you even with my advice. I am sorry."

He turned his head towards her and regarded her critically, as though making some test of her sincerity.

"Helene," he said gravely, "it is for your own sake that I do not explain further, that I do not make things clearer to you. Only I wanted you to understand why I once more set foot in Europe. I wanted you to understand why I am here. It is to win back Lucille. It is like that with me, Helene. I, who once schemed and plotted for an empire, am once more a schemer and a worker, but for no other purpose than to recover possession of the woman whom I love. You do not recognise me, Helene. I do not recognise myself. Nevertheless, I would have you know the truth. I am here for that, and for no other purpose."

He rose slowly to his feet. She held out both her hands and grasped his.

"Let me help you," she begged. "Do! This is not a matter of politics or anything compromising. I am sure that I could be useful to you."

"So you can," he answered quietly. "Do as I have asked you. Watch Mr. Brott!"

XVI

M r. Brott and Mr. Sabin dined together—not, as it happened, at the House of Commons, but at the former's club in Pall Mall. For Mr. Sabin it was not altogether an enjoyable meal. The club was large, gloomy and political; the cooking was exactly of that order which such surroundings seemed to require. Nor was Mr. Brott a particularly brilliant host. Yet his guest derived a certain amount of pleasure from the entertainment, owing to Brott's constant endeavours to bring the conversation round to Lucille.

"I find," he said, as they lit their cigarettes, "that I committed an indiscretion the other day at Camperdown House!"

Mr. Sabin assumed the puzzled air of one endeavouring to pin down an elusive memory.

"Let me see," he murmured doubtfully. "It was in connection with—"

"The Countess Radantz. If you remember, I told you that it was her desire just now to remain incognito. I, however, unfortunately forgot this during the course of our conversation."

"Yes, I remember. You told me where she was staying. But the Countess and I are old acquaintances. I feel sure that she did not object to your having given me her address. I could not possibly leave London without calling upon her."

Mr. Brott moved in his chair uneasily.

"It seems presumption on my part to make such a suggestion perhaps," he said slowly, "but I really believe that the Countess is in earnest with reference to her desire for seclusion just at present. I believe that she is really very anxious that her presence in London, just now should not be generally known."

"I am such a very old friend," Mr. Sabin said. "I knew her when she was a child."

Mr. Brott nodded.

"It is very strange," he said, "that you should have come together again in such a country as America, and in a small town too."

"Lenox," Mr. Sabin said, "is a small place, but a great center. By the bye, is there not some question of an impending marriage on the part of the Countess?"

"I have heard—of nothing of the sort," Mr. Brott said, looking up startled. Then, after a moment's pause, during which he studied closely his companion's imperturbable face, he added the question which forced its way to his lips.

"Have you?"

Mr. Sabin looked along his cigarette and pinched it affectionately. It was one of his own, which he had dexterously substituted for those which his host had placed at his disposal.

"The Countess is a very charming, a very beautiful, and a most attractive woman," he said slowly. "Her marriage has always seemed to me a matter of certainty."

Mr. Brott hesitated, and was lost.

"You are an old friend of hers," he said. "You perhaps know more of her recent history than I do. For a time she seemed to drop out of my life altogether. Now that she has come back I am very anxious to persuade her to marry me."

A single lightning-like flash in Mr. Sabin's eyes for a moment disconcerted his host. But, after all, it was gone with such amazing suddenness that it left behind it a sense of unreality. Mr. Brott decided that after all it must have been fancy.

"May I ask," Mr. Sabin said quietly, "whether the Countess appears to receive your suit with favour?"

Mr. Brott hesitated.

"I am afraid I cannot go so far as to say that she does," he said regretfully. "I do not know why I find myself talking on this matter to you. I feel that I should apologise for giving such a personal turn to the conversation."

"I beg that you will do nothing of the sort," Mr. Sabin protested. "I am, as a matter of fact, most deeply interested."

"You encourage me," Mr. Brott declared, "to ask you a question—to me a very important question."

"It will give me great pleasure," Mr. Sabin assured him, "if I am able to answer it."

"You know," Mr. Brott said, "of that portion of her life concerning which I have asked no questions, but which somehow, whenever I think of it, fills me with a certain amount of uneasiness. I refer to the last three years which the Countess has spent in America."

Mr. Sabin looked up, and his lips seemed to move, but he said nothing. Mr. Brott felt perhaps that he was on difficult ground.

"I recognise the fact," he continued slowly, "that you are the friend of the Countess, and that you and I are nothing more than the merest acquaintances. I ask my question therefore with some diffidence. Can you tell me from your recent, more intimate knowledge of the Countess and her affairs, whether there exists any reason outside her own inclinations why she should not accept my proposals of marriage?"

Mr. Sabin had the air of a man gravely surprised. He shook his head very slightly.

"You must not ask me such a question as that, Mr. Brott," he said. "It is not a subject which I could possibly discuss with you. But I have no objection to going so far as this. My experience of the Countess is that she is a woman of magnificent and effective will power. I think if she has any desire to marry you there are or could be no obstacles existing which she would not easily dispose of."

"There are obstacles, then?"

"You must not ask me that," Mr. Sabin said, with a certain amount of stiffness. "The Countess is a very dear friend of mine, and you must forgive me now if I say that I prefer not to discuss her any longer."

A hall servant entered the room, bearing a note for Mr. Brott. He received it at first carelessly, but his expression changed the moment he saw the superscription. He turned a little away, and Mr. Sabin noticed that the fingers which tore open the envelope were trembling. The note seemed short enough, but he must have read it half a dozen times before at last he turned round to the messenger.

"There is no answer," he said in a low tone.

He folded the note and put it carefully into his breast pocket. Mr. Sabin subdued an insane desire to struggle with him and discover, by force, if necessary, who was the sender of those few brief lines. For Mr. Brott was a changed man.

"I am afraid," he said, turning to his guest, "that this has been a very dull evening for you. To tell you the truth, this club is not exactly the haunt of pleasure-seekers. It generally oppresses me for the first hour or so. Would you like a hand at bridge, or a game of billiards? I am wholly at your service—until twelve o'clock."

Mr. Sabin glanced at the clock.

"You are very good," he said, "but I was never much good at indoor games. Golf has been my only relaxation for many years. Besides, I too have an engagement for which I must leave in a very few minutes."

"It is very good of you," Mr. Brott said, "to have given me the pleasure of your company. I have the greatest possible admiration for your niece,

Mr. Sabin, and Camperdown is a thundering good fellow. He will be our leader in the House of Lords before many years have passed."

"He is, I believe," Mr. Sabin remarked, "of the same politics as yourself."

"We are both," Mr. Brott answered, with a smile, "I am afraid outside the pale of your consideration in this respect. We are both Radicals."

Mr. Sabin lit another cigarette and glanced once more at the clock.

"A Radical peer!" he remarked. "Isn't that rather an anomaly? The principles of Radicalism and aristocracy seem so divergent."

"Yet," Mr. Brott said, "they are not wholly irreconcilable. I have often wished that this could be more generally understood. I find myself at times very unpopular with people, whose good opinion I am anxious to retain, simply owing to this too general misapprehension."

Mr. Sabin smiled gently.

"You were referring without doubt—" he began.

"To the Countess," Brott admitted. "Yes, it is true. But after all," he added cheerfully, "I believe that our disagreements are mainly upon the surface. The Countess is a woman of wide culture and understanding. Her mind, too, is plastic. She has few prejudices."

Mr. Sabin glanced at the clock for the third time, and rose to his feet. He was quite sure now that the note was from her. He leaned on his stick and took his leave quietly. All the time he was studying his host, wondering at his air of only partially suppressed excitement.

"I must thank you very much, Mr. Brott," he said, "for your entertainment. I trust that you will give me an opportunity shortly of reciprocating your hospitality."

The two men parted finally in the hall. Mr. Sabin stepped into his hired carriage.

"Dorset House!" he directed.

E. PHILLIPS OPPENHEIM

XVII

"This little difference of opinion," the Prince remarked, looking thoughtfully through the emerald green of his liqueur, "interests me. Our friend Dolinski here thinks that he will not come because he will be afraid. De Brouillac, on the contrary, says that he will not come because he is too sagacious. Felix here, who knows him best, says that he will not come because he prefers ever to play the game from outside the circle, a looker-on to all appearance, yet sometimes wielding an unseen force. It is a strong position that."

Lucille raised her head and regarded the last speaker steadily.

"And I, Prince!" she exclaimed, "I say that he will come because he is a man, and because he does not know fear."

The Prince of Saxe Leinitzer bowed low towards the speaker.

"Dear Lucille," he said, so respectfully that the faint irony of his tone was lost to most of those present, "I, too, am of your opinion. The man who has a right, real or fancied, to claim you must indeed be a coward if he suffered dangers of any sort to stand in the way. After all, dangers from us! Is it not a little absurd?"

Lucille looked away from the Prince with a little shudder. He laughed softly, and drank his liqueur. Afterwards he leaned back for a moment in his chair and glanced thoughtfully around at the assembled company as though anxious to impress upon his memory all who were present. It was a little group, every member of which bore a well-known name. Their host, the Duke of Dorset, in whose splendid library they were assembled, was, if not the premier duke of the United Kingdom, at least one of those whose many hereditary offices and ancient family entitled him to a foremost place in the aristocracy of the world. Raoul de Brouillac, Count of Orleans, bore a name which was scarcely absent from a single page of the martial history of France. The Prince of Saxe Leinitzer kept up still a semblance of royalty in the State which his ancestors had ruled with despotic power. Lady Muriel Carey was a younger daughter of a ducal house, which had more than once intermarried with Royalty. The others, too, had their claims to be considered amongst the greatest families of Europe.

The Prince glanced at his watch, and then at the bridge tables ready set out.

"I think," he said, "that a little diversion—what does our hostess say?"

"Two sets can start at least," the Duchess said. "Lucille and I will stay out, and the Count de Brouillac does not play."

The Prince rose.

"It is agreed," he said. "Duke, will you honour me? Felix and Dolinski are our ancient adversaries. It should be an interesting trial of strength."

There was a general movement, a re-arrangement of seats, and a little buzz of conversation. Then silence. Lucille sat back in a great chair, and Lady Carey came over to her side.

"You are nervous to-night, Lucille," she said.

"Yes, I am nervous," Lucille admitted. "Why not? At any moment he may be here."

"And you care—so much?" Lady Carey said, with a hard little laugh.

"I care so much," Lucille echoed.

Lady Carey shook out her amber satin skirt and sat down upon a low divan. She held up her hands, small white hands, ablaze with jewels, and looked at them for a moment thoughtfully.

"He was very much in earnest when I saw him at Sherry's in New York," she remarked, "and he was altogether too clever for Mr. Horser and our friends there. After all their talk and boasting too. Why, they are ignorant of the very elements of intrigue."

Lucille sighed.

"Here," she said, "it is different. The Prince and he are ancient rivals, and Raoul de Brouillac is no longer his friend. Muriel, I am afraid of what may happen."

Lady Carey shrugged her shoulders.

"He is no fool," she said in a low tone. "He will not come here with a magistrate's warrant and a policeman to back it up, nor will he attempt to turn the thing into an Adelphi drama. I know him well enough to be sure that he will attempt nothing crude. Lucille, don't you find it exhilarating?"

"Exhilarating? But why?"

"It will be a game played through to the end by masters, and you, my dear woman, are the inspiration. I think that it is most fascinating."

Lucille looked sadly into the fire.

"I think," she said, "that I am weary of all these things. I seem to have lived such a very long time. At Lenox I was quite happy. Of my own will I would never have left it."

Lady Carey's thin lips curled a little, her blue eyes were full of scorn.

E. PHILLIPS OPPENHEIM

She was not altogether a pleasant woman to look upon. Her cheeks were thin and hollow, her eyes a little too prominent, some hidden expression which seemed at times to flit from one to the other of her features suggested a sensuality which was a little incongruous with her somewhat angular figure and generally cold demeanour. But that she was a woman of courage and resource history had proved.

"How idyllic!" she exclaimed. "Positively medieval! Fancy living with one man three years."

Lucille smiled.

"Why, not? I never knew a woman yet however cold however fond of change, who had not at some time or other during her life met a man for whose sake she would have done—what I did. I have had as many admirers—as many lovers, I suppose, as most women. But I can truthfully say that during the last three years no thought of one of them has crossed my mind."

Lady Carey laughed scornfully.

"Upon my word," she said. "If the Prince had not a temper, and if they were not playing for such ruinous points, I would entertain them all with these delightful confidences. By the bye, the Prince himself was once one of those who fell before your chariot wheels, was he not? Look at him now—sideways. What does he remind you of?"

Lucille raised her eyes.

"A fat angel," she answered, "or something equally distasteful. How I hate those mild eyes and that sweet, slow smile. I saw him thrash a poor beater once in the Saxe Leinitzer forests. Ugh!"

"I should not blame him for that," Lady Carey said coldly. "I like masterful men, even to the point of cruelty. General Dolinski there fascinates me. I believe that he keeps a little private knout at home for his wife and children. A wicked little contrivance with an ivory handle. I should like to see him use it."

Lucille shuddered. This tete-a-tete did not amuse her. She rose and looked over one of the bridge tables for a minute. The Prince, who was dealing, looked up with a smile.

"Be my good angel, Countess," he begged. "Fortune has deserted me to-night. You shall be the goddess of chance, and smile your favours upon me."

A hard little laugh came from the chair where Lady Carey sat. She turned her head towards them, and there was a malicious gleam in her eyes.

"Too late, Prince," she exclaimed. "The favours of the Countess are all given away. Lucille has become even as one of those flaxen-haired dolls of your mountain villages. She has given her heart away, and she is sworn to perpetual constancy."

The Prince smiled.

"The absence," he said, glancing up at the clock, "of that most fortunate person should surely count in our favour."

Lucille followed his eyes. The clock was striking ten. She shrugged her shoulders.

"If the converse also is true, Prince," she said, "you can scarcely have anything to hope for from me. For by half-past ten he will be here."

The Prince picked up his cards and sorted them mechanically.

"We shall see," he remarked. "It is true, Countess, that you are here, but in this instance you are set with thorns."

"To continue the allegory, Prince," she answered, passing on to the next table, "also with poisonous berries. But to the hand which has no fear, neither are harmful."

The Prince laid down his hand.

"Now I really believe," he said gently, "that she meant to be rude. Partner, I declare hearts!"

Felix was standing out from the next table whilst his hand was being played by General Dolinski, his partner. He drew her a little on one side.

"Do not irritate Saxe Leinitzer," he whispered. "Remember, everything must rest with him. Twice to-night you have brought that smile to his lips, and I never see it without thinking of unpleasant things."

"You are right," she answered; "but I hate him so. He and Muriel Carey seem to have entered into some conspiracy to lead me on to say things which I might regret."

"Saxe Leinitzer," he said, "has never forgotten that he once aspired to be your lover."

"He has not failed to let me know it," she answered. "He has even dared—ah!"

There was a sudden stir in the room. The library door was thrown open. The solemn-visaged butler stood upon the threshold.

"His Grace the Duke of Souspennier!" he announced.

XVIII

There was for the moment a dead silence. The soft patter of cards no longer fell upon the table. The eyes of every one were turned upon the newcomers. And he, leaning upon his stick, looked only for one person, and having found her, took no heed of any one else.

"Lucille!"

She rose from her seat and stood with hands outstretched towards him, her lips parted in a delightful smile, her eyes soft with happiness.

"Victor, welcome! It is like you to have found me, and I knew that you would come."

He raised her fingers to his lips—tenderly—with the grace of a prince, but all the affection of a lover. What he said to her none could hear, for his voice was lowered almost to a whisper. But the colour stained her cheeks, and her blush was the blush of a girl.

A movement of the Duchess recalled him to a sense of his social duty. He turned courteously to her with extended hand.

"I trust," he said, "that I may be forgiven my temporary fit of aberration. I cannot thank you sufficiently, Duchess, for your kind invitation."

Her answering smile was a little dubious.

"I am sure," she said "that we are delighted to welcome back amongst us so old and valued a friend. I suppose you know every one?"

Mr. Sabin looked searchingly around, exchanging bows with those whose faces were familiar to him. But between him and the Prince of Saxe Leinitzer there passed no pretense at any greeting. The two men eyed one another for a moment coldly. Each seemed to be trying to read the other through.

"I believe," Mr. Sabin said, "that I have that privilege. I see, however, that I am interrupting your game. Let me beg you to continue. With your permission, Duchess, I will remain a spectator. There are many things which my wife and I have to say to one another."

The Prince of Saxe Leinitzer laid his cards softly upon the table. He smiled upon Mr. Sabin—a slow, unpleasant smile.

"I think," he said slowly, "that our game must be postponed. It is a pity, but I think it had better be so."

"It must be entirely as you wish," Mr. Sabin answered. "I am at your service now or later."

The Prince rose to his feet.

"Monsieur le Due de Souspennier," he said, "what are we to conclude from your presence here this evening?"

"It is obvious," Mr. Sabin answered. "I claim my place amongst you."

"You claim to be one of us?"

"I do!"

"Ten years ago," the Prince continued, "you were granted immunity from all the penalties and obligations which a co-membership with us might involve. This privilege was extended to you on account of certain great operations in which you were then engaged, and the object of which was not foreign to our own aims. You are aware that the period of that immunity is long since past."

Mr. Sabin leaned with both hands upon his stick, and his face was like the face of a sphinx. Only Lucille, who knew him best of all those there, saw him wince for a moment before this reminder of his great failure.

"I am not accustomed," Mr. Sabin said quietly, "to shirk my share of the work in any undertaking with which I am connected. Only in this case I claim to take the place of the Countess Lucille, my wife. I request that the task, whatever it may be which you have imposed upon her, may be transferred to me."

The Prince's smile was sweet, but those who knew him best wondered what evil it might betoken for his ancient enemy.

"You offer yourself, then, as a full member?"

"Assuredly!"

"Subject," he drawled, "to all the usual pains and privileges?"

"Certainly!"

The Prince played with the cards upon the table. His smooth, fair face was unruffled, almost undisturbed. Yet underneath he was wondering fiercely, eagerly, how this might serve his ends.

"The circumstances," he said at last, "are peculiar. I think that we should do well to consult together—you and I, Felix, and Raoul here."

The two men named rose up silently. The Prince pointed to a small round table at the farther end of the apartment, half screened off by a curtained recess.

"Am I also," Mr. Sabin asked, "of your company?"

The Prince shook his head.

"I think not," he said. "In a few moments we will return."

Mr. Sabin moved away with a slight enigmatic gesture. Lucille gathered up her skirts, making room for him by her side on a small sofa.

"It is delightful to see you, Victor," she murmured. "It is delightful to know that you trusted me."

Mr. Sabin looked at her, and the smile which no other woman had ever seen softened for a moment his face.

"Dear Lucille," he murmured, "how could you ever doubt it? There was a day, I admit, when the sun stood still, when, if I had felt inclined to turn to light literature, I should have read aloud the Book of Job. But afterwards—well, you see that I am here."

She laughed.

"I knew that you would come," she said, "and yet I knew that it would be a struggle between you and them. For—the Prince—" she murmured, lowering her voice, "had pledged his word to keep us apart."

Mr. Sabin raised his head, and his eyes traveled towards the figure of the man who sat with his back to them in the far distant corner of the room.

"The Prince," he said softly, "is faithful to his ancient enmities."

Lucille's face was troubled. She turned to her companion with a little grimace.

"He would have me believe," she murmured, "that he is faithful to other things besides his enmities."

Mr. Sabin smiled.

"I am not jealous," he said softly, "of the Prince of Saxe Leinitzer!"

As though attracted by the mention of his name, which must, however, have been unheard by him, the Prince at that moment turned round and looked for a moment towards them. He shot a quick glance at Lady Carey. Almost at once she rose from her chair and came across to them.

"The Prince's watch-dog," Lucille murmured. "Hateful woman! She is bound hand and foot to him, and yet—"

Her eyes met his, and he laughed.

"Really," he said, "you and I in our old age might be hero and heroine of a little romance—the undesiring objects of a hopeless affection!"

Lady Carey sank into a low chair by their side. "You two," she said, with a slow, malicious smile, "are a pattern to this wicked world. Don't you know that such fidelity is positively sinful, and after three years in such a country too?"

"It is the approach of senility," Mr. Sabin answered her. "I am an old man, Lady Muriel!"

She shrugged her shoulders.

"You are like Ulysses," she said. "The gods, or rather the goddesses, have helped you towards immortality."

"It is," Mr. Sabin answered, "the most delicious piece of flattery I have ever heard."

"Calypso," she murmured, nodding towards Lucille, "is by your side."

"Really," Mr. Sabin interrupted, "I must protest. Lucille and I were married by a most respectable Episcopalian clergyman. We have documentary evidence. Besides, if Lucille is Calypso, what about Penelope?"

Lady Carey smiled thoughtfully.

"I have always thought," she said, "that Penelope was a myth. In your case I should say that Penelope represents a return to sanity—to the ordinary ways of life."

Mr. Sabin and Lucille exchanged swift glances. He raised his eyebrows.

"Our little idyll," he said, "seems to be the sport and buffet of every one. You forget that I am of the old world. I do not understand modernity."

"Ulysses," she answered, "was of the old world, yet he was a wanderer in more senses of the word than one. And there have been times—"

Her eyes sought his. He ignored absolutely the subtlety of meaning which lurked beneath the heavy drooping eyelids.

"One travels through life," he answered, "by devious paths, and a little wandering in the flower-gardens by the way is the lot of every one. But when the journey is over, one's taste for wandering has gone—well, Ulysses finished his days at the hearth of Penelope."

She rose and walked away. Mr. Sabin sat still and watched her as though listening to the soft sweep of her gown upon the carpet.

"Hateful woman!" Lucille exclaimed lightly. "To make love, and such love, to one's lawful husband before one's face is a little crude, don't you think?"

He shook his head.

"Too obvious," he answered. "She is playing the Prince's game. Dear me, how interesting this will be soon."

She nodded. A faint smile of bitterness had stolen into her tone.

"Already," she said, "you are beginning to scent the delight of the atmosphere. You are stiffening for the fight. Soon—"

"Ah, no! Don't say it," he whispered, taking her hand. "I shall never forget. If the fight seems good to me it is because you are the prize, and after all, you know, to fight for one's womenkind is amongst the primeval instincts."

Lady Carey, who had been pacing the room restlessly, touching an ornament here, looking at a picture there, came back to them and stood before Mr. Sabin. She had caught his last words.

"Primeval instincts!" she exclaimed mockingly. "What do you know about them, you of all men, a bundle of nerves and brains, with a motor for a heart, and an automatic brake upon your passions? Upon my word, I believe that I have solved the mystery of your perennial youth. You have found a way of substituting machinery for the human organ, and you are wound up to go for ever."

"You have found me out," he admitted. "Professor Penningram of Chicago will supply you too with an outfit. Mention my name if you like. It is a wonderful country America."

The Prince came over to them, fair and bland with no trace upon his smooth features or in his half-jesting tone of any evil things.

"Souspennier," he said, holding out his hand, "welcome back once more to your old place. I am happy to say that there appears to be no reason why your claim should not be fully admitted."

Mr. Sabin rose to his feet.

"I presume," he said, "that no very active demands are likely to be made upon my services. In this country more than any other I fear that the possibilities of my aid are scanty."

The Prince smiled.

"It is a fact," he said, "which we all appreciate. Upon you at present we make no claim."

There was a moment's intense silence. A steely light glittered in Mr. Sabin's eyes. He and the Prince alone remained standing. The Duchess of Dorset watched them through her lorgnettes; Lady Carey watched too with an intense eagerness, her eyes alight with mingled cruelty and excitement. Lucille's eyes were so bright that one might readily believe the tears to be glistening beneath.

XIX

I will not pretend," Mr. Sabin said, "to misunderstand you. My help is not required by you in this enterprise, whatever it may be, in which you are engaged. On the contrary, you have tried by many and various ways to keep me at a distance. But I am here, Prince—here to be dealt with and treated according to my rights."

The Prince stroked his fair moustache.

"I am a little puzzled," he admitted, "as to this—shall I not call it self-assertiveness?—on the part of my good friend Souspennier."

"I will make it quite clear then," Mr. Sabin answered. "Lucille, will you favour me by ringing for your maid. The carriage is at the door."

The Prince held out his hand.

"My dear Souspennier," he said, "you must not think of taking Lucille away from us."

"Indeed," Mr. Sabin answered coolly. "Why not?"

"It must be obvious to you," the Prince answered, "that we did not send to America for Lucille without an object. She is now engaged in an important work upon our behalf. It is necessary that she should remain under this roof."

"I demand," Mr. Sabin said, "that the nature of that necessity should be made clear to me."

The Prince smiled with the air of one disposed to humour a wilful child.

"Come!" he said. "You must know very well that I cannot stand here and tell you the bare outline, much less the details of an important movement. To-morrow, at any hour you choose, one from amongst us shall explain the whole matter—and the part to be borne in it by the Countess!"

"And to-night?" Mr. Sabin asked.

The Prince shrugged his shoulders and glanced at the clock.

"To-night, my dear friend," he said, "all of us, I believe, go on to a ball at Carmarthen House. It would grieve me also, I am sure, Duke, to seem inhospitable, but I am compelled to mention the fact that the hour for which the carriages have been ordered is already at hand."

Mr. Sabin reflected for a few moments.

"Did I understand you to say," he asked, "that the help to be given to you by my wife, Lucille, Duchess of Souspennier, entailed her remaining under this roof?"

The Prince smiled seraphically.

"It is unfortunate," he murmured, "since you have been so gallant as to follow her, but it is true! You will understand this perfectly—to-morrow."

"And why should I wait until to-morrow?" Mr. Sabin asked coolly.

"I fear," the Prince said, "that it is a matter of necessity."

Mr. Sabin glanced for a moment in turn at the faces of all the little company as though seeking to discover how far the attitude of his opponent met with their approval. Lady Carey's thin lips were curved in a smile, and her eyes met his mockingly. The others remained imperturbable. Last of all he looked at Lucille.

"It seems," he said, smiling towards her, "that I am called upon to pay a heavy entrance fee on my return amongst your friends. But the Prince of Saxe Leinitzer forgets that he has shown me no authority, or given me no valid reason why I should tolerate such flagrant interference with my personal affairs."

"To-morrow—to-morrow, my good sir!" the Prince interrupted.

"No! To-night!" Mr. Sabin answered sharply. "Lucille, in the absence of any reasonable explanation, I challenge the right of the Prince of Saxe Leinitzer to rob me even for an hour of my dearest possession. I appeal to you. Come with me and remain with me until it has been proved, if ever it can be proved, that greater interests require our separation. If there be blame I will take it. Will you trust yourself to me?"

Lucille half rose, but Lady Carey's hand was heavy upon her shoulder. As though by a careless movement General Dolinski and Raoul de Brouillac altered their positions slightly so as to come between the two. The Duke of Dorset had left the room. Then Mr. Sabin knew that they were all against him.

"Lucille," he said, "have courage! I wait for you."

She looked towards him, and her face puzzled him. For there flashed across the shoulders of these people a glance which was wholly out of harmony with his own state of barely subdued passion—a glance half tender, half humorous, full of subtle promise. Yet her words were a blow to him.

"Victor, how is it possible? Believe me, I should come if I could. To-morrow—very soon, it may be possible. But now. You hear what the Prince says. I fear that he is right!"

To Mr. Sabin the shock was an unexpected one. He had never doubted but that she at least was on his side. Her words found him unprepared, and a moment he showed his discomfiture. His recovery however, was swift and amazing. He bowed to Lucille, and by the time he raised his head even the reproach had gone from his eyes.

"Dear lady," he said, "I will not venture to dispute your decision. Prince, will you appoint a time to-morrow when this matter shall be more fully explained to me?"

The Prince's smile was sweetness itself, and his tone very gentle. But Mr. Sabin, who seldom yielded to any passionate impulse, kept his teeth set and his hand clenched, lest the blow he longed to deal should escape him.

"At midday to-morrow I shall be pleased to receive you," he said. "The Countess, with her usual devotion and good sense, has, I trust, convinced you that our action is necessary!"

"To-morrow at midday," Mr. Sabin said, "I will be here. I have the honour to wish you all good-night."

His farewell was comprehensive. He did not even single out Lucille for a parting glance. But down the broad stairs and across the hall of Dorset House he passed with weary steps, leaning heavily upon his stick. It was a heavy blow which had fallen upon him. As yet he scarcely realised it.

His carriage was delayed for a few moments, and just as he was entering it a young woman, plainly dressed in black, came hurrying out and slipped a note into his hand.

"Pardon, monsieur," she exclaimed, with a smile. "I feared that I was too late."

Mr. Sabin's fingers closed over the note, and he stepped blithely into the carriage. But when he tore it open and saw the handwriting he permitted himself a little groan of disappointment. It was not from her. He read the few lines and crushed the sheet of paper in his hand.

"I am having supper at the Carlton with some friends on our way to C. H. I want to speak to you for a moment. Be in the Palm Court at 12.15, but do not recognise me until I come to you. If possible keep out of sight. If you should have left my maid will bring this on to your hotel.

M. C.

Mr. Sabin leaned back in his carriage, and a frown of faint perplexity contracted his forehead.

E. PHILLIPS OPPENHEIM

"If I were a younger man," he murmured to himself, "I might believe that this woman was really in earnest, as well as being Saxe Leinitzer's jackal. We were friendly enough in Paris that year. She is unscrupulous enough, of course. Always with some odd fancy for the grotesque or unlikely. I wonder—"

He pulled the check-string, and was driven to Camperdown House. A great many people were coming and going. Mr. Sabin found Helene's maid, and learnt that her mistress was just going to her room, and would be alone for a few minutes. He scribbled a few words on the back of a card, and was at once taken up to her boudoir.

"My dear UNCLE," Helene exclaimed, "you have arrived most opportunely. We have just got rid of a few dinner people, and we are going on to Carmarthen House presently. Take that easy-chair, please, and, light a cigarette. Will you have a liqueur? Wolfendon has some old brandy which every one seems to think wonderful."

"You are very kind, Helene," Mr. Sabin said. "I cannot refuse anything which you offer in so charming a manner. But I shall not keep you more than a few minutes."

"We need not leave for an hour," Helene said, "and I am dressed except for my jewels. Tell me, have you seen Lucille? I am so anxious to know."

"I have seen Lucille this evening," Mr. Sabin answered.

"At Dorset House!"

"Yes."

Helene sat down, smiling.

"Do tell me all about it."

"There is very little to tell," Mr. Sabin answered.

"She is with you—she returns at least!"

Mr. Sabin shook his head.

"No," he answered. "She remains at Dorset House."

Helene was silent. Mr. Sabin smoked pensively a moment or two, and sipped the liqueur which Camperdown's own servant had just brought him.

"It is very hard, Helene," he said, "to make you altogether understand the situation, for there are certain phases of it which I cannot discuss with you at all. I have made my first effort to regain Lucille, and it has failed. It is not her fault. I need not say that it is not mine. But the struggle has commenced, and in the end I shall win."

"Lucille herself—" Helene began hesitatingly.

"Lucille is, I firmly believe, as anxious to return to me as I am anxious to have her," Mr. Sabin said.

Helene threw up her hands.

"It is bewildering," she exclaimed.

"It must seem so to you," Mr. Sabin admitted.

"I wish that Lucille were anywhere else," Helene said. "The Dorset House set, you know, although they are very smart and very exclusive, have a somewhat peculiar reputation. Lady Carey, although she is such a brilliant woman, says and does the most insolent, the most amazing things, and the Prince of Saxe Leinitzer goes everywhere in Europe by the name of the Royal libertine. They are powerful enough almost to dominate society, and we poor people who abide by the conventions are absolutely nowhere beside them. They think that we are bourgeois because we have virtue, and prehistoric because we are not decadent."

"The Duke—" Mr. Sabin remarked.

"Oh, the Duke is quite different, of course," Helene admitted. "He is a fanatical Tory, very stupid, very blind to anything except his beloved Primrose League. How he came to lend himself to the vagaries of such a set I cannot imagine."

Mr. Sabin smiled.

"C'est la femme toujours!" he remarked. "His Grace is, I fear, henpecked, and the Duchess herself is the sport of cleverer people. And now, my dear niece, I see that the time is going. I came to know if you could get me a card for the ball at Carmarthen House to-night."

Helene laughed softly.

"Very easily, my dear Uncle. Lady Carmarthen is Wolfendon's cousin, you know, and a very good friend of mine. I have half a dozen blank cards here. Shall I really see you there?"

"I believe so," Mr. Sabin answered.

"And Lucille?"

"It is possible."

"There is nothing I suppose which I can do in the way of intervention, or anything of that sort?"

Mr. Sabin shook his head.

"Lucille and I are the best of friends," he answered. "Talk to her, if you will. By the bye, is that twelve o'clock? I must hurry. Doubtless we shall meet again at the ball."

But Carmarthen House saw nothing of Mr. Sabin that night.

E. PHILLIPS OPPENHEIM

XX

M r. Sabin from his seat behind a gigantic palm watched her egress from the supper-room with a little group of friends.

They came to a halt in the broad carpeted way only a few feet from him. Lady Carey, in a wonderful green gown, her neck and bosom ablaze with jewels, seemed to be making her farewells.

"I must go in and see the De Lausanacs," she exclaimed. "They are in the blue room supping with the Portuguese Ambassador. I shall be at Carmarthen House within half an hour—unless my headache becomes unbearable. Au revoir, all of you. Good-bye, Laura!"

Her friends passed on towards the great swing doors. Lady Carey retraced her steps slowly towards the supper-room, and made some languid inquiries of the head waiter as to a missing handkerchief. Then she came again slowly down the broad way and reached Mr. Sabin. He rose to his feet.

"I thank you very much for your note," he said. "You have something, I believe, to say to me."

She stood before him for a moment in silence, as though not unwilling that he should appreciate the soft splendour of her toilette. The jewels which encircled her neck were priceless and dazzling; the soft material of her gown, the most delicate shade of sea green, seemed to foam about her feet, a wonderful triumph of allegoric dressmaking. She saw that he was studying her, and she laughed a little uneasily, looking all the time into his eyes.

"Shockingly overdressed, ain't I?" she said. "We were going straight to Carmarthen House, you know. Come and sit in this corner for a moment, and order me some coffee. I suppose there isn't any less public place!"

"I fear not," he answered. "You will perhaps be unobserved behind this palm."

She sank into a low chair, and he seated himself beside her. She sighed contentedly.

"Dear me!" she said. "Do men like being run after like this?"

Mr. Sabin raised his eyebrows.

"I understood," he said, "that you had something to say to me of importance."

She shot a quick look up at him.

"Don't be horrid," she said in a low tone. "Of course I wanted to see you. I wanted to explain. Give me one of your cigarettes."

He laid his case silently before her. She took one and lit it, watching him furtively all the time. The man brought their coffee. The place was almost empty now, and some of the lights were turned down.

"It is very kind of you," he said slowly, "to honour me by so much consideration, but if you have much to say perhaps it would be better if you permitted me to call upon you to-morrow. I am afraid of depriving you of your ball—and your friends will be getting impatient."

"Bother the ball—and my friends," she exclaimed, a certain strained note in her tone which puzzled him. "I'm not obliged to go to the thing, and I don't want to. I've invented a headache, and they won't even expect me. They know my headaches."

"In that case," Mr. Sabin said, "I am entirely at your service."

She sighed, and looked up at him through a little cloud of tobacco smoke.

"What a wonderful man you are," she said softly. "You accept defeat with the grace of a victor. I believe that you would triumph as easily with a shrug of the shoulders. Haven't you any feeling at all? Don't you know what it is like to feel?"

He smiled.

"We both come," he said, "of a historic race. If ancestry is worth anything it should at least teach us to go about without pinning our hearts upon our sleeves."

"But you," she murmured, "you have no heart."

He looked down upon her then with still cold face and steady eyes.

"Indeed," he said, "you are mistaken."

She moved uneasily in her chair. She was very pale, except for a faint spot of pink colour in her cheeks.

"It is very hard to find, then," she said, speaking quickly, her bosom rising and falling, her eyes always seeking to hold his. "To-night you see what I have done—I have, sent away my friends—and my carriage. They may know me here—you see what I have risked. And I don't care. You thought to-night that I was your enemy—and I am not. I am not your enemy at all."

Her hand fell as though by accident upon his, and remained there. Mr. Sabin was very nearly embarrassed. He knew quite well that if she were not his enemy at that moment she would be very shortly.

E. PHILLIPS OPPENHEIM

"Lucille," she continued, "will blame me too. I cannot help it. I want to tell you that for the present your separation from her is a certain thing. She acquiesces. You heard her. She is quite happy. She is at the ball to-night, and she has friends there who will make it pleasant for her. Won't you understand?"

"No," Mr. Sabin answered.

She beat the ground with her foot.

"You must understand," she murmured. "You are not like these fools of Englishmen who go to sleep when they are married, and wake in the divorce court. For the present at least you have lost Lucille. You heard her choose. She's at the ball to-night—and I have come here to be with you. Won't you, please," she added, with a little nervous laugh, "show some gratitude?"

The interruption which Mr. Sabin had prayed for came at last. The musicians had left, and many of the lights had been turned down. An official came across to them.

"I beg your pardon, sir," he said, addressing Mr. Sabin, "but we are closing now, unless you are a guest in the hotel."

"I am staying here," Mr. Sabin answered, rising, "but the lady—"

Lady Carey interrupted him.

"I am staying here also," she said to the man.

He bowed at once and withdrew. She rose slowly to her feet and laid her fingers upon his arm. He looked steadily away from her.

"Fortunately," he said, "I have not yet dismissed my own carriage. Permit me."

Mr. Sabin leaned heavily upon his stick as he slowly made his way along the corridor to his rooms. Things were going ill with him indeed. He was not used to the fear of an enemy, but the memory of Lady Carey's white cheeks and indrawn lips as she had entered his carriage chilled him. Her one look, too, was a threat worse than any which her lips could have uttered. He was getting old indeed, he thought, wearily, when disappointment weighed so heavily upon him. And Lucille? Had he any real fears of her? He felt a little catch in his throat at the bare thought—in a moment's singular clearness of perception he realised that if Lucille were indeed lost the world was no longer a place for him. So his feet fell wearily upon the thickly carpeted floor of the corridor, and his face was unusually drawn and haggard as he opened the door of his sitting-room.

And then—a transformation, amazing, stupefying. It was Lucille who was smiling a welcome upon him from the depths of his favourite easy-chair—Lucille sitting over his fire, a novel in her hand, and wearing a delightful rose-pink dressing-gown. Some of her belongings were scattered about his room, giving it a delicate air of femininity. The faint odour of her favourite and only perfume gave to her undoubted presence a wonderful sense of reality.

She held out her hands to him, and the broad sleeves of her dressing-gown fell away from her white rounded arms. Her eyes were wonderfully soft, the pink upon her cheeks was the blush of a girl.

"Victor," she murmured, "do not look so stupefied. Did you not believe that I would risk at least a little for you, who have risked so much for me? Only come to me! Make the most of me. All sorts of things are sure to happen directly I am found out."

He took her into his arms. It was one of the moments of his lifetime.

"Tell me," he murmured, "how have you dared to do this?"

She laughed.

"You know the Prince and his set. You know the way they bribe. Intrigues everywhere, new and old overlapping. They have really some reason for keeping you and me apart, but as regards my other movements, I am free enough. And they thought, Victor—don't be angry—but I let them think it was some one else. And I stole away from the ball, and they think—never mind what they think. But you, Victor, are my intrigue, you, my love, my husband!"

Then all the fatigue and all the weariness, died away from Mr. Sabin's face. Once more the fire of youth burned in his heart. And Lucille laughed softly as her lips met his, and her head sank upon his shoulder.

XXI

L ady Carey suddenly dropped her partner's arm. She had seen a man standing by himself with folded arms and moody face at the entrance to the ball-room. She raised her lorgnettes. His identity was unquestionable.

"Will you excuse me for a moment, Captain Horton," she said to her escort. "I want particularly to speak to Mr. Brott."

Captain Horton bowed with the slight disappointment of a hungry man on his way to the supper-room.

"Don't be long," he begged. "The places are filling up."

Lady Carey nodded and walked swiftly across to where Brott was standing. He moved eagerly forward to meet her.

"Not dancing, Mr. Brott?"

He shrugged his shoulders.

"This sort of thing isn't much in my way," he answered. "I was rather hoping to see the Countess here. I trust that she is not indisposed."

She looked at him steadily.

"Do you mean," she said, "that you do not know where she is?"

"I?" he answered in amazement. "How should I? I have not seen her at all this evening. I understood that she was to be here."

Lady Carey hesitated. The man was too honest to be able to lie like this, even in a good cause. She stood quite still for a moment thinking. Several of her dearest friends had already told her that she was looking tired and ill this evening. At that moment she was positively haggard.

"I have been down at Ranelagh this afternoon," she said slowly, "and dining out, so I have not seen Lucille. She was complaining of a headache yesterday, but I quite thought that she was coming here. Have you seen the Duchess?"

He shook his head.

"No. There is such a crowd."

Lady Carey glanced towards her escort and turned away.

"I will try and find out what has become of her," she said. "Don't go away yet."

She rejoined her escort.

"When we have found a table," she said, "I want you to keep my place for a few moments while I try and find some of my party."

They passed into the supper-room, and appropriated a small table. Lady Carey left her partner, and made her way to the farther end of the apartment, where the Prince of Saxe Leinitzer was supping with half a dozen men and women. She touched him on the shoulder.

"I want to speak to you for a moment, Ferdinand," she whispered.

He rose at once, and she drew him a little apart.

"Brott is here," she said slowly.

"Brott here!" he repeated. "And Lucille?"

"He is asking for her—expected to find her here. He is downstairs now, looking the picture of misery."

He looked at her inquiringly. There was a curious steely light in her eyes, and she was showing her front teeth, which were a little prominent.

"Do you think," he asked, "that she has deceived us?"

"What else? Where are the Dorsets?"

"The Duchess is with the Earl of Condon, and some more people at the round table under the balcony."

"Give me your arm," she whispered. "We must go and ask her."

They crossed the room together. Lady Carey sank into a vacant chair by the side of the Duchess and talked for a few minutes to the people whom she knew. Then she turned and whispered in the Duchess's ear.

"Where is Lucille?"

The Duchess looked at her with a meaning smile.

"How should I know? She left when we did."

"Alone?"

"Yes. It was all understood, wasn't it?"

Lady Carey laughed unpleasantly.

"She has fooled us," she said. "Brott is here alone. Knows nothing of her."

The Duchess was puzzled.

"Well, I know nothing more than you do," she answered. "Are you sure the man is telling the truth?"

"Of course. He is the image of despair."

"I am sure she was in earnest," the Duchess said. "When I asked her whether she should come on here she laughed a little nervously, and said perhaps or something of that sort."

"The fool may have bungled it," Lady Carey said thoughtfully. "I will go back to him. There's that idiot of a partner of mine. I must go and pretend to have some supper."

Captain Horton found his vis-a-vis a somewhat unsatisfactory companion. She drank several glasses of champagne, ate scarcely anything, and rushed him away before he had taken the edge off his appetite. He brought her to the Duchess and went back in a huff to finish his supper alone. Lady Carey went downstairs and discovered Mr. Brott, who had scarcely moved.

"Have you seen anything of her?" she asked.

He shook his head gloomily.

"No! It is too late for her to come now, isn't it?"

"Take me somewhere where we can talk," she said abruptly. "One of those seats in the recess will do."

He obeyed her, and they found a retired corner. Lady Carey wasted no time in fencing.

"I am Lucille's greatest friend, Mr. Brott, and her confidante," she said.

He nodded.

"So I have understood."

"She tells me everything."

He glanced towards her a little uneasily.

"That is comprehensive!" he remarked.

"It is true," she answered. "Lucille has told me a great deal about your friendship! Come, there is no use in our mincing words. Lucille has been badly treated years ago, and she has a perfect right to seek any consolation she may find. The old fashioned ideas, thank goodness, do not hold any longer amongst us. It is not necessary to tie yourself for life to a man in order to procure a little diversion."

"I will not pretend to misunderstand you, Lady Carey," he said gravely, "but I must decline to discuss the Countess of Radantz in connection with such matters."

"Oh, come!" she declared impatiently; "remember that I am her friend. Yours is quite the proper attitude, but with me it doesn't matter. Now I am going to ask you a plain question. Had you any engagement with Lucille to-night?"

She watched him mercilessly. He was colouring like a boy. Lady Carey's thin lips curled. She had no sympathy with such amateurish love-making. Nevertheless, his embarrassment was a great relief to her.

"She promised to be here," he answered stiffly.

"Everything depends upon your being honest with me," she continued. "You will see from my question that I know. Was there not something said about supper at your rooms before or after the dance?"

"I cannot discuss this matter with you or any living person," he answered. "If you know so much why ask me?"

Lady Carey could have shaken the man, but she restrained herself.

"It is sufficient!" she declared. "What I cannot understand is why you are here—when Lucille is probably awaiting for you at your rooms."

He started from his chair as though he had been shot.

"What do you mean?" he exclaimed. "She was to—"

He stopped short. Lady Carey shrugged her shoulders.

"Oh, written you or something, I suppose!" she exclaimed. "Trust an Englishman for bungling a love affair. All I can tell you is that she left Dorset House in a hansom without the others, and said some thing about having supper with some friends."

Brott sprang to his feet and took a quick step towards the exit.

"It is not possible!" he exclaimed.

She took his arm. He almost dragged her along.

"Well, we are going to see," she said coolly. "Tell the man to call a hansom."

They drove almost in silence through the Square to Pall Mall. Brott leaped out onto the pavement directly the cab pulled up.

"I will wait here," Lady Carey said. "I only want to know that Lucille is safe."

He disappeared, and she sat forward in the cab drumming idly with her forefingers upon the apron. In a few minutes he came back. His appearance was quite sufficient. He was very pale. The change in him was so ludicrous that she laughed.

"Get in," she said. "I am going round to Dorset House. We must find out if we can what has become of her."

He obeyed without comment. At Dorset House Lady Carey summoned the Duchess's own maid.

"Marie," she said, "you were attending upon the Countess Radantz to-night?"

"Yes, my lady."

"At what time did she leave?"

"At about, eleven, my lady."

"Alone?"

"Yes, my lady."

Lady Carey looked steadily at the girl.

"Did she take anything with her?"

The girl hesitated. Lady Carey frowned.

"It must be the truth, remember, Marie."

"Certainly, my lady! She took her small dressing-case."

Lady Carey set her teeth hard. Then with a movement of her head she dismissed the maid. She walked restlessly up and down the room. Then she stopped short with a hard little laugh.

"If I give way like this," she murmured, "I shall be positively hideous, and after all, if she was there it was not possible for him—"

She stopped short, and suddenly tearing the handkerchief which she had been carrying into shreds threw the pieces upon the floor, and stamped upon them. Then she laughed shortly, and turned towards the door.

"Now I must go and get rid of that poor fool outside," she said. "What a bungler!"

Brott was beside himself with impatience.

"Lucille is here," she announced, stepping in beside him. "She has a shocking headache and has gone to bed. As a matter of fact, I believe that she was expecting to hear from you."

"Impossible!" he answered shortly. He was beginning to distrust this woman.

"Never mind. You can make it up with her to-morrow. I was foolish to be anxious about her at all. Are you coming in again?"

They were at Carmarthen House. He handed her out.

"No, thanks! If you will allow me I will wish you good-night."

She made her way into the ball-room, and found the Prince of Saxe Leinitzer, who was just leaving.

"Do you know where Lucille is?" she asked.

He looked up at her sharply. "Where?"

"At the Carlton Hotel—with him."

He rose to his feet with slow but evil promptitude. His face just then was very unlike the face of an angel. Lady Carey laughed aloud.

"Poor man," she said mockingly. "It is always the same when you and Souspennier meet."

He set his teeth.

"This time," he muttered, "I hold the trumps."

She pointed at the clock. It was nearly four. "She was there at eleven," she remarked drily.

XXII

H is Highness, the Prince of Saxe Leinitzer!"
Duson stood away from the door with a low bow. The Prince—in the buttonhole of whose frock-coat was a large bunch of Russian violets, passed across the threshold. Mr. Sabin rose slowly from his chair.

"I fear," the Prince said suavely, "that I am an early visitor. I can only throw myself upon your indulgence and plead the urgency of my mission."

His arrival appeared to have interrupted a late breakfast of the Continental order. The small table at which Lucille and Mr. Sabin were seated was covered with roses and several dishes of wonderful fruit. A coffee equipage was before Lucille. Mr. Sabin, dressed with his usual peculiar care and looking ten years younger, had just lit a cigarette.

"We have been anticipating your visit, Prince," Mr. Sabin remarked, with grim courtesy. "Can we offer you coffee or a liqueur?"

"I thank you, no," the Prince answered. "I seldom take anything before lunch. Let me beg that you do not disturb yourselves. With your permission I will take this easy-chair. So! That is excellent. We can now talk undisturbed."

Mr. Sabin bowed.

"You will find me," he said, "an excellent listener."

The Prince smiled in an amiable manner. His eyes were fixed upon Lucille, who had drawn her chair a little away from the table. What other woman in the world who had passed her first youth could sit thus in the slanting sunlight and remain beautiful?

"I will ask you to believe," the Prince said slowly, "how sincerely I regret this unavoidable interference in a domestic happiness so touching. Nevertheless, I have come for the Countess. It is necessary that she returns to Dorset House this morning."

"You will oblige me," Mr. Sabin remarked, "by remembering that my wife is the Duchesse de Souspennier, and by so addressing her."

The Prince spread out his hands—a deprecating gesture.

"Alas!" he said, "for the present it is not possible. Until the little affair upon which we are now engaged is finally disposed of it is necessary that Lucille should be known by the title which she bears in her own right, or by the name of her late husband, Mr. James B. Peterson."

"That little affair," Mr. Sabin remarked, "is, I presume, the matter which you have come to explain to me."

The Prince smiled and shook his head.

"Explain! My dear Duke, that is not possible. It is not within your rights to ask questions or to require any explanation as to anything which Lucille is required to do by us. You must remember that our claim upon her comes before yours. It is a claim which she cannot evade or deny. And in pursuance of it, Countess, I deeply regret having to tell you that your presence at Dorset House within the next hour is demanded."

Lucille made no answer, but looked across the table at Mr. Sabin with a little grimace.

"It is a comedy," she murmured. "After all, it is a comedy!"

Mr. Sabin fingered his cigarette thoughtfully.

"I believe," he said, "that the Duchess realises her responsibilities in this matter. I myself have no wish to deny them. As ordinary members we are both pledged to absolute obedience. I therefore place no embargo upon the return of my wife to Dorset House. But there are certain conditions, Prince, that considering the special circumstances of the case I feel impelled to propose."

"I can recognise," the Prince said, "no conditions."

"They are very harmless," Mr. Sabin continued calmly. "The first is that in a friendly way, and of course under the inviolable law of secrecy, you explain to me for what part Lucille is cast in this little comedy; the next that I be allowed to see her at reasonable intervals, and finally that she is known by her rightful name as Duchesse de Souspennier."

The forced urbanity which the Prince had assumed fell away from him without warning. The tone of his reply was almost a sneer.

"I repeat," he said, "that I can recognise no conditions."

"It is perhaps," Mr. Sabin continued, "the wrong word to use. We submit to your authority, but you and I are well aware that your discretionary powers are large. I ask you to use them."

"And I," the Prince said, "refuse. Let me add that I intend to prevent any recurrence of your little adventure of last night. Lucille shall not see you again until her task is over. And as for you, my dear Duke, I desire only your absence. I do not wish to hurt your feelings, but your name has been associated in the past with too many failures to inspire us with any confidence in engaging you as an ally. Countess, a carriage from Dorset House awaits you."

But Lucille sat still, and Mr. Sabin rose slowly to his feet.

"I thank you, Prince," he said, "for throwing away the mask. Fighting is always better without the buttons. It is true that I have failed more than once, but it is also true that my failures have been more magnificent than your waddle across the plain of life. As for your present authority, I challenge you to your face that you are using it to gain your private ends. What I have said to you I shall repeat to those whose place is above yours. Lucille shall go to Dorset House, but I warn you that I hold my life a slight thing where her welfare is concerned. Your hand is upon the lever of a great organization, I am only a unit in the world. Yet I would have you remember that more than once, Prince, when you and I have met with the odds in your favour the victory has been mine. Play the game fairly, and you have nothing to fear from me but the open opposition I have promised you. Bring but the shadow of evil upon her, misuse your power but ever so slightly against her, and I warn you that I shall count the few years of life left to me a trifle—of less than no account—until you and I cry quits."

The Prince smiled, a fat, good-natured smile, behind which the malice was indeed well hidden.

"Come, come, my dear Souspennier," he declared. "This is unworthy of you. It is positively melodramatic. It reminds me of the plays of my Fatherland, and of your own Adelphi Theatre. We should be men of the world, you and I. You must take your defeats with your victories. I can assure you that the welfare of the Countess Lucille shall be my special care."

Lucille for the first time spoke. She rose from her chair and rested her hands affectionately upon her husband's shoulder.

"Dear Victor," she said, "remember that we are in London, and, need I add, have confidence in me. The Prince of Saxe Leinitzer and I understand one another, I believe. If we do not it is not my fault. My presence here at this moment should prove to you how eagerly I shall look forward to the time when our separation is no longer necessary."

She passed away into the inner room with a little farewell gesture tender and regretful. Mr. Sabin resumed his seat.

"I believe, Prince," he said, "that no good can come of any further conference between you and me. We understand one another too well. Might I suggest therefore that you permit me to ring?"

The Prince rose to his feet.

"You are right," he said. "The bandying of words between you and me is a waste of time. We are both of us too old at the game. But come, before I go I will do you a good turn. I will prove that I am in a generous mood."

Mr. Sabin shrugged his shoulders.

"If anything in this world could inspire me with fear," he remarked, "it would be the generosity of the Prince of Saxe Leinitzer."

The Prince sighed.

"You always misunderstand me," he murmured. "However, I will prove my words. You spoke of an appeal."

"Certainly," Mr. Sabin answered. "I intend to impeach you for making use of the powers entrusted to you for your own private ends—in other words, for making an arbitrary misuse of your position."

The Prince nodded.

"It is very well put," he said. "I shall await the result of your appeal in fear and trembling. I confess that I am very much afraid. But, come now, I am going to be generous. I am going to help you on a little. Do you know to whom your appeal must be made?"

"To the Grand Duke!" Mr. Sabin replied.

The Prince shook his head.

"Ah me!" he said, "how long indeed you have been absent from the world. The Grand Duke is no longer the head of our little affair. Shall I tell you who has succeeded him?"

"I can easily find out," Mr. Sabin answered.

"Ah, but I warned you that I was in a generous mood," the Prince said, with a smile. "I will save you the trouble. With your permission I will whisper the name in your ear. It is not one which we mention lightly."

He stepped forward and bent his head for a moment. Afterwards, as he drew back, the smile upon his lips broadened until he showed all his teeth. It was a veritable triumph. Mr. Sabin, taken wholly by surprise, had not been able to conceal his consternation.

"It is not possible," he exclaimed hoarsely. "He would not dare."

But in his heart he knew that the Prince had spoken the truth.

XXIII

"A fter all," said the Prince, looking up from the wine list, "why cannot I be satisfied with you? And why cannot you be satisfied with me? It would save so much trouble."

Lady Carey, who was slowly unwinding the white veil from her picture hat, shrugged her shoulders.

"My dear man," she said, "you could not seriously expect me to fall in love with you."

The Prince sipped his wine—a cabinet hock of rare vintage—and found it good. He leaned over towards his companion.

"Why not?" he asked. "I wish that you would try—in earnest, I mean. You are capable of great things, I believe—perhaps of the great passion itself."

"Perhaps," she murmured derisively.

"And yet," he continued, "there has always been in our love-making a touch of amateurishness. It is an awkward word, but I do not know how better to explain myself."

"I understand you perfectly," she answered. "I can also, I think, explain it. It is because I never cared a rap about you."

The Prince did not appear altogether pleased. He curled his fair moustache, and looked deprecatingly at his companion. She had so much the air of a woman who has spoken the truth.

"My dear Muriel!" he protested.

She looked at him insolently.

"My good man," she said, "whatever you do don't try and be sentimental. You know quite well that I have never in my life pretended to care a rap about you—except to pass the time. You are altogether too obvious. Very young girls and very old women would rave about you. You simply don't appeal to me. Perhaps I know you too well. What does it matter!"

He sighed and examined a sauce critically. They were lunching at Prince's alone, at a small table near the wall.

"Your taste," he remarked a little spitefully, "would be considered a trifle strange. Souspennier carries his years well, but he must be an old man."

She sipped her wine thoughtfully.

"Old or young," she said, "he is a man, and all my life I have loved men,—strong men. To have him here opposite to me at this moment, mine, belonging to me, the slave of my will, I would give—well, I would give—a year of my life—my new tiara—anything!"

"What a pity," he murmured, "that we cannot make an exchange, you and I, Lucille and he!"

"Ah, Lucille!" she murmured. "Well, she is beautiful. That goes for much. And she has the grand air. But, heavens, how stupid!"

"Stupid!" he repeated doubtfully.

She drummed nervously upon the tablecloth with her fingers.

"Oh, not stupid in the ordinary way, of course, but yet a fool. I should like to see man or devil try and separate us if I belonged to him—until I was tired of him. That would come, of course. It comes always. It is the hideous part of life."

"You look always," he said, "a little too far forward. It is a mistake. After all, it is the present only which concerns us."

"Admirable philosophy," she laughed scornfully, "but when one is bored to death in the present one must look forward or backward for consolation."

He continued his lunch in silence for a while.

"I am rebuked!" he said.

There came a pause in the courses. He looked at her critically. She was very handsomely dressed in a walking costume of dove-coloured grey. The ostrich feathers which drooped from her large hat were almost priceless. She had the undeniable air of being a person of breeding. But she was paler even than usual, her hair, notwithstanding its careful arrangement, gave signs of being a little thin in front. There were wrinkles at the corners of her eyes. She knew these things, but she bore his inspection with indifference.

"I wonder," he said reflectively, "what we men see in you. You have plenty of admirers. They say that Grefton got himself shot out at the front because you treated him badly. Yet—you are not much to look at, are you?"

She laughed at him. Hers was never a pleasant laugh, but this time it was at least natural.

"How discriminating," she declared. "I am an ugly woman, and men of taste usually prefer ugly women. Then I am always well dressed. I know how to wear my clothes. And I have a shocking reputation. A really wicked woman, I once heard pious old Lady Surbiton call me! Dear old thing! It did me no end of good. Then I have the very great advantage of never caring for any one more than a few days together. Men find that annoying."

"You have violent fancies," he remarked, "and strange ones."

"Perhaps," she admitted. "They concern no one except myself."

"This Souspennier craze, for instance!"

She nodded.

"Well, you can't say that I'm not honest. It is positively my only virtue. I adore the truth. I loathe a lie. That is one reason, I daresay, why I can only barely tolerate you. You are a shocking—a gross liar."

"Muriel!"

"Oh, don't look at me like that," she exclaimed irritably. "You must hear the truth sometimes. And now, please remember that I came to lunch with you to hear about your visit this morning."

The Prince gnawed his moustache, and the light in his eyes was not a pleasant thing to see. This woman with her reckless life, her odd fascination, her brusque hatred of affectations, was a constant torment to him. If only he could once get her thoroughly into his power.

"My visit," he said, "was wholly successful. It could not well be otherwise. Lucille has returned to Dorset House. Souspennier is confounded altogether by a little revelation which I ventured to make. He spoke of an appeal. I let him know with whom he would have to deal. I left him nerveless and crushed. He can do nothing save by open revolt. And if he tries that—well, there will be no more of this wonderful Mr. Sabin."

"Altogether a triumph to you," she remarked scornfully. "Oh, I know the sort of thing. But, after all, my dear Ferdinand, what of last night. I hate the woman, but she played the game, and played it well. We were fooled, both of us. And to think that I—"

She broke off with a short laugh. The Prince looked at her curiously.

"Perhaps," he said, "you had some idea of consoling the desolate husband?"

"Perhaps I had," she answered coolly. "It didn't come off, did it? Order me some coffee, and give me a cigarette, my friend. I have something else to say to you."

He obeyed her, and she leaned back in the high chair.

"Listen to me," she said. "I have nothing whatever to do with you and Lucille. I suppose you will get your revenge on Souspennier through her. It won't be like you if you don't try, and you ought to have the game pretty well in your own hands. But I won't have Souspennier harmed. You understand?"

He shrugged his shoulders.

"Souspennier," he said, "must take care. If he oversteps the bounds he must pay the penalty."

She leaned forward. There was a look in her face which he knew very well.

"You and I understand one another," she said coolly. "If you want me for an enemy you can have me. Very likely I shall tell you before long that you can do what you like with the man. But until I do it will be very dangerous for you if harm comes to him."

"It is no use," he answered doggedly. "If he attacks he must be silenced."

"If he attacks," she answered, "you must give me twenty-four hours clear notice before you move a hand against him. Afterwards—well, we will discuss that."

"You had better," he said, looking at her with an ugly gleam in his eyes, "persuade him to take you for a little tour on the Continent. It would be safer."

"If he would come," she said coolly, "I would go to-morrow. But he won't—just yet. Never mind. You have heard what I wanted to say. Now shall we go? I am going to get some sleep this afternoon. Everybody tells me that I look like a ghost."

"Why not come to Grosvenor Square with me?" he leaning a little across the table. "Patoff shall make you some Russian tea, and afterwards you shall sleep as long as you like."

"How idyllic!" she answered, with a faint sarcastic smile. "It goes to my heart to decline so charming an invitation. But, to tell you the truth, it would bore me excessively."

He muttered something under his breath which startled the waiter at his elbow. Then he followed her out of the room. She paused for a few moments in the portico to finish buttoning her gloves.

"Many thanks for my lunch," she said, nodding to him carelessly. "I'm sure I've been a delightful companion."

"You have been a very tormenting one," he answered gloomily as he followed her out on to the pavement.

"You should try Lucille," she suggested maliciously.

He stood by her side while they waited for her carriage, and looked at her critically. Her slim, elegant figure had never seemed more attractive to him. Even the insolence of her tone and manner had an odd sort of fascination. He tried to hold for a moment the fingers which grasped her skirt.

"I think," he whispered, "that after you Lucille would be dull!"

She laughed.

"That is because Lucille has morals and a conscience," she said, "and I have neither. But, dear me, how much more comfortably one gets on without them. No, thank you, Prince. My coupe is only built for one. Remember."

She flung him a careless nod from the window. The Prince remained on the pavement until after the little brougham had driven away. Then he smiled softly to himself as he turned to follow it.

"No!" he said. "I think not! I think that she will not get our good friend Souspennier. We shall see!"

XXIV

A barely furnished man's room, comfortable, austere, scholarly. The refuge of a busy man, to judge by the piles of books and papers which littered the large open writing-table. There were despatch boxes turned upside down, a sea of parchment and foolscap. In the midst of it all a man deep in thought.

A visitor, entering with the freedom of an old acquaintance, laid his hand upon his shoulder and greeted him with an air of suppressed enthusiasm.

"Planning the campaign, eh, Brott? Or is that a handbook to Court etiquette? You will need it within the week. There are all sorts of rumours at the clubs."

Brott shook himself free from his fit of apathetic reflection. He would not have dared to tell his visitor where his thoughts had been for the last half hour.

"Somehow," he said, "I do not think that little trip to Windsor will come just yet. The King will never send for me unless he is compelled."

His visitor, an ex-Cabinet Minister, a pronounced Radical and a lifelong friend of Brott's, shrugged his shoulders.

"That time," he said, "is very close at hand. He will send for Letheringham first, of course, and great pressure will be brought to bear upon him to form a ministry. But without you he will be helpless. He has not the confidence of the people."

"Without me," Brott repeated slowly. "You think then that I should not accept office with Letheringham?"

His visitor regarded him steadily for a moment, open-mouthed, obviously taken aback.

"Brott, are you in your right senses?" he asked incredulously. "Do you know what you are saying?"

Brott laughed a little nervously.

"This is a great issue, Grahame," he said. "I will confess that I am in an undecided state. I am not sure that the country is in a sufficiently advanced state for our propaganda. Is this really our opportunity, or is it only the shadow of what is to come thrown before? If we show our hand too soon all is lost for this generation. Don't look at me as though I were insane, Grahame. Remember that the country is only just free from a long era of Conservative rule."

"The better our opportunity," Grahame answered vigorously. "Two decades of puppet government are enervating, I admit, but they only pave the way more surely to the inevitable reaction. What is the matter with you, Brott? Are you ill? This is the great moment of our lives. You must speak at Manchester and Birmingham within this week. Glasgow is already preparing for you. Everything and everybody waits for your judgment. Good God, man, it's magnificent! Where's your enthusiasm? Within a month you must be Prime Minister, and we will show the world the way to a new era."

Brott sat quite still. His friend's words had stirred him for the moment. Yet he seemed the victim of a curious indecision. Grahame leaned over towards him.

"Brott, old friend," he said, "you are not ill?"

Brott shook his head.

"I am perfectly well," he said.

Grahame hesitated.

"It is a delicate thing to mention," he said. "Perhaps I shall pass even the bounds of our old comradeship. But you have changed. Something is wrong with you. What is it?"

"There is nothing," Brott answered, looking up. "It is your fancy. I am well enough."

Grahame's face was dark with anxiety.

"This is no idle curiosity of mine," he said. "You know me better than that. But the cause which is nearer my heart than life itself is at stake. Brott, you are the people's man, their promised redeemer. Think of them, the toilers, the oppressed, God's children, groaning under the iniquitous laws of generations of evil statesmanship. It is the dawn of their new day, their faces are turned to you. Man, can't you hear them crying? You can't fail them. You mustn't. I don't know what is the matter with you, Brott, but away with it. Free yourself, man."

Brott sighed wearily, but already there was a change in him. His face was hardening—the lines in his face deepened. Grahame continued hastily—eagerly.

"Public men," he said, "are always at the mercy of the halfpenny press, but you know, Brott, your appearance so often in Society lately has set men's tongues wagging. There is no harm done, but it is time to stop them. You are right to want to understand these people. You must go down amongst them. It has been slumming in Mayfair for you, I know. But have done with it now. It is these people we are going to fight. Let it be open war. Let them hear your programme at Glasgow. We don't want another French Revolution, but it is going to be war against the drones, fierce, merciless war! You must break with them, Brott, once and for ever. And the time is now."

Brott held out his hand across the table. No one but this one man could have read the struggle in his face.

"You are right, Grahame. I thank you. I thank you as much for what you have left unsaid as for what you have said. I was a fool to think of compromising. Letheringham is a nerveless leader. We should have gone pottering on for another seven years. Thank God that you came when you did. See here!"

He tossed him over a letter. Grahame's cheek paled as he read.

"Already!" he murmured.

Brott nodded.

"Read it!"

Grahame devoured every word. His eyes lit up with excitement.

"My prophecy exactly," he exclaimed, laying it down. "It is as I said. He cannot form the ministry without you. His letter is abject. He gives himself away. It is an entreaty. And your answer?"

"Has not yet gone," Brott said. "You shall write it yourself if you like. I am thankful that you came when you did."

"You were hesitating?" Grahame exclaimed.

"I was."

Grahame looked at him in wonder, and Brott faced him sturdily.

"It seems like treason to you, Grahame!" he said. "So it does to me now. I want nothing in the future to come between us," he continued more slowly, "and I should like if I can to expunge the memory of this interview. And so I am going to tell you the truth." Grahame held out his hand.

"Don't!" he said. "I can forget without."

Brott shook his head.

"No," he said. "You had better understand everything. The halfpenny press told the truth. Yet only half the truth. I have been to all these places, wasted my time, wasted their time, from a purely selfish reason— to be near the only woman I have ever cared for, the woman, Grahame!"

"I knew it," Grahame murmured. "I fought against the belief, I thought that I had stifled it. But I knew it all the time."

"If I have seemed lukewarm sometimes of late," Brott said, "there is the cause. She is an aristocrat, and my politics are hateful to her. She has told me so seriously, playfully, angrily. She has let me feel it in a hundred ways. She has drawn me into discussions and shown the utmost horror of my views. I have cared for her all my life, and she knows it. And I think, Grahame, that lately she has been trying constantly, persistently, to tone down my opinions. She has let me understand that they are a bar between us. And it is a horrible confession, Grahame, but I believe that I was wavering. This invitation from Letheringham seemed such a wonderful opportunity for compromise."

"This must never go out of the room," Grahame said hoarsely. "It would ruin your popularity. They would never trust you again."

"I shall tell no one else," Brott said.

"And it is over?" Grahame demanded eagerly.

"It is over."

THE DUKE OF DORSET, WHO entertained for his party, gave a great dinner that night at Dorset House, and towards its close the Prince of Saxe Leinitzer, who was almost the only non-political guest, moved up to his host in response to an eager summons. The Duke was perturbed.

"You have heard the news, Saxe Leinitzer?"

"I did not know of any news," the Prince answered. "What is it?"

"Brott has refused to join with Letheringham in forming a ministry. It is rumoured even that a coalition was proposed, and that Brott would have nothing to do with it."

The Prince looked into his wineglass.

"Ah!" he said.

"This is disturbing news," the Duke continued. "You do not seem to appreciate its significance."

The Prince looked up again.

"Perhaps not," he said. "You shall explain to me."

"Brott refuses to compromise," the Duke said. "He stands for a ministry of his own selection. Heaven only knows what mischief this may mean. His doctrines are thoroughly revolutionary. He is an iconoclast with a genius for destruction. But he has the ear of the people. He is to-day their Rienzi."

The Prince nodded.

"And Lucille?" he remarked. "What does she say?"

"I have not spoken to her," the Duke answered. "The news has only just come."

"We will speak to her," the Prince said, "together."

Afterwards in the library there was a sort of informal meeting, and their opportunity came.

"So you have failed, Countess," her host said, knitting his grey brows at her.

She smilingly acknowledged defeat.

"But I can assure you," she said, "that I was very near success. Only on Monday he had virtually made up his mind to abandon the extreme party and cast in his lot with Letheringham. What has happened to change him I do not know."

The Prince curled his fair moustache.

"It is a pity," he said, "that he changed his mind. For one thing is very certain. The Duke and I are agreed upon it. A Brott ministry must never be formed."

She looked up quickly.

"What do you mean?"

The Prince answered her without hesitation.

"If one course fails," he said, "another must be adopted. I regret having to make use of means which are somewhat clumsy and obvious. But our pronouncement on this one point is final. Brott must not be allowed to form a ministry."

She looked at him with something like horror in her soft full eyes.

"What would you do?" she murmured.

The Prince shrugged his shoulders.

"Well," he said, "we are not quite medieval enough to adopt the only really sensible method and remove Mr. Brott permanently from the face of the earth. We should stop a little short of that, but I can assure you that Mr. Brott's health for the next few months is a matter for grave uncertainty. It is a pity for his sake that you failed."

She bit her lip.

"Do you know if he is still in London?" she asked.

"He must be on the point of leaving for Scotland," the Duke answered. "If he once mounts the platform at Glasgow there will be no further chance of any compromise. He will be committed irretrievably to his campaign of anarchy."

"And to his own disaster," the Prince murmured.

Lucille remained for a moment deep in thought. Then she looked up.

"If I can find him before he starts," she said hurriedly, "I will make one last effort."

XXV

He peered forward over his desk at the tall graceful figure whose entrance had been so noiseless, and whose footsteps had been so light that she stood almost within a few feet of him before he was even aware of her presence. Then his surprise was so great that he could only gasp out her name.

"You! Lucille!"

She smiled upon him delightfully.

"Me! Lucille! Don't blame your servant. I assured him that I was expected, so he allowed me to enter unannounced. His astonishment was a delightful testimony to your reputation, by the bye. He was evidently not used to these invasions."

Brott had recovered himself by this time, and if any emotion still remained he was master of it.

"You must forgive my surprise!" he said. "You have of course something important to say to me. Will you not loosen your cloak?"

She unfastened the clasp and seated herself in his most comfortable chair. The firelight flashed and glittered on the silver ornaments of her dress; her neck and arms, with their burden of jewels, gleamed like porcelain in the semi-darkness outside the halo of his student lamp. And he saw that her dark hair hung low behind in graceful folds as he had once admired it. He stood a little apart, and she noted his traveling clothes and the various signs of a journey about the room.

"You may be glad to see me," she remarked, looking at him with a smile. "You don't look it."

"I am anxious to hear your news," he answered. "I am convinced that you have something important to say to me."

"Supposing," she answered, still looking at him steadily, "supposing I were to say that I had no object in coming here at all—that it was merely a whim? What should you say then?"

"I should take the liberty," he answered quietly, "of doubting the evidence of my senses."

There was a moment's silence. She felt his aloofness. It awoke in her some of the enthusiasm with which this mission itself had failed to inspire her. This man was measuring his strength against hers.

"It was not altogether a whim," she said, her eyes falling from his, "and yet—now I am here—it does not seem easy to say what was in my mind."

He glanced towards the clock.

"I fear," he said, "that it may sound ungallant, but in case this somewhat mysterious mission of yours is of any importance I had better perhaps tell you that in twenty minutes I must leave to catch the Scotch mail."

She rose at once to her feet, and swept her cloak haughtily around her.

"I have made a mistake," she said. "Be so good as to pardon my intrusion. I shall not trouble you again."

She was half-way across the room. She was at the door, her hand was upon the handle. He was white to the lips, his whole frame was shaking with the effort of intense repression. He kept silence, till only a flutter of her cloak was to be seen in the doorway. And then the cry which he had tried so hard to stifle broke from his lips.

"Lucille! Lucille!"

She hesitated, and came back—looking at him, so he thought, with trembling lips and eyes soft with unshed tears.

"I was a brute," he murmured. "I ought to be grateful for this chance of seeing you once more, of saying good-bye to you."

"Good-bye!" she repeated.

"Yes," he said gravely. "It must be good-bye. I have a great work before me, and it will cut me off completely from all association with your world and your friends. Something wider and deeper than an ocean will divide us. Something so wide that our hands will never reach across."

"You can talk about it very calmly," she said, without looking at him.

"I have been disciplining myself," he answered.

She rested her face upon her hand, and looked into the fire.

"I suppose," she said, "this means that you have refused Mr. Letheringham's offer."

"I have refused it," he answered.

"I am sorry," she said simply.

She rose from her chair with a sudden start, began to draw on her cloak, and then let it fall altogether from her shoulders.

"Why do you do this?" she asked earnestly. "Is it that you are so ambitious? You used not to be so—in the old days."

He laughed bitterly.

"You too, then," he said, "can remember. Ambitious! Well, why not? To be Premier of England, to stand for the people, to carry through to its logical consummation a bloodless revolution, surely this is worth while. Is there anything in the world better worth having than power?"

"Yes," she answered, looking him full in the eyes.

"What is it then? Let me know before it is too late."

"Love!"

He threw his arms about her. For a moment she was powerless in his grasp.

"So be it then," he cried fiercely. "Give me the one, and I will deny the other. Only no half measures! I will drink to the bottom of the cup or not at all."

She shook herself free from him, breathless, consumed with an anger to which she dared not give voice. For a moment or two she was speechless. Her bosom rose and fell, a bright streak of colour flared in her cheeks. Brott stood away from her, white and stern.

"You—are clumsy!" she said. "You frighten me!"

Her words carried no conviction. He looked at her with a new suspicion.

"You talk like a child," he answered roughly, "or else your whole conduct is a fraud. For months I have been your slave. I have abandoned my principles, given you my time, followed at your heels like a tame dog. And for what? You will not marry me, you will not commit yourself to anything. You are a past mistress in the art of binding fools to your chariot wheels. You know that I love you—that there breathes on this earth no other woman for me but you. I have told you this in all save words a hundred times. And now—now it is my turn. I have been played with long enough. You are here unbidden—unexpected. You can consider that door locked. Now tell me why you came."

Lucille had recovered herself. She stood before him, white but calm.

"Because," she said, "I am a woman."

"That means that you came without reason—on impulse?" he asked.

"I came," she said, "because I heard that you were about to take a step which must separate us for ever."

"And that," he asked, "disturbed you?"

"Yes!"

"Come, we are drawing nearer together," he said, a kindling light in his eyes. "Now answer me this. How much do you care if this eternal separation does come? Here am I on the threshold of action. Unless

I change my mind within ten minutes I must throw in my lot with those whom you and your Order loathe and despise. There can be no half measures. I must be their leader, or I must vanish from the face of the political world. This I will do if you bid me. But the price must be yourself—wholly, without reservation—yourself, body and soul."

"You care—as much as that?" she murmured.

"Ask me no questions, answer mine!" he cried fiercely. "You shall stay with me here—or in five minutes I leave on my campaign."

She laughed musically.

"This is positively delicious," she exclaimed. "I am being made love to in medieval fashion. Other times other manners, sir! Will you listen to reason?"

"I will listen to nothing—save your answer, yes or no," he declared, drawing on his overcoat.

She laid her hand upon his shoulder.

"Reginald," she said, "you are like the whirlwind—and how can I answer you in five minutes!"

"You can answer me in one," he declared fiercely. "Will you pay my price if I do your bidding? Yes or no! The price is yourself. Now! Yes or no?"

She drew on her own cloak and fastened the clasp with shaking fingers. Then she turned towards the door.

"I wish you good-bye and good fortune, Reginald," she said. "I daresay we may not meet again. It will be better that we do not."

"This then is your answer?" he cried.

She looked around at him. Was it his fancy, or were those tears in her eyes? Or was she really so wonderful an actress?

"Do you think," she said, "that if I had not cared I should have come here?"

"Tell me that in plain words," he cried. "It is all I ask."

The door was suddenly opened. Grahame stood upon the threshold. He looked beyond Lucille to Brott.

"You must really forgive me," he said, "but there is barely time to catch the train, Brott. I have a hansom waiting, and your luggage is on."

Brott answered nothing. Lucille held out her hands to him.

"Yes or no?" he asked her in a low hoarse tone.

"You must—give me time! I don't want to lose you. I—"

He caught up his coat.

"Coming, Grahame," he said firmly. "Countess, I must beg your pardon ten thousand times for this abrupt departure. My servants will call your carriage."

She leaned towards him, beautiful, anxious, alluring.

"Reginald!"

"Yes or no," he whispered in her ear.

"Give me until to-morrow," she faltered.

"Not one moment," he answered. "Yes—now, this instant—or I go!"

"Brott! My dear man, we have not a second to lose."

"You hear!" he muttered. "Yes or no?"

She trembled.

"Give me until to-morrow," she begged. "It is for your own sake. For your own safety."

He turned on his heel! His muttered speech was profane, but inarticulate. He sprang into the hansom by Grahame's side.

"Euston!" the latter cried through the trap-door. "Double fare, cabby. We must catch the Scotchman."

Lucille came out a few moments later, and looked up and down the street as her brougham drove smartly up. The hansom was fast disappearing in the distance. She looked after it and sighed.

XXVI

L ucille gave a little start of amazement as she realised that she was not alone in the brougham. She reached out for the check-cord, but a strong hand held hers.

"My dear Lucille," a familiar voice exclaimed, "why this alarm? Is it your nerves or your eyesight which is failing you?"

Her hand dropped. She turned towards him.

"It is you, then, Prince!" she said. "But why are you here? I do not understand."

The Prince shrugged his shoulders.

"It is so simple," he said. "We are all very anxious indeed to hear the result of your interview with Brott—and apart from that, I personally have too few opportunities to act as your escort to let a chance go by. I trust that my presence is not displeasing to you?"

She laughed a little uneasily.

"It is at any rate unnecessary," she answered. "But since you are here I may as well make my confession. I have failed."

"It is incredible," the Prince murmured.

"As you will—but it is true," she answered. "I have done my very best, or rather my worst, and the result has been failure. Mr. Brott has a great friend—a man named Grahame, whose influence prevailed against mine. He has gone to Scotland."

"That is serious news," the Prince said quietly.

Lucille leaned back amongst the cushions.

"After all," she declared, "we are all out of place in this country. There is no scope whatever for such schemes and intrigues as you and all the rest of them delight in. In France and Russia, even in Austria, it is different. The working of all great organisation there is underground— it is easy enough to meet plot by counterplot, to suborn, to deceive, to undermine. But here all the great games of life seem to be played with the cards upon the table. We are hopelessly out of place. I cannot think, Prince, what ill chance led you to ever contemplate making your headquarters in London."

The Prince stroked his long moustache.

"That is all very well, Lucille," he said, "but you must remember that in England we have very large subscriptions to the Order. These people will not go on paying for nothing. There was a meeting of the London branch a few months ago, and it was decided that unless some practical work was done in this country all English subscriptions should cease. We had no alternative but to come over and attempt something. Brott is of course the bete noire of our friends here. He is distinctly the man to be struck at."

"And what evil stroke of fortune," Lucille asked, "induced you to send for me?"

"That is a very cruel speech, dear lady," the Prince murmured.

"I hope," Lucille said, "that you have never for a moment imagined that I find any pleasure in what I am called upon to do."

"Why not? It must be interesting. You can have had no sympathy with Brott—a hopeless plebeian, a very paragon of Anglo-Saxon stupidity?"

Lucille laughed scornfully.

"Reginald Brott is a man, at any rate, and an honest one," she answered. "But I am too selfish to think much of him. It is myself whom I pity. I have a home, Prince, and a husband. I want them both."

"You amaze me," the Prince said slowly. "Lucille, indeed, you amaze me. You have been buried alive for three years. Positively we believed that our summons would sound to you like a message from Heaven."

Lucille was silent for a moment. She rubbed the mist from the carriage window and looked out into the streets.

"Well," she said, "I hope that you realise now how completely you have misunderstood me. I was perfectly happy in America. I have been perfectly miserable here. I suppose that I have grown too old for intrigues and adventures."

"Too old, Lucille," the Prince murmured, leaning a little towards her. "Lucille, you are the most beautiful woman in London. Many others may have told you so, but there is no one, Lucille, who is so devotedly, so hopelessly your slave as I."

She drew her hand away, and sat back in her corner. The man's hot breath fell upon her cheek, his eyes seemed almost phosphorescent in the darkness. Lucille could scarcely keep the biting words from her tongue.

"You do not answer me, Lucille. You do not speak even a single kind word to me. Come! Surely we are old friends. We should understand one another. It is not a great deal that I ask from your kindness—not a great deal to you, but it is all the difference between happiness and misery for me."

"This is a very worn-out game, Prince," Lucille said coldly. "You have been making love to women in very much the same manner for twenty years, and I—well, to be frank, I am utterly weary of being made love to like a doll. Laugh at me as you will, my husband is the only man who interests me in the slightest. My failure to-day is almost welcome to me. It has at least brought my work here to a close. Come, Prince, if you want to earn my eternal gratitude, tell me now that I am a free woman."

"You give me credit," the Prince said slowly, "for great generosity. If I let you go it seems to me that I shall lose you altogether. You will go to your husband. He will take you away!"

"Why not?" Lucille asked. "I want to go. I am tired of London. You cannot lose what you never possessed—what you never had the slightest chance of possessing."

The Prince laughed softly—not a pleasant laugh, not even a mirthful one.

"Dear lady," he said, "you speak not wisely. For I am very much in earnest when I say that I love you, and until you are kinder to me I shall not let you go."

"That is rather a dangerous threat, is it not?" Lucille asked. "You dare to tell me openly that you will abuse your position, that you will keep me bound a servant to the cause, because of this foolish fancy of yours?"

The Prince smiled at her through the gloom—a white, set smile.

"It is no foolish fancy, Lucille. You will find that out before long. You have been cold to me all your life. Yet you would find me a better friend than enemy."

"If I am to choose," she said steadily, "I shall choose the latter."

"As you will," he answered. "In time you will change your mind."

The carriage had stopped. The Prince alighted and held out his hand. Lucille half rose, and then with her foot upon the step she paused and looked around.

"Where are we?" she exclaimed. "This is not Dorset House."

"No, we are in Grosvenor Square," the Prince answered. "I forgot to tell you that we have a meeting arranged for here this evening. Permit me." But Lucille resumed her seat in the carriage.

"It is your house, is it not?" she asked.

"Yes. My house assuredly."

"Very well," Lucille said. "I will come in when the Duchess of Dorset shows herself at the window or the front door—or Felix, or even De Brouillae."

The Prince still held open the carriage door.

"They will all be here," he assured her. "We are a few minutes early."

"Then I will drive round to Dorset House and fetch the Duchess. It is only a few yards."

The Prince hesitated. His cheeks were very white, and something like a scowl was blackening his heavy, insipid face.

"Lucille," he said, "you are very foolish. It is not much I ask of you, but that little I will have or I pledge my word to it that things shall go ill with you and your husband. There is plain speech for you. Do not be absurd. Come within, and let us talk. What do you fear? The house is full of servants, and the carriage can wait for you here."

Lucille smiled at him—a maddening smile.

"I am not a child," she said, "and such conversations as I am forced to hold with you will not be under your own roof. Be so good as to tell the coachman to drive to Dorset House."

The Prince turned on his heel with a furious oath.

"He can drive you to Hell," he answered thickly.

Lucille found the Duchess and Lady Carey together at Dorset House. She looked from one to the other.

"I thought that there was a meeting to-night," she remarked.

The Duchess shook her head.

"Not to-night," she answered. "It would not be possible. General Dolinski is dining at Marlborough House, and De Broullae is in Paris. Now tell us all about Mr. Brott."

"He has gone to Scotland," Lucille answered. "I have failed."

Lady Carey looked up from the depths of the chair in which she was lounging.

"And the prince?" she asked. "He went to meet you!"

"He also failed," Lucille answered.

XXVII

M r. Sabin drew a little breath, partly of satisfaction because he had discovered the place he sought, and partly of disgust at the neighbourhood in which he found himself. Nevertheless, he descended three steps from the court into which he had been directed, and pushed open the swing door, behind which Emil Sachs announced his desire to supply the world with dinners at eightpence and vin ordinaire at fourpence the small bottle.

A stout black-eyed woman looked up at his entrance from behind the counter. The place was empty.

"What does monsieur require she asked, peering forward through the gloom with some suspicion. For the eightpenny dinners were the scorn of the neighbourhood, and strangers were rare in the wine shop of Emil Sachs."

Mr. Sabin smiled.

"One of your excellent omelettes, my good Annette," he answered, "if your hand has not lost its cunning!"

She gave a little cry.

"It is monsieur!" she exclaimed. "After all these years it is monsieur! Ah, you will pardon that I did not recognise you. This place is a cellar. Monsieur has not changed. In the daylight one would know him anywhere."

The woman talked fast, but even in that dim light Mr. Sabin knew quite well that she was shaking with fear. He could see the corners of her mouth twitch. Her black eyes rolled incessantly, but refused to meet his. Mr. Sabin frowned.

"You are not glad to see me, Annette!"

She leaned over the counter.

"For monsieur's own sake," she whispered, "go!"

Mr. Sabin stood quite still for a short space of time.

"Can I rest in there for a few minutes?" he asked, pointing to the door which led into the room beyond.

The woman hesitated. She looked up at the clock and down again.

"Emil will return," she said, "at three. Monsieur were best out of the neighbourhood before then. For ten minutes it might be safe."

Mr. Sabin passed forward. The woman lifted the flap of the counter and followed him. Within was a smaller room, far cleaner and better appointed than the general appearance of the place promised. Mr. Sabin seated himself at one of the small tables. The linen cloth, he noticed, was spotless, the cutlery and appointments polished and clean.

"This, I presume," he remarked, "is not where you serve the eightpenny table d'hote?"

The woman shrugged her shoulders.

"But it would not be possible," she answered. "We have no customers for that. If one arrives we put together a few scraps. But one must make a pretense. Monsieur understands?"

Mr. Sabin nodded.

"I will take," he said, "a small glass of fin champagne."

She vanished, and reappeared almost immediately with the brandy in a quaintly cut liqueur glass. A glance at the clock as she passed seemed to have increased her anxiety.

"If monsieur will drink his liqueur and depart," she prayed. "Indeed, it will be for the best."

Mr. Sabin set down his glass. His steadfast gaze seemed to reduce Annette into a state of nervous panic.

"Annette," he said, "they have placed me upon the list."

"It is true, monsieur," she answered. "Why do you come here?"

"I wanted to know first for certain that they had ventured so far," Mr. Sabin said. "I believe that I am only the second person in this country who has been so much honoured."

The woman drew nearer to him.

"Monsieur," she said, "your only danger is to venture into such parts as these. London is so safe, and the law is merciless. They only watch. They will attempt nothing. Do not leave England. There is here no machinery of criminals. Besides, the life of monsieur is insured."

"Insured?" Mr. Sabin remarked quietly. "That is good news. And who pays the premium?"

"A great lady, monsieur! I know no more. Monsieur must go indeed. He has found his way into the only place in London where he is not safe."

Mr. Sabin rose.

"You are expecting, perhaps," he said, "one of my friends from the—"

She interrupted him.

"It is true," she declared. "He may be here at any instant. The time is already up. Oh, monsieur, indeed, indeed it would not do for him to find you."

Mr. Sabin moved towards the door.

"You are perhaps right," he said regretfully, "although I should much like to hear about this little matter of life insurance while I am here."

"Indeed, monsieur," Annette declared, "I know nothing. There is nothing which I can tell monsieur."

Mr. Sabin suddenly leaned forward. His gaze was compelling. His tone was low but terrible.

"Annette," he said, "obey me. Send Emil here."

The woman trembled, but she did not move. Mr. Sabin lifted his forefinger and pointed slowly to the door. The woman's lips parted, but she seemed to have lost the power of speech.

"Send Emil here!" Mr. Sabin repeated slowly.

Annette turned and left the room, groping her way to the door as though her eyesight had become uncertain. Mr. Sabin lit a cigarette and looked for a moment carefully into the small liqueur glass out of which he had drunk.

"That was unwise," he said softly to himself. "Just such a blunder might have cost me everything."

He held it up to the light and satisfied himself that no dregs remained. Then he took from his pocket a tiny little revolver, and placing it on the table before him, covered it with his handkerchief. Almost immediately a door at the farther end of the room opened and closed. A man in dark clothes, small, unnaturally pale, with deep-set eyes and nervous, twitching mouth, stood before him. Mr. Sabin smiled a welcome at him.

"Good-morning, Emil Sachs," he said. "I am glad that you have shown discretion. Stand there in the light, please, and fold your arms. Thanks. Do not think that I am afraid of you, but I like to talk comfortably."

"I am at monsieur's service," the man said in a low tone.

"Exactly. Now, Emil, before starting to visit you I left a little note behind addressed to the chief of the police here—no, you need not start—to be sent to him only if my return were unduly delayed. You can guess what that note contained. It is not necessary for us to revert to—unpleasant subjects."

The man moistened his dry lips.

"It is not necessary," he repeated. "Monsieur is as safe here—from me—as at his own hotel."

"Excellent!" Mr. Sabin said. "Now listen, Emil. It has pleased me chiefly, as you know, for the sake of your wife, the good Annette, to be very merciful to you as regards the past. But I do not propose to allow you to run a poison bureau for the advantage of the Prince of Saxe Leinitzer and his friends—more especially, perhaps, as I am at present upon his list of superfluous persons."

The man trembled.

"Monsieur," he said, "the Prince knows as much as you know, and he has not the mercy that one shows to a dog."

"You will find," Mr. Sabin said, "that if you do not obey me, I myself can develop a similar disposition. Now answer me this! You have within the last few days supplied several people with that marvelous powder for the preparation of which you are so justly famed."

"Several—no, monsieur! Two only."

"Their names?"

The man trembled.

"If they should know!"

"They will not, Emil. I will see to that."

"The first I supplied to the order of the Prince."

"Good! And the second?"

"To a lady whose name I do not know."

Mr. Sabin raised his eyebrows.

"Is not that," he remarked, "a little irregular?"

"The lady wrote her request before me in the yellow crayon. It was sufficient."

"And you do not know her name, Emil?"

"No, monsieur. She was dark and tall, and closely veiled. She was here but a few minutes since."

"Dark and tall!" Mr. Sabin repeated to himself thoughtfully. "Emil, you are telling me the truth?"

"I do not dare to tell you anything else, monsieur," the man answered.

Mr. Sabin did not continue his interrogations for a few moments. Suddenly he looked up.

"Has that lady left the place yet, Emil?"

"No, monsieur!"

Mr. Sabin smiled.

"Have you a back exit?" he asked.

"None that the lady would know of," Emil answered. "She must pass along the passage which borders this apartment, and enter the bar by a door from behind. If monsieur desires it, it is impossible for her to leave unobserved."

"That is excellent, Emil," Mr. Sabin said. "Now there is one more question—quite a harmless one. Annette spoke of my life being in some way insured."

"It is true, monsieur," Emil admitted. "A lady who also possessed the yellow crayon came here the day that—that monsieur incurred the displeasure of—of his friends. She tried to bribe me to blow up my laboratory and leave the country, or that I should substitute a harmless powder for any required by the Prince. I was obliged to refuse."

"And then?"

"Then she promised me a large sum if you were alive in six months, and made me at once a payment.

"Dear me," Mr. Sabin said, "this is quite extraordinary."

"I can tell monsieur the lady's name," Emil continued, "for she raised her veil, and everywhere the illustrated papers have been full of her picture. It was the lady who was besieged in a little town of South Africa, and who carried despatches for the general, disguised as a man."

"Lady Carey!" Mr. Sabin remarked quietly.

"That was the lady's name," Emil agreed.

Mr. Sabin was thoughtful for a few moments. Then he looked up.

"Emil Sachs," he said sternly, "you have given out at least one portion of your abominable concoction which is meant to end my days. Whether I shall escape it or not remains to be seen. I am forced at the best to discharge my servant, and to live the life of a hunted man. Now you have done enough mischief in the world. To-morrow morning a messenger will place in your hands two hundred pounds. A larger sum will await you at Baring's Bank in New York. You will go there and buy a small restaurant in the business quarter. This is your last chance, Emil. I give it to you for the sake of Annette."

"And I accept it, monsieur, with gratitude."

"For the present—"

Mr. Sabin stopped short. His quick ears had caught the swish of woman's gown passing along the passage outside. Emil too had heard it.

"It is the dark lady," he whispered, "who purchased from me the other powder. See, I open gently this door. Monsieur must both see and hear."

The door at the end of the passage was opened. A woman stepped out into the little bar and made her way towards the door. Here she was met by a man entering. Mr. Sabin held up his forefinger to stop the terrified exclamation which trembled on Emil's lips. The woman was Lucille, the man the Prince. It was Lucille who was speaking.

"You have followed me, Prince. It is intolerable."

"Dear Lucille, it is for your own sake. These are not fit parts for you to visit alone."

"It is my own business," she answered coldly.

The Prince appeared to be in a complaisant mood.

"Come," he said, "the affair is not worth a quarrel. I ask you no questions. Only since we are here I propose that we test the cooking of the good Annette. We will lunch together."

"What, here?" she answered. "Absurd."

"By no means," he answered. "As you doubtless know, the exterior of the place is entirely misleading. These people are old servants of mine. I can answer for the luncheon."

"You can also eat it," came the prompt reply. "I am returning to the carriage."

"But—"

Mr. Sabin emerged through the swing door. "Your discretion, my dear Lucille," he said, smiling, "is excellent. The place is indeed better than it seems, and Annette's cookery may be all that the Prince claims. Yet I think I know better places for a luncheon party, and the ventilation is not of the best. May I suggest that you come with me instead to the Milan?"

"Victor! You here?"

Mr. Sabin smiled as he admitted the obvious fact. The Prince's face was as black as night.

"Believe me," Mr. Sabin said, turning to the Prince, "I sympathise entirely with your feelings at the present moment. I myself have suffered in precisely the same manner. The fact is, intrigue in this country is almost an impossibility. At Paris, Vienna, Pesth, how different! You raise your little finger, and the deed is done. Superfluous people—like myself—are removed like the hairs from your chin. But here intrigue seems indeed to exist only within the pages of a shilling novel, or in a comic opera. The gentleman with a helmet there, who regards us so benignly, will presently earn a shilling by calling me a hansom. Yet in effect he does me a far greater service. He stands for a multitude of cold Anglo-Saxon laws, adamant, incorruptible, inflexible—as certain as the laws of Nature herself. I am quite aware that by this time I ought to be lying in a dark cellar with a gag in my mouth, or perhaps in the river with a dagger in my chest. But here in England, no!"

The Prince smiled—to all appearance a very genial smile.

"You are right, my dear friend," he said, "yet what you say possesses, shall we call it, a somewhat antediluvian flavour. Intrigue is no longer a clumsy game of knife and string and bowl. It becomes to-day a game of finesse. I can assure you that I have no desire to give a stage whistle and have you throttled at my feet. On the contrary, I beg you to use my carriage, which you will find in the street. You will lunch at the Milan with Lucille, and I shall retire discomfited to eat alone at my club. But the game is a long one, my dear friend. The new methods take time."

"This conversation," Mr. Sabin said to Lucille, "is interesting, but it is a little ungallant. I think that we will resume it at some future occasion. Shall we accept the Prince's offer, or shall we be truly democratic and take a hansom."

Lucille passed her arm through his and laughed.

"You are robbing the Prince of me," she declared. "Let us leave him his carriage."

She nodded her farewells to Saxe Leinitzer, who took leave of them with a low bow. As they waited at the corner for a hansom Mr. Sabin glanced back. The Prince had disappeared through the swing doors.

"I want you to promise me one thing," Lucille said earnestly.

"It is promised," Mr. Sabin answered.

"You will not ask me the reason of my visit to this place?"

"I have no curiosity," Mr. Sabin answered. "Come!"

XXVIII

M r. Sabin, contrary to his usual custom, engaged a private room at the Milan. Lucille was in the highest spirits.

"If only this were a game instead of reality!" she said, flashing a brilliant smile at him across the table, "I should find it most fascinating. You seem to come to me always when I want you most. And do you know, it is perfectly charming to be carried off by you in this manner."

Mr. Sabin smiled at her, and there was a look in his eyes which shone there for no other woman.

"It is in effect," he said, "keeping me young. Events seem to have enclosed us in a curious little cobweb. All the time we are struggling between the rankest primitivism and the most delicate intrigue. To-day is the triumph of primitivism."

"Meaning that you, the medieval knight, have carried me off, the distressed maiden, on your shoulder."

"Having confounded my enemy," he continued, smiling, "by an embarrassing situation, a little argument, and the distant view of a policeman's helmet."

"This," she remarked, with a little satisfied sigh as she selected an ortolan, "is a very satisfactory place to be carried off to. And you," she added, leaning across the table and touching his fingers for a moment tenderly, "are a very delightful knight-errant."

He raised the fingers to his lips—the waiter had left the room. She blushed, but yielded her hand readily enough.

"Victor," she murmured, "you would spoil the most faithless woman on earth for all her lovers. You make me very impatient."

"Impatience, then," he declared, "must be the most infectious of fevers. For I too am a terrible sufferer."

"If only the Prince," she said, "would be reasonable."

"I am afraid," Mr. Sabin answered, "that from him we have not much to hope for."

"Yet," she continued, "I have fulfilled all the conditions. Reginald Brott remains the enemy of our cause and Order. Yet some say that his influence upon the people is lessened. In any case, my work is over. He began to mistrust me long ago. To-day I believe that mistrust is the only feeling he has in connection with me. I shall demand my release."

"I am afraid," Mr. Sabin said, "that Saxe Leinitzer has other reasons for keeping you at Dorset House."

She shrugged her shoulders.

"He has been very persistent even before I left Vienna. But he must know that it is hopeless. I have never encouraged him."

"I am sure of it," Mr. Sabin said. "It is the incorrigible vanity of the man which will not be denied. He has been taught to believe himself irresistible. I have never doubted you for a single moment, Lucille. I could not. But you have been the slave of these people long enough. As you say, your task is over. Its failure was always certain. Brott believes in his destiny, and it will be no slight thing which will keep him from following it. They must give you back to me."

"We will go back to America," she said. "I have never been so happy as at Lenox."

"Nor I," Mr. Sahin said softly.

"Besides," she continued, "the times have changed since I joined the Society. In Hungary you know how things were. The Socialists were carrying all before them, a united solid body. The aristocracy were forced to enter into some sort of combination against them. We saved Austria, I am not sure that we did not save Russia. But England is different. The aristocracy here are a strong resident class. They have their House of Lords, they own the land, and will own it for many years to come, their position is unassailable. It is the worst country in Europe for us to work in. The very climate and the dispositions of the people are inimical to intrigue. It is Muriel Carey who brought the Society here. It was a mistake. The country is in no need of it. There is no scope for it."

"If only one could get beyond Saxe Leinitzer," Mr. Sabin said.

She shook her head.

"Behind him," she said, "there is only the one to whom all reference is forbidden. And there is no man in the world who would be less likely to listen to an appeal from you—or from me."

"After all," Mr. Sabin said, "though Saxe Leinitzer is our enemy, I am not sure that he can do us any harm. If he declines to release you— well, when the twelve months are up you are free whether he wishes it or not. He has put me outside the pale. But this is not, or never was, a vindictive Society. They do not deal in assassinations. In this country at least anything of the sort is rarely attempted. If I were a young man with my life to live in the capitals of Europe I should be more or less a social outcast, I suppose. But I am proof against that sort of thing."

Lucille looked a little doubtful.

"The Prince," she said, "is an intriguer of the old school. I know that in Vienna he has more than once made use of more violent means than he would dare to do here. And there is an underneath machinery very seldom used, I believe, and of which none of us who are ordinary members know anything at all, which gives him terrible powers."

Mr. Sabin nodded grimly.

"It was worked against me in America," he said, "but I got the best of it. Here in England I do not believe that he would dare to use it. If so, I think that before now it would have been aimed at Brott. I have just read his Glasgow speech. If he becomes Premier it will lead to something like a revolution."

She sighed.

"Brott is a clever man, and a strong man," she said. "I am sorry for him, but I do not believe that he will never become Prime Minister of England."

Mr. Sabin sipped his wine thoughtfully.

"I believe," he said, "that intrigue is the resource of those who have lived their lives so quickly that they have found weariness. For these things to-day interest me very little. I am only anxious to have you back again, Lucille, to find ourselves on our way to our old home."

She laughed softly.

"And I used to think," she said, "that after all I could only keep you a little time—that presently the voices from the outside world would come whispering in your ears, and you would steal back again to where the wheels of life were turning."

"A man," he answered, "is not easily whispered out of Paradise."

She laughed at him.

"Ah, it is so easy," she said, "to know that your youth was spent at a court."

"There is only one court," he answered, "where men learn to speak the truth."

She leaned back in her chair.

"Oh, you are incorrigible," she said softly. "The one role in life in which I fancied you ill at ease you seem to fill to perfection."

"And that?"

"You are an adorable husband!"

"I should like," he said, "a better opportunity to prove it!"

"Let us hope," she murmured, "that our separation is nearly over. I shall appeal to the Prince to-night. My remaining at Dorset House is no longer necessary."

"I shall come," he said, "and demand you in person."

She shook her head.

"No! They would not let you in, and it would make it more difficult. Be patient a little longer."

He came and sat by her side. She leaned over to meet his embrace.

"You make patience," he murmured, "a torture!"

MR. SABIN WALKED HOME TO HIS rooms late in the afternoon, well content on the whole with his day. He was in no manner prepared for the shock which greeted him on entering his sitting-room. Duson was leaning back in his most comfortable easy-chair.

"Duson!" Mr. Sabin said sharply. "What does this mean?"

There was no answer. Mr. Sabin moved quickly forward, and then stopped short. He had seen dead men, and he knew the signs. Duson was stone dead.

Mr. Sabin's nerve answered to this demand upon it. He checked his first impulse to ring the bell, and looked carefully on the table for some note or message from the dead man. He found it almost at once—a large envelope in Duson's handwriting. Mr. Sabin hastily broke the seal and read:

Monsieur,

I kill myself because it is easiest and best. The poison was given me for you, but I have not the courage to become a murderer, or afterwards to conceal my guilt. Monsieur has been a good master to me, and also Madame la Comtesse was always indulgent and kind. The mistake of my life has been the joining the lower order of the Society. The money which I have received has been but a poor return for the anxiety and trouble which have come upon me since Madame la Comtesse left America. Now that I seek shelter in the grave I am free to warn Monsieur that the Prince of S. L. is his determined and merciless enemy, and that he has already made an unlawful use of his position in the Society for the sake of private vengeance. If monsieur would make a powerful friend he should seek the Lady Muriel Carey.

"Monsieur will be so good as to destroy this when read. My will is in my trunk.

Your Grace's faithful servant,
Jules Duson

Mr. Sabin read this letter carefully through to the end. Then he put it into his pocket-book and quickly rang the bell.

"You had better send for a doctor at once," he said to the waiter who appeared. "My servant appears to have suffered from some sudden illness. I am afraid that he is quite dead."

XXIX

You spoke, my dear Lucille," the Duchess of Dorset said, "of your departure. Is not that a little premature?"

Lucille shrugged her beautiful shoulders, and leaned back in her corner of the couch with half-closed eyes. The Duchess, who was very Anglo-Saxon, was an easy person to read, and Lucille was anxious to know her fate.

"Why premature?" she asked. "I was sent for to use my influence with Reginald Brott. Well, I did my best, and I believe that for days it was just a chance whether I did not succeed. However, as it happened, I failed. One of his friends came and pulled him away just as he was wavering. He has declared himself now once and for all. After his speech at Glasgow he cannot draw back. I was brought all the way from America, and I want to go back to my husband."

The Duchess pursed her lips.

"When one has the honour, my dear," she said, "of belonging to so wonderful an organisation as this we must not consider too closely the selfish claims of family. I am sure that years ago I should have laughed at any one who had told me that I, Georgina Croxton, should ever belong to such a thing as a secret society, even though it had some connection with so harmless and excellent an organisation as the Primrose League."

"It does seem remarkable," Lucille murmured.

"But look what terrible times have come upon us," the Duchess continued, without heeding the interruption. "When I was a girl a Radical was a person absolutely without consideration. Now all our great cities are hot-beds of Socialism and—and anarchism. The whole country seems banded together against the aristocracy and the landowners. Combination amongst us became absolutely necessary in some shape or form. When the Prince came and began to drop hints about the way the spread of Socialism had been checked in Hungary and Austria, and even Germany, I was interested from the first. And when he went further, and spoke of the Society, it was I who persuaded Dorset to join. Dear man, he is very earnest, but very slow, and very averse to anything at all secretive. I am sure the reflection that he is a member of a secret society, even although it is simply a linking together of the aristocracy of Europe in their own defence, has kept him awake for many a night."

Lucille was a little bored.

"The Society," she said, "is an admirable one enough, but just now I am beginning to feel it a little exacting. I think that the Prince expects a good deal of one. I shall certainly ask for my release to-night."

The Duchess looked doubtful.

"Release!" she repeated. "Come, is that not rather an exaggerated expression? I trust that your stay at Dorset House has not in any way suggested an imprisonment."

"On the contrary," Lucille answered; "you and the Duke have been most kind. But you must remember that I have home of my own—and a husband of my own."

"I have no doubt," the Duchess said, "that you will be able to return to them some day. But you must not be impatient. I do not think that the Prince has given up all hopes of Reginald Brott yet."

Lucille was silent. So her emancipation was to be postponed. After all, it was what she had feared. She sat watching idly the Duchess's knitting needles. Lady Carey came sweeping in, wonderful in a black velvet gown and a display of jewels almost barbaric.

"On my way to the opera," she announced. "The Maddersons sent me their box. Will any of you good people come? What do you say, Lucille?"

Lucille shook her head.

"My toilette is deficient," she said; "and besides, I am staying at home to see the Prince. We expect him this evening."

"You'll probably be disappointed then," Lady Carey remarked, "for he's going to join us at the opera. Run and change your gown. I'll wait."

"Are you sure that the Prince will be there?" Lucille asked.

"Certain."

"Then I will come," she said, "if the Duchess will excuse me."

The Duchess and Lady Carey were left alone for a few minutes. The former put down her knitting.

"Why do we keep that woman here," she asked, "now that Brott has broken away from her altogether?"

Lady Carey laughed meaningly.

"Better ask the Prince," she remarked.

The Duchess frowned.

"My dear Muriel," she said, "I think that you are wrong to make such insinuations. I am sure that the Prince is too much devoted to our cause to allow any personal considerations to intervene."

Lady Carey yawned.

"Rats!" she exclaimed.

The Duchess took up her knitting, and went on with it without remark. Lady Carey burst out laughing.

"Don't look so shocked," she exclaimed. "It's funny. I can't help being a bit slangy. You do take everything so seriously. Of course you can see that the Prince is waiting to make a fool of himself over Lucille. He has been trying more or less all his life."

"He may admire her," the Duchess said. "I am sure that he would not allow that to influence him in his present position. By the bye, she is anxious to leave us now that the Brott affair is over. Do you think that the Prince will agree?"

Lady Carey's face hardened.

"I am sure that he will not," she said coolly. "There are reasons why she may not at present be allowed to rejoin her husband."

The Duchess used her needles briskly.

"For my part," she said, "I can see no object in keeping her here any longer. Mr. Brott has shown himself quite capable of keeping her at arm's length. I cannot see what further use she is."

Lady Carey heard the flutter of skirts outside and rose.

"There are wheels within wheels," she remarked. "My dear Lucille, what a charming toilette. We shall have the lady journalists besieging us in our box. Paquin, of course. Good-night, Duchess. Glad to see you're getting on with the socks, or stockings, do you call them?"

Insolent aristocratic, now and then attractive in some strange suggestive way, Lady Carey sat in front of the box and exchanged greetings with her friends. Presently the Prince came in and took the chair between the two women. Lady Carey greeted him with a nod.

"Here's Lucille dying to return to her lawful husband," she remarked. "Odd thing, isn't it? Most of the married women I ever knew are dying to get away from theirs. You can make her happy or miserable in a few moments."

The Prince leaned over between them, but he looked only at Lucille.

"I wish that I could," he murmured. "I wish that that were within my power."

"It is," she answered coolly. "Muriel is quite right. I am most anxious to return to my husband."

The Prince said nothing. Lady Carey, glancing towards him at that moment, was surprised at certain signs of disquietude in his face which startled her.

"What is the matter with you?" she asked almost roughly.

"Matter with me? Nothing," he answered. "Why this unaccustomed solicitude?"

Lady Carey looked into his face fiercely. He was pale, and there was a strained look about his eyes. He seemed, too, to be listening. From outside in the street came faintly to their ears the cry of a newsboy.

"Get me an evening paper," she whispered in his ear.

He got up and left the box. Lucille was watching the people below and had not appreciated the significance of what had been passing between the two. Lady Carey leaned back in the box with half-closed eyes. Her fingers were clenched nervously together, her bosom was rising and falling quickly. If he had dared to defy her! What was it the newsboys were calling? What a jargon! Why did not Saxe Leinitzer return? Perhaps he was afraid! Her heart stood still for a moment, and a little half-stifled cry broke from her lips. Lucille looked around quickly.

"What is the matter, Muriel?" she asked. "Are you faint?"

"Faint, no," Lady Carey answered roughly. "I'm quite well. Don't take any notice of me. Do you hear? Don't look at me."

Lucille obeyed. Lady Carey sat quite still with her hand pressed to her side. It was a stifling pain. She was sure that she had heard at last. "Sudden death of a visitor at the Carlton Hotel." The place was beginning to go round.

Saxe Leinitzer returned. His face to her seemed positively ghastly. He carried an evening paper in his hand. She snatched it away from him. It was there before her in bold, black letters:

"Sudden death in the Carlton Hotel."

Her eyes, dim a moment ago, suddenly blazed fire upon him.

"It shall be a life for a life," she whispered. "If you have killed him you shall die."

Lucille looked at them bewildered. And just then came a sharp tap at the box door. No one answered it, but the door was softly opened. Mr. Sabin stood upon the threshold.

"Pray, don't let me disturb you," he said. "I was unable to refrain from paying you a brief visit. Why, Prince, Lady Carey! I can assure you that I am no ghost."

He glanced from one to the other with a delicate smile of mockery parting his thin lips. For upon the Prince's forehead the perspiration stood out like beads, and he shrank away from Mr. Sabin as from some unholy thing. Lady Carey had fallen back across her chair. Her hand was still pressed to her side, and her face was very pale. A nervous little laugh broke from her lips.

XXX

Mr. Sabin found a fourth chair, and calmly seated himself by Lucille's side. But his eyes were fixed upon Lady Carey. She was slowly recovering herself, but Mr. Sabin, who had never properly understood her attitude towards him, was puzzled at the air of intense relief which almost shone in her face.

"You seem—all of you," he remarked suavely, "to have found the music a little exciting. Wagner certainly knew how to find his way to the emotions. Or perhaps I interrupted an interesting discussion?"

Lucille smiled gently upon him.

"These two," she said, looking from the Prince to Lady Carey, "seem to have been afflicted with a sudden nervous excitement, and yet I do not think that they are, either of them, very susceptible to music."

Lady Carey leaned forward, and looked at him from behind the large fan of white feathers which she was lazily fluttering before her face.

"Your entrance," she murmured, "was most opportune, besides being very welcome. The Prince and I were literally—on the point of flying at one another's throats."

Mr. Sabin glanced at his neighbour and smiled.

"You are certainly a little out of sorts, Saxe Leinitzer," he remarked. "You look pale, and your hands are not quite steady. Nerves, I suppose. You should see Dr. Carson in Brook Street."

The Prince shrugged his shoulders.

"My health," he said, "was never better. It is true that your coming was somewhat of a surprise," he added, looking steadily at Mr. Sabin. "I understood that you had gone for a short journey, and I was not expecting to see you back again so soon."

"Duson," Mr. Sabin said, "has taken that short journey instead. It was rather a liberty, but he left a letter for me fully explaining his motives. I cannot blame him."

The Prince stroked his moustache.

"Ah!" he remarked. "That is a pity. You may, however, find it politic, even necessary, to join him very shortly."

Mr. Sabin smiled grimly.

"I shall go when I am ready," he said, "not before!"

Lucille looked from one to the other with protesting eyebrows.

　　　　　　　　　　　　　　　E. PHILLIPS OPPENHEIM

"Come," she said, "it is very impolite of you to talk in riddles before my face. I have been flattering myself, Victor, that you were here to see me. Do not wound my vanity."

He whispered something in her ear, and she laughed softly back at him. The Prince, with the evening paper in his hand, escaped from the box, and found a retired spot where he could read the little paragraph at his leisure. Lady Carey pretended to be absorbed by the music.

"Has anything happened, Victor?" Lucille whispered.

He hesitated.

"Well, in a sense, yes," he admitted. "I appear to have become unpopular with our friend, the Prince. Duson, who has always been a spy upon my movements, was entrusted with a little sleeping draught for me, which he preferred to take himself. That is all."

"Duson is—"

He nodded.

"He is dead!"

Lucille went very pale.

"This is horrible!" she murmured

"The Prince is a little annoyed, naturally," Mr. Sabin said. "It is vexing to have your plans upset in such a manner."

She shuddered.

"He is hateful! Victor, I fear that he does not mean to let me leave Dorset House just yet. I am almost inclined to become, like you, an outcast. Who knows—we might go free. Bloodshed is always avoided as much as possible, and I do not see how else they could strike at me. Social ostracism is their chief weapon. But in America that could not hurt us."

He shook his head.

"Not yet," he said. "I am sure that Saxe Leinitzer is not playing the game. But he is too well served here to make defiance wise."

"You run the risk yourself," she protested.

He smiled.

"It is a different matter. By the bye, we are overheard."

Lady Carey had forgotten to listen any more to the music. She was watching them both, a steely light in her eyes, her fingers nervously entwined. The Prince was still absent.

"Pray do not consider me," she begged. "So far as I am concerned, your conversation is of no possible interest. But I think you had better remember that the Prince is in the corridor just outside."

"We are much obliged to you," Mr. Sabin said. "The Prince may hear every word I have to say about him. But all the same, I thank you for your warning."

"I fear that we are very unsociable, Muriel," Lucille said, "and, after all, I should never have been here but for you."

Lady Carey turned her left shoulder upon them.

"I beg," she said, "that you will leave me alone with the music. I prefer it."

The Prince suddenly stood upon the threshold. His hand rested lightly upon the arm of another man.

"Come in, Brott," he said. "The women will be charmed to see you. And I don't suppose they've read your speeches. Countess, here is the man who counts all equal under the sun, who decries class, and recognises no social distinctions. Brott was born to lead a revolution. He is our natural enemy. Let us all try to convert him."

Brott was pale, and deep new lines were furrowed on his face. Nevertheless he smiled faintly as he bowed over Lucille's fingers.

"My introduction," he remarked, "is scarcely reassuring. Yet here at least, if anywhere in the world, we should all meet upon equal ground. Music is a universal leveler."

"And we haven't a chance," Lady Carey remarked with uplifted eyebrows, "of listening to a bar of it."

Lucille welcomed the newcomer coldly. Nevertheless, he manoeuvred himself into the place by her side. She took up her fan and commenced swinging it thoughtfully.

"You are surprised to see me here?" he murmured.

"Yes!" she admitted.

He looked wearily away from the stage up into her face.

"And I too," he said. "I am surprised to find myself here!"

"I pictured you," she remarked, "as immersed in affairs. Did I not hear something of a Radical ministry with you for Premier?"

"It has been spoken of," he admitted.

"Then I really cannot see," she said, "what you are doing here."

"Why not?" he asked doggedly.

She shrugged her shoulders.

"In the first place," she said, "you ought to be rushing about amongst your supporters, keeping them up to the mark, and all that sort of thing. And in the second—"

"Well?"

"Are we not the very people against whom you have declared war?"

"I have declared war against no people," he answered. "It is systems and classes, abuses, injustice against which I have been forced to speak. I would not deprive your Order of a single privilege to which they are justly entitled. But you must remember that I am a people's man. Their cause is mine. They look to me as their mouthpiece."

Lucille shrugged her shoulders.

"You cannot evade the point," she said. "If you are the, what do you call it, the mouthpiece of the people, I do not see how you can be anything else than the enemy of the aristocracy."

"The aristocracy? Who are they?" he asked. "I am the enemy of all those who, because they possess an ancient name and inherited wealth, consider themselves the God-appointed bullies of the poor, dealing them out meagre charities, lordly patronage, an unspoken but bitter contempt. But the aristocracy of the earth are not of such as these. Your class are furnishing the world with advanced thinkers every year, every month! Inherited prejudices can never survive the next few generations. The fusion of classes must come."

She shook her head.

"You are sanguine, my friend," she said. "Many generations have come and gone since the wonderful pages of history were opened to us. And during all these years how much nearer have the serf and the aristocrat come together? Nay, have they not rather drifted apart? . . . But listen! This is the great chorus. We must not miss it."

"So the Prince has brought back the wanderer," Lady Carey whispered to Mr. Sabin behind her fan. "Hasn't he rather the air of a sheep who has strayed from the fold?"

Mr. Sabin raised the horn eyeglass, which he so seldom used, and contemplated Brott steadily.

"He reminds me more than ever," he remarked, "of Rienzi. He is like a man torn asunder by great causes. They say that his speech at Glasgow was the triumph of a born orator."

Lady Carey shrugged her shoulders.

"It was practically the preaching a revolution to the people," she said. "A few more such, and we might have the red flag waving. He left Glasgow in a ferment. If he really comes into power, what are we to expect?"

"To the onlookers," Mr. Sabin remarked, "a revolution in this country would possess many interesting features. The common people lack the ferocity of our own rabble, but they are even more determined. I may yet live to see an English Duke earning an honest living in the States."

"It depends very much upon Brott," Lady Carey said. "For his own sake it is a pity that he is in love with Lucille."

Mr. Sabin agreed with her blandly.

"It is," he affirmed, "a most regrettable incident."

She leaned a little towards him. The box was not a large one, and their chairs already touched.

"Are you a jealous husband?" she asked.

"Horribly," he answered.

"Your devotion to Lucille, or rather the singleness of your devotion to Lucille," she remarked, "is positively the most gauche thing about you. It is—absolutely callow!"

He laughed gently.

"Did I not always tell you," he said, "that when I did marry I should make an excellent husband?"

"You are at least," she answered sharply, "a very complaisant one."

The Prince leaned forward from the shadows of the box.

"I invite you all," he said, "to supper with me. It is something of an occasion, this! For I do not think that we shall all meet again just as we are now for a very long time."

"Your invitation," Mr. Sabin remarked, "is most agreeable. But your suggestion is, to say the least of it, nebulous. I do not see what is to prevent your all having supper with me to-morrow evening."

Lady Carey laughed as she rose, and stretched out her hand for her cloak.

"To-morrow evening," she said, "is a long way off. Let us make sure of to-night—before the Prince changes his mind."

Mr. Sabin bowed low.

"To-night by all means," he declared. "But my invitation remains—a challenge!"

XXXI

The Prince, being host, arranged the places at his supper-table. Mr. Sabin found himself, therefore, between Lady Carey and a young German attache, whom they had met in the ante-room of the restaurant. Lucille had the Prince and Mr. Brott on either side of her.

Lady Carey monopolised at first the greater part of the conversation. Mr. Sabin was unusually silent. The German attache, whose name was Baron von Opperman, did not speak until the champagne was served, when he threw a bombshell into the midst of the little party.

"I hear," he said, with a broad and seraphic smile, "that in this hotel there has to-day a murder been committed."

Baron von Opperman was suddenly the cynosure of several pairs of eyes. He was delighted with the success of his attempt towards the general entertainment.

"The evening papers," he continued, "they have in them news of a sudden death. But in the hotel here now they are speaking of something—what you call more—mysterious. There has been ordered an examination post-mortem!"

"It is a case of poisoning then, I presume?" the Prince asked, leaning forward.

"It is so supposed," the attache answered. "It seems that the doctors could find no trace of disease, nothing to have caused death. They were not able to decide anything. The man, they said, was in perfect health—but dead."

"It must have been, then," the Prince remarked, "a very wonderful poison."

"Without doubt," Baron Opperman answered.

The Prince sighed gently.

"There are many such," he murmured. "Indeed the science of toxicology was never so ill-understood as now. I am assured that there are many poisons known only to a few chemists in the world, a single grain of which is sufficient to destroy the strongest man and leave not the slightest trace behind. If the poisoner be sufficiently accomplished he can pursue his—calling without the faintest risk of detection."

Mr. Sabin sipped his wine thoughtfully.

"The Prince is, I believe, right," he remarked. "It is for that reason, doubtless, that I have heard of men whose lives have been threatened, who have deposited in safe places a sealed statement of the danger in which they find themselves, with an account of its source, so that if they should come to an end in any way mysterious there may be evidence against their murderers."

"A very reasonable and judicious precaution," the Prince remarked with glittering eyes. "Only if the poison was indeed of such a nature that it was not possible to trace it nothing worse than suspicion could ever be the lot of any one."

Mr. Sabin helped himself carefully to salad, and resumed the discussion with his next course.

"Perhaps not," he admitted. "But you must remember that suspicion is of itself a grievous embarrassment. No man likes to feel that he is being suspected of murder. By the bye, is it known whom the unfortunate person was?"

"The servant of a French nobleman who is staying in the hotel," Mr. Brott remarked. "I heard as much as that."

Mr. Sabin smiled. Lady Carey glanced at him meaningly.

"You have worried the Prince quite sufficiently," she whispered. "Change the subject."

Mr. Sabin bowed.

"You are very considerate—to the Prince," he said.

"It is perhaps for your sake," she answered. "And as for the Prince—well, you know, or you should know, for how much he counts with me."

Mr. Sabin glanced at her curiously. She was a little flushed as though with some inward excitement. Her eyes were bright and soft. Despite a certain angularity of figure and her hollow cheeks she was certainly one of the most distinguished-looking women in the room.

"You are so dense," she whispered in his ear, "wilfully dense, perhaps. You will not understand that I wish to be your friend."

He smiled with gentle deprecation.

"Do you blame me," he murmured, "if I seem incredulous? For I am an old man, and you are spoken of always as the friend of my enemy, the friend of the Prince."

"I wonder," she said thoughtfully, "if this is really the secret of your mistrust? Do you indeed fear that I have no other interest in life save to serve Saxe Leinitzer?"

"As to that," he answered, "I cannot say. Yet I know that only a few months ago you were acting under orders from him. It is you who brought Lucille from America. It was through you that the first blow was struck at my happiness."

"Cannot I atone?" she murmured under her breath. "If I can I will. And as for the present, well, I am outside his schemes now. Let us be friends. You would find me a very valuable ally."

"Let it be so," he answered without emotion. "You shall help me, if you will, to regain Lucille. I promise you then that my gratitude shall not disappoint you."

She bit her lip.

"And are you sure," she whispered, "that Lucille is anxious to be won back? She loves intrigue, excitement, the sense of being concerned in important doings. Besides—you must have heard what they say about her—and Brott. Look at her now. She wears her grass widowhood lightly enough."

Mr. Sabin looked across the table. Lucille had indeed all the appearance of a woman thoroughly at peace with the world and herself. Brott was talking to her in smothered and eager undertones. The Prince was waiting for an opportunity to intervene. Mr. Sabin looked into Brott's white strong face, and was thoughtful.

"It is a great power—the power of my sex," Lady Carey continued, with a faint, subtle smile. "A word from Lucille, and the history book of the future must be differently written."

"She will not speak that word," Mr. Sabin said. Lady Carey shrugged her shoulders. The subtlety of her smile faded away. Her whole face expressed a contemptuous and self-assured cynicism.

"You know her very well," she murmured. "Yet she and I are no strangers. She is one who loves to taste—no, to drink—deeply of all the experiences of life. Why should we blame her, you and I? Have we not the same desire?"

Mr. Sabin lit a cigarette.

"Once, perhaps," he remarked. "You must not forget that I am no longer a young man."

She leaned towards him.

"You will die young," she murmured. "You are not of the breed of men who grow old."

"Do you mean to turn my head?" he asked her, with a humorous smile.

"It would be easier," she answered, "than to touch your heart."

Then Lucille looked across at them—and Mr. Sabin suddenly remembered that Reginald Brott knew them both only as strangers.

"Muriel," she said, "you are behaving disgracefully."

"I am doing my best," Lady Carey answered, "to keep you in countenance."

The eyes of the two women met for a moment, and though the smiles lingered still upon their faces Lady Carey at any rate was not able to wholly conceal her hatred. Lucille shrugged her shoulders.

"I am doing my best," she said, "to convert Mr. Brott."

"To what?" Lady Carey asked.

"To a sane point of view concerning the holiness of the aristocracy," Lucille answered. "I am afraid though that I have made very little impression. In his heart I believe Mr. Brott would like to see us all working for our living, school-teachers and dressmakers, and that sort of thing, you know."

Mr. Brott protested.

"I am not even," he declared, "moderately advanced in my views as regards matters of your sex. To tell you the truth, I do not like women to work at all outside their homes."

Lady Carey laughed.

"My dear," she said to Lucille, "you and I may as well retire in despair. Can't you see the sort of woman Mr. Brott admires? She isn't like us a bit. She is probably a healthy, ruddy-cheeked young person who lives in the country, gets up to breakfast to pour out the coffee for some sort of a male relative, goes round the garden snipping off roses in big gloves and a huge basket, interviews the cook, orders the dinner, makes fancy waistcoats for her husband, and failing a sewing maid, does the mending for the family. You and I, Lucille, are not like that."

"Well, you have mentioned nothing which I couldn't do, if it seemed worth while," Lucille objected. "It sounds very primitive and delightful. I am sure we are all too luxurious and too lazy. I think we ought to turn over a new leaf."

"For you, dear Lucille," Lady Carey said with suave and deadly satire, "what improvement is possible? You have all that you could desire. It is much less fortunate persons, such as myself, to whom Utopia must seem such a delightful place."

A frock-coated and altogether immaculate young man approached their table and accosted Mr. Sabin.

"I beg your pardon, sir," he said, "but the manager would be much obliged if you would spare him a moment or two in his private room as soon as possible."

Mr. Sabin nodded.

"In a few minutes," he answered.

The little party broke up almost immediately. Coffee was ordered in the palm court, where the band was playing. Mr. Sabin and the Prince fell a little behind the others on the way out of the room.

"You heard my summons?" Mr. Sabin asked.

"Yes!"

"I am going to be cross-examined as regards Duson. I am no longer a member of the Order. What is to prevent my setting them upon the right track?"

"The fact," the Prince said coolly, "that you are hoping one day to recover Lucille."

"I doubt," Mr. Sabin said, "whether you are strong enough to keep her from me."

The Prince smiled. All his white teeth were showing.

"Come," he said, "you know better than—much better than that. Lucille must wait her release. You know that."

"I will buy it," Mr. Sabin said, "with a lie to the manager here, or I will tell the truth and still take her from you."

The Prince stood upon the topmost step of the balcony. Below was the palm court, with many little groups of people dotted about.

"My dear friend," he said, "Duson died absolutely of his own free will. You know that quite well. We should have preferred that the matter had been otherwise arranged. But as it is we are safe, absolutely safe."

"Duson's letter!" Mr. Sabin remarked.

"You will not show it," the Prince answered. "You cannot. You have kept it too long. And, after all, you cannot escape from the main fact. Duson committed suicide."

"He was incited to murder. His letter proves it."

The Prince shrugged his shoulders.

"By whom? Ah, how your story would excite ridicule. I seem to hear the laughter now. No, my dear Souspennier, you would bargain for me with Lucille. Look below. Are we likely to part with her just yet?"

In a corner, behind a gigantic palm, Lucille and Brott were talking together. Lady Carey had drawn Opperman a little distance away. Brott was talking eagerly, his cheeks flushed, his manner earnest. Mr. Sabin turned upon his heel and walked away.

XXXII

M r. Sabin, although he had registered at the hotel under his accustomed pseudonym, had taken no pains to conceal his identity, and was well known to the people in authority about the place. He was received with all the respect due to his rank.

"Your Grace will, I trust, accept my most sincere apologies for disturbing you," Mr. Hertz, the manager, said, rising and bowing at his entrance. "We have here, however, an emissary connected with the police come to inquire into the sad incident of this afternoon. He expressed a wish to ask your Grace a question or two with a view to rendering your Grace's attendance at the inquest unnecessary."

Mr. Sabin nodded.

"I am perfectly willing," he said, "to answer any questions you may choose to put to me."

A plain, hard-featured little man, in a long black overcoat, and holding a bowler hat in his hand, bowed respectfully to Mr. Sabin.

"I am much obliged to you, sir," he said. "My name is John Passmore. We do not of course appear in this matter unless the post-mortem should indicate anything unusual in the circumstances of Duson's death, but it is always well to be prepared, and I ventured to ask Mr. Hertz here to procure for me your opinion as regards the death of your servant."

"You have asked me," Mr. Sabin said gravely, "a very difficult question."

The eyes of the little detective flashed keenly.

"You do not believe then, sir, that he died a natural death?"

"I do not," Mr. Sabin answered.

Mr. Hertz was startled. The detective controlled his features admirably.

"May I ask your reasons, sir?"

Mr. Sabin lightly shrugged his shoulders.

"I have never known the man to have a day's illness in his life," he said. "Further, since his arrival in England he has been acting in a strange and furtive manner, and I gathered that he had some cause for fear which he was indisposed to talk about."

"This," the detective said, "is very interesting."

"Doubtless," Mr. Sabin answered. "But before I say anything more I must clearly understand my position. I am giving you personally a few friendly hints, in the interests of justice perhaps, but still quite informally.

E. PHILLIPS OPPENHEIM

I am not in possession of any definite facts concerning Duson, and what I say to you here I am not prepared to say at the inquest, before which I presume I may have to appear as a witness. There, I shall do nothing more save identify Duson and state the circumstances under which I found him."

"I understand that perfectly, sir," the man answered. "The less said at the inquest the better in the interests of justice."

Mr. Sabin nodded.

"I am glad," he said, "that you appreciate that. I do not mind going so far then as to tell you that I believe Duson died of poison."

"Can you give me any idea," the detective asked, "as to the source?"

"None," Mr. Sabin answered. "That you must discover for yourselves. Duson was a man of silent and secretive habits, and it has occurred to me more than once that he might possibly be a member of one of those foreign societies who have their headquarters in Soho, and concerning which you probably know more than I do."

The detective smiled. It was a very slight flicker of the lips, but it attracted Mr. Sabin's keen attention.

"Your suggestions," the detective said, "are making this case a very interesting one. I have always understood, however, that reprisals of this extreme nature are seldom resorted to in this country. Besides, the man's position seems scarcely to indicate sufficient importance— perhaps—"

"Well?" Mr. Sabin interjected.

"I notice that Duson was found in your sitting-room. It occurs to me as a possibility that he may have met with a fate intended for some one else—for yourself, for instance, sir!"

"But I," Mr. Sabin said smoothly, "am a member of no secret society, nor am I conscious of having enemies sufficiently venomous to desire my life."

The detective sat for a moment with immovable face.

"We, all of us, know our friends, sir," he said. "There are few of us properly acquainted with our enemies."

Mr. Sabin lit a cigarette. His fingers were quite steady, but this man was making him think.

"You do not seriously believe," he asked, "that Duson met with a death which was intended for me?"

"I am afraid," the detective said thoughtfully, "that I know no more about it than you do."

"I see," Mr. Sabin said, "that I am no stranger to you."

"You are very far from being that, sir," the man answered. "A few years ago I was working for the Government—and you were not often out of my sight."

Mr. Sabin smiled.

"It was perhaps judicious," he remarked, "though I am afraid it proved of very little profit to you. And what about the present time?"

"I see no harm in telling you, sir, that a general watch is kept upon your movements. Duson was useful to us. . . but now Duson is dead."

"It is a fact," Mr. Sabin said impressively, "that Duson was a genius. My admiration for him continually increases."

"Duson made harmless reports to us as we desired them," the detective said. "I have an idea, however, that if this course had at any time been inimical to your interests that Duson would have deceived us."

"I am convinced of it," Mr. Sabin declared.

"And Duson is dead!"

Mr. Sabin nodded gravely.

The little hard-visaged man looked steadily for a moment upon the carpet.

"Duson died virtually whilst accepting pay from if not actually in the employ of our Secret Service Department. You will understand, therefore, that we, knowing of this complication in his life, naturally incline towards the theory of murder. Shall I be taking a liberty, sir, if I give you an unprofessional word of warning?"

Mr. Sabin raised his eyebrows.

"By no means," he answered. "But surely you cannot—"

The man smiled.

"No, sir," he said drily. "I do not for one moment suspect you. The man was our spy upon your movements, but I am perfectly aware that there has been nothing worth reporting, and I also know that you would never run such a risk for the removal of so insignificant a person. No, my warning comes to you from a different point of view. It is, if you will pardon my saying so, none the less personal, but wholly friendly. The case of Duson will be sifted to the dregs, but unless I am greatly mistaken, and I do not see room for the possibility of a mistake, I know the truth already."

"You will share your knowledge?" Mr. Sabin asked quietly.

The detective shook his head.

E. PHILLIPS OPPENHEIM

"You shall know," he said, "before the last moment. But I want to warn you that when you do know it—it will be a shock to you."

Mr. Sabin stood perfectly still for several moments. This little man believed what he was saying. He was certainly deceived. Yet none the less Mr. Sabin was thoughtful.

"You do not feel inclined," he said slowly, "to give me your entire confidence."

"Not at present, sir," the man answered. "You would certainly intervene, and my case would be spoilt."

Mr. Sabin glanced at the clock.

"If you care to call on me to-morrow," he said, "I could perhaps show you something which might change your opinion."

The detective bowed.

"I am always open, sir," he said, "to conviction. I will come about twelve o'clock."

Mr. Sabin went back to the palm lounge. Lucille and Reginald Brott were sitting together at a small table, talking earnestly to one another. The Prince and Lady Carey had joined another party who were all talking together near the entrance. The latter, directly she saw them coming, detached herself from them and came to him.

"Your coffee is almost cold," she said, "but the Prince has found some brandy of wonderful age, somewhere in the last century, I believe."

Mr. Sabin glanced towards Lucille. She appeared engrossed in her conversation, and had not noticed his approach. Lady Carey shrugged.

"You have only a few minutes," she said, "before that dreadful person comes and frowns us all out. I have kept you a chair."

Mr. Sabin sat down. Lady Carey interposed herself between him and the small table at which Lucille was sitting.

"Have they discovered anything?" she asked.

"Nothing!" Mr. Sabin answered.

She played with her fan for a moment. Then she looked him steadily in the face.

"My friend?"

He glanced towards her.

"Lady Carey!"

"Why are you so obstinate?" she exclaimed in a low, passionate whisper. "I want to be your friend, and I could be very useful to you. Yet you keep me always at arm's length. You are making a mistake. Indeed you are. I suppose you do not trust me. Yet reflect. Have I ever told you anything that was not true? Have I ever tried to deceive you? I don't pretend to be a paragon of the virtues. I live my life to please myself. I admit it. Why not? It is simply applying the same sort of philosophy to my life as you have applied to yours. My enemies can find plenty to say about me—but never that I have been false to a friend. Why do you keep me always at arm's length, as though I were one of those who wished you evil?"

"Lady Carey," Mr. Sabin said, "I will not affect to misunderstand you, and I am flattered that you should consider my good will of any importance. But you are the friend of the Prince of Saxe Leinitzer. You are one of those even now who are working actively against me. I am not blaming you, but we are on opposite sides."

Lady Carey looked for a moment across at the Prince, and her eyes were full of venom.

"If you knew," she murmured, "how I loathe that man. Friends! That is all long since past. Nothing would give me so much pleasure as never to see his face again."

"Nevertheless," Mr. Sabin reminded her, "whatever your private feelings may be, he has claims upon you which you cannot resist."

"There is one thing in the world," she said in a low tone, "for which I would risk even the abnegation of those claims."

"You would perjure your honour?"

"Yes—if it came to that."

Mr. Sabin moved uneasily in his chair. The woman was in earnest. She offered him an invaluable alliance; she could show him the way to hold his own against even the inimical combination by which he was surrounded. If only he could compromise. But her eyes were seeking his eagerly, even fiercely.

"You doubt me still," she whispered. "And I thought that you had genius. Listen, I will prove myself. The Prince has one of his foolish passions for Lucille. You know that. So far she has shown herself able to resist his fascinations. He is trying other means. Lucille is in danger! Duson!—but after all, I was never really in danger, except the time when I carried the despatches for the colonel and rode straight into a Boer ambush."

Mr. Sabin saw nothing, but he did not move a muscle of his face. A moment later they heard the Prince's voice from behind them.

"I am very sorry," he said, "to interrupt these interesting reminiscences, but you see that every one is going. Lucille is already in the cloak-room."

E. PHILLIPS OPPENHEIM

Lady Carey rose at once, but the glance she threw at the Prince was a singularly malicious one. They walked down the carpeted way together, and Lady Carey left them without a word. In the vestibule Mr. Sabin and Reginald Brott came face to face.

XXXIII

The greeting between the two men was cold, and the Prince almost immediately stepped between them. Nevertheless, Brott seemed to have a fancy to talk with Mr. Sabin.

"I was at Camperdown House yesterday," he remarked. "Her Ladyship was regretting that she saw you so seldom."

"I have been a little remiss," Mr. Sabin answered. "I hope to lunch there to-morrow."

"You have seen the evening paper, Brott?" the Prince asked.

"I saw the early editions," Brott answered. "Is there anything fresh?"

The Prince dropped his voice a little. He drew Brott on one side.

"The Westminster declared that you had left for Windsor by an early train this afternoon, and gives a list of your Cabinet. The Pall Mall, on the other hand, declares that Letheringham will assuredly be sent for to-morrow."

Brott shrugged his shoulders.

"There are bound to be a crop of such reports at a time like this," he remarked.

The Prince dropped his voice almost to a whisper.

"Brott," he said, "there is something which I have had it in my mind to say to you for the last few days. I am not perhaps a great politician, but, like many outsiders, I see perhaps a good deal of the game. I know fairly well what the feeling is in Vienna and Berlin. I can give you a word of advice."

"You are very kind, Prince," Brott remarked, looking uneasily over his shoulder. "But—"

"It is concerning Brand. There is no man more despised and disliked abroad, not only because he is a Jew and ill-bred, but because of his known sympathy with some of these anarchists who are perfect firebrands in Europe."

"I am exceedingly obliged to you," Brott answered hurriedly. "I am afraid, however, that you anticipate matters a good deal. I have not yet been asked to form a Cabinet. It is doubtful whether I ever shall. And, beyond that, it is also doubtful whether even if I am asked I shall accept."

"I must confess," the Prince said, "that you puzzle me. Every one says that the Premiership of the country is within your reach. It is surely the Mecca of all politicians."

"There are complications," Brott muttered. "You—"

He stopped short and moved towards the door. Lucille, unusually pale and grave, had just issued from the ladies' ante-room, and joined Lady Carey, who was talking to Mr. Sabin. She touched the latter lightly on the arm.

"Help us to escape," she said quickly. "I am weary of my task. Can we get away without their seeing us?"

Mr. Sabin offered his arm. They passed along the broad way, and as they were almost the last to leave the place, their carriage was easily found. The Prince and Mr. Brott appeared only in time to see Mr. Sabin turning away, hat in hand, from the curb-stone. Brott's face darkened.

"Prince," he said, "who is that man?"

The Prince shrugged his shoulders.

"A man," he said, "who has more than once nearly ruined your country. His life has been a splendid failure. He would have given India to the Russians, but they mistrusted him and trifled away their chance. Once since then he nearly sold this country to Germany; it was a trifle only which intervened. He has been all his life devoted to one cause."

"And that?" Brott asked.

"The restoration of the monarchy to France. He, as you of course know, is the Duc de Souspennier, the sole living member in the direct line of one of the most ancient and historical houses in England. My friend," he added, turning to Mr. Sabin, "you have stolen a march upon us. We had not even an opportunity of making our adieux to the ladies."

"I imagine," Mr. Sabin answered, "that the cause of quarrel may rest with them. You were nowhere in sight when they came out."

"These fascinating politics," the Prince remarked. "We all want to talk politics to Mr. Brott just now."

"I will wish you good-night, gentlemen," Mr. Sabin said, and passed into the hotel.

The Prince touched Brott on the arm.

"Will you come round to the club, and take a hand at bridge?" he said.

Brott laughed shortly.

"I imagine," he said, "that I should be an embarrassing guest to you just now at, say the Mallborough, or even at the St. James. I believe the aristocracy are looking forward to the possibility of my coming into power with something like terror."

"I am not thoroughly versed; in the politics of this country," the Prince said, "but I have always understood that your views were very much advanced. Dorset solemnly believes that you are pledged to exterminate the large landed proprietors, and I do not think he would be surprised to hear that you had a guillotine up your sleeve."

The two men were strolling along Pall Mall. The Prince had lit a large cigar, and was apparently on the best of terms with himself and the world in general. Brott, on the contrary, was most unlike himself, preoccupied, and apparently ill at ease.

"The Duke and his class are, of course, my natural opponents," Brott said shortly. "By the bye, Prince," he added, suddenly turning towards him, and with a complete change of tone, "it is within your power to do me a favour."

"You have only to command," the Prince assured him good-naturedly.

"My rooms are close here," Brott continued. "Will you accompany me there, and grant me the favour of a few minutes' conversation?"

"Assuredly!" the Prince answered, flicking the end off his cigar. "It will be a pleasure."

They walked on towards their destination in silence. Brott's secretary was in the library with a huge pile of letters and telegrams before him. He welcomed Brott with relief.

"We have been sending all over London for you, sir," he said.

Brott nodded.

"I am better out of the way for the present," he answered. "Deny me to everybody for an hour, especially Letheringham. There is nothing here, I suppose, which cannot wait so long as that?"

The secretary looked a little doubtful.

"I think not, sir," he decided.

"Very good. Go and get something to eat. You look fagged. And tell Hyson to bring up some liqueurs, will you! I shall be engaged for a short time."

The secretary withdrew. A servant appeared with a little tray of liqueurs, and in obedience to an impatient gesture from his master, left them upon the table. Brott closed the door firmly.

"Prince," he said, resuming his seat, "I wished to speak with you concerning the Countess."

Saxe Leinitzer nodded.

"All right," he said. "I am listening!"

"I understand," Brott continued, "that you are one of her oldest friends, and also one of the trustees of her estates. I presume that you stand to her therefore to some extent in the position of an adviser?"

"It is perfectly true," the Prince admitted.

"I, too, am an old friend, as she has doubtless told you," Brott said. "All my life she has been the one woman whom I have desired to call my wife. That desire has never been so strong as at the present moment."

The Prince removed his cigar from his mouth and looked grave.

"But, my dear Brott," he said, "have you considered the enormous gulf between your—views? The Countess owns great hereditary estates, she comes from a family which is almost Royal, she herself is an aristocrat to the backbone. It is a class against which you have declared war. How can you possibly come together on common ground?"

Brott was silent for a moment. Looking at him steadily the Prince was surprised at the change in the man's appearance. His cheeks seemed blanched and his skin drawn. He had lost flesh, his eyes were hollow, and he frequently betrayed in small mannerisms a nervousness wholly new and unfamiliar to him.

"You speak as a man of sense, Prince," he said after a while. "You are absolutely correct. This matter has caused me a great deal of anxious thought. To falter at this moment is to lose, politically, all that I have worked for all my life. It is to lose the confidence of the people who have trusted me. It is a betrayal, the thought of which is a constant shame to me. But, on the other hand, Lucille is the dearest thing to me in life."

The Prince's expression was wholly sympathetic. The derision which lurked behind he kept wholly concealed. A strong man so abjectly in the toils, and he to be chosen for his confidant! It was melodrama with a dash of humour.

"If I am to help you," the Prince said, "I must know everything. Have you made any proposals to Lucille? In plain words, how much of your political future are you disposed to sacrifice?"

"All!" Brott said hoarsely. "All for a certainty of her. Not one jot without."

"And she?"

Brott sprang to his feet, white and nervous.

"It is where I am at fault," he exclaimed. "It is why I have asked for your advice, your help perhaps. I do not find it easy to understand Lucille. Perhaps it is because I am not well versed in the ways of her sex. I find her elusive. She will give me no promise. Before I went to Glasgow

I talked with her. If she would have married me then my political career was over—thrown on one side like an old garment. But she would give me no promise. In everything save the spoken words I crave she has promised me her love. Again there comes a climax. In a few hours I must make my final choice. I must decline to join Letheringham, in which case the King must send for me, or accept office with him, and throw away the one great chance of this generation. Letheringham's Cabinet, of course, would be a moderate Liberal one, a paragon of milk and water in effectiveness. If I go in alone we make history. The moment of issue has come. And, Prince, although I have pleaded with all the force and all the earnestness I know, Lucille remains elusive. If I choose for her side—she promises me—reward. But it is vague to me. I don't, I can't understand! I want her for my wife, I want her for the rest of my life—nothing else. Tell me, is there any barrier to this? There are no complications in her life which I do not know of? I want your assurance. I want her promise. You understand me?"

"Yes, I understand you," the Prince said gravely. "I understand more than you do. I understand Lucille's position."

Brott leaned forward with bright eyes.

"Ah!"

"Lucille, the Countess of Radantz, is at the present moment a married woman."

Brott was speechless. His face was like a carved stone image, from which the life had wholly gone.

"Her husband—in name only, let me tell you, is the Mr. Sabin with whom we had supper this evening."

"Great God!"

"Their marriage had strange features in it which are not my concern, or even yours," the Prince said deliberately. "The truth is, that they have not lived together for years, they never will again, for their divorce proceedings would long ago have been concluded but for the complications arising from the difference between the Hungarian and the American laws. Here, without doubt, is the reason why the Countess has hesitated to pledge her word directly."

"It is wonderful," Brott said slowly. "But it explains everything."

There was a loud knock at the door. The secretary appeared upon the threshold. Behind him was a tall, slim young man in traveling costume.

"The King's messenger!" Brott exclaimed, rising to his feet.

XXXIV

The Prince presented himself with a low bow. Lucille had a copy of the morning paper in her hand.

"I congratulate you, Countess," he said. "You progress admirably. It is a great step gained."

Lucille, who was looking pale and nervous, regarded him with anxiety.

"A step! But it is everything. If these rumours are true, he refuses the attempt to form a Cabinet. He takes a subordinate position under Letheringham. Every paper this morning says that if this is so his political career is over. It is true, is it not?"

"It is a great gain," the Prince said slowly.

"But it is everything," Lucille declared, with a rising note of passion in her tone. "It was my task. It is accomplished. I demand my release."

The Prince was silent for a moment.

"You are in a great hurry, Lucille," he said.

"What if I am!" she replied fiercely. "Do you suppose that this life of lies and deceit is pleasant to me? Do you suppose that it is a pleasant task to lure a brave man on to his ruin?"

The Prince raised his eyebrows.

"Come," he said, "you can have no sympathy with Reginald Brott, the sworn enemy of our class, a Socialist, a demagogue who would parcel out our lands in allotments, a man who has pledged himself to nothing more nor less than a revolution."

"The man's views are hateful enough," she answered, "but he is in earnest, and however misguided he may be there is something noble in his unselfishness, in his, steady fixedness of purpose."

The Prince's face indicated his contempt.

"Such men," he declared, "are only fit to be crushed like vermin under foot. In any other country save England we should have dealt with him differently."

"This is all beside the question," she declared. "My task was to prevent his becoming Prime Minister, and I have succeeded."

The Prince gave vent to a little gesture of dissent. "Your task," he said, "went a little farther than that. We require his political ruin."

She pointed to the pile of newspapers upon the table.

"Read what they say!" she exclaimed. "There is not one who does not use that precise term. He has missed his opportunity. The people will never trust him again."

"That, at any rate, is not certain," the Prince said. "You must remember that before long he will realise that he has been your tool. What then? He will become more rabid than ever, more also to be feared. No, Lucille, your task is not yet over. He must be involved in an open and public scandal, and with you."

She was white almost to the lips with passion.

"You expect a great deal!" she exclaimed. "You expect me to ruin my life, then, to give my honour as well as these weary months, this constant humiliation."

"You are pleased to be melodramatic," he said coldly. "It is quite possible to involve him without actually going to extremes."

"And what of my husband?" she asked.

The Prince laughed unpleasantly.

"If you have not taught him complaisance," he said, "it is possible, of course, that Mr. Sabin might be unkind. But what of it? You are your own mistress. You are a woman of the world. Without him there is an infinitely greater future before you than as his wife you could ever enjoy."

"You are pleased," she said, "to be enigmatic."

The Prince looked hard at her. Her face was white and set. He sighed.

"Lucille," he said, "I have been very patient for many years. Yet you know very well my secret, and in your heart you know very well that I am one of those who generally win the thing upon which they have set their hearts. I have always loved you, Lucille, but never more than now. Fidelity is admirable, but surely you have done your duty. He is an old man, and a man who has failed in the great things of life. I, on the other hand, can offer you a great future. Saxe Leinitzer, as you know, is a kingdom of its own, and, Lucille, I stand well with the Emperor. The Socialist party in Berlin are strong and increasing. He needs us. Who can say what honours may not be in store for us? For I, too, am of the Royal House, Lucille. I am his kinsman. He never forgets that. Come, throw aside this restlessness. I will tell you how to deal with Brott, and the publicity, after all, will be nothing. We will go abroad directly afterwards."

"Have you finished?" she asked.

"You will be reasonable!" he begged.

"Reasonable!" She turned upon him with flashing eyes. "I wonder how you ever dared to imagine that I could tolerate you for one moment as a lover or a husband. Wipe it out of your mind once and for all. You are repellent to me. Positively the only wish I have in connection with you is never to see your face again. As for my duty, I have done it. My conscience is clear. I shall leave this house to-day."

"I hope," the Prince said softly, "that you will do nothing rash!"

"In an hour," she said, "I shall be at the Carlton with my husband. I will trust to him to protect me from you."

The Prince shook his head.

"You talk rashly," he said. "You do not think. You are forbidden to leave this house. You are forbidden to join your husband."

She laughed scornfully, but underneath was a tremor of uneasiness.

"You summoned me from America," she said, "and I came. . . I was forced to leave my husband without even a word of farewell. I did it! You set me a task—I have accomplished it. I claim that I have kept my bond, that I have worked out my own freedom. If you require more of me, I say that you are overstepping your authority, and I refuse. Set the black cross against my name if you will. I will take the risk."

The Prince came a little nearer to her. She held her own bravely enough, but there was a look in his face which terrified her.

"Lucille," he said, "you force me to disclose something which I have kept so far to myself. I wished to spare you anxiety, but you must understand that your safety depends upon your remaining in this house, and in keeping apart from all association with—your husband."

"You will find it difficult," she said, "to convince me of that."

"On the contrary," he said, "I shall find it easy—too easy, believe me. You will remember my finding you at the wine-shop of Emil Sachs?"

"Yes!"

"You refused to tell me the object of your visit. It was foolish, for of course I was informed. You procured from Emil a small quantity of the powder prepared according to the recipe of Herr Estentrauzen, and for which we paid him ten thousand marks. It is the most silent, the most secret, the most swift poison yet discovered."

"I got it for myself," she said coldly. "There have been times when I have felt that the possession of something of that sort was an absolute necessity."

"I do not question you as to the reason for your getting it," he answered. "Very shortly afterwards you left your carriage in Pall Mall, and without even asking for your husband you called at his hotel—you stole up into his room."

"I took some roses there and left them," she said "What of that?"

"Only that you were the last person seen to enter Mr. Sabin's rooms before Duson was found there dead. And Duson died from a dose of that same poison, a packet of which you procured secretly from Emil Sachs. An empty wineglass was by his side—it was one generally used by Mr. Sabin. I know that the English police, who are not so foolish as people would have one believe, are searching now for the woman who was seen to enter the sitting-room shortly before Mr. Sabin returned and found Duson there dead."

She laughed scornfully.

"It is ingenious," she admitted, "and perhaps a little unfortunate for me. But the inference is ridiculous. What interest had I in the man's death?"

"None, of course!" the Prince said. "But, Lucille, in all cases of poisoning it is the wife of whom one first thinks!"

"The wife? I did not even know that the creature had a wife."

"Of course not! But Duson drank from Mr. Sabin's glass, and you are Mr. Sabin's wife. You are living apart from him. He is old and you are young. And for the other man—there is Reginald Brott. Your names have been coupled together, of course. See what an excellent case stands there. You procure the poison—secretly. You make your way to your husband's room—secretly. The fatal dose is taken from your husband's wineglass. You leave no note, no message. The poison of which the man died is exactly the same as you procured from Sachs. Lucille, after all, do you wonder that the police are looking for a woman in black with an ermine toque? What a mercy you wore a thick veil!"

She sat down suddenly.

"This is hideous," she said.

"Think it over," he said, "step by step. It is wonderful how all the incidents dovetail into one another."

"Too wonderful," she cried. "It sounds like some vile plot to incriminate me. How much had you to do with this, Prince?"

"Don't be a fool!" he answered roughly. "Can't you see for yourself that your arrest would be the most terrible thing that could happen for us? Even Sachs might break down in cross-examination, and you—well, you are a woman, and you want to live. We should all be in the most deadly peril. Lucille, I would have spared you this anxiety if I could, but your defiance made it necessary. There was no other way of getting you away from England to-night except by telling you the truth."

"Away from England to-night," she repeated vaguely. "But I will not go. It is impossible."

"It is imperative," the Prince declared, with a sharp ring of authority in his tone. "It is your own folly, for which you have to pay. You went secretly to Emil Sachs. You paid surreptitious visits to your husband, which were simply madness. You have involved us all in danger. For our own sakes we must see that you are removed."

"It is the very thing to excite suspicion—flight abroad," she objected.

"Your flight," he said coolly, "will be looked upon from a different point of view, for Reginald Brott must follow you. It will be an elopement, not a flight from justice."

"And in case I should decline?" Lucille asked quietly.

The Prince shrugged his shoulders.

"Well, we have done the best we can for ourselves," he said. "Come, I will be frank with you. There are great interests involved here, and, before all things, I have had to consider the welfare of our friends. That is my duty! Emil Sachs by this time is beyond risk of detection. He has left behind a letter, in which he confesses that he has for some time supplemented the profits of his wine-shop by selling secretly certain deadly poisons of his own concoctions. Alarmed at reading of the death of Duson immediately after he had sold a poison which the symptoms denoted he had fled the country. That letter is in the hands of the woman who remains in the wine-shop, and will only be used in case of necessity. By other means we have dissociated ourselves from Duson and all connection with him. I think I could go so far as to say that it would be impossible to implicate us. Our sole anxiety now, therefore, is to save you."

Lucille rose to her feet.

"I shall go at once to my husband," she said. "I shall tell him everything. I shall act on his advice."

The Prince stood over by the door, and she heard the key turn.

"You will do nothing of the sort," he said quietly. "You are in my power at last, Lucille. You will do my bidding, or—"

"Or what?"

"I shall myself send for the police and give you into custody!"

XXXV

The Prince crossed the hall and entered the morning-room. Felix was there and Raoul de Brouillac. The Duchess sat at her writing-table, scribbling a note. Lady Carey, in a wonderful white serge costume, and a huge bunch of Neapolitan violets at her bosom, was lounging in an easy-chair, swinging her foot backwards and forwards. The Duke, in a very old tweed coat, but immaculate as to linen and the details of his toilet, stood a little apart, with a frown upon his forehead, and exactly that absorbed air which in the House of Lords usually indicated his intention to make a speech. The entrance of the Prince, who carefully closed the door behind him, was an event for which evidently they were all waiting.

"My good people," he said blandly, "I wish you all a very good-morning."

There was a little murmur of greetings, and before they had all subsided the Duke spoke.

"Saxe Leinitzer," he said, "I have a few questions to ask you."

The Prince looked across the room at him.

"By all means, Duke," he said. "But is the present an opportune time?"

"Opportune or no, it is the time which I have selected," the Duke answered stiffly. "I do not altogether understand what is going on in this house. I am beginning to wonder whether I have been misled."

The Prince, as he twirled his fair moustache, glanced carelessly enough across at the Duchess. She was looking the other way.

"I became a—er—general member of this Society," the Duke continued, "sympathising heartily with its objects as explained to me by you, Prince, and believing, although to confess it is somewhat of a humiliation, that a certain amount of—er—combination amongst the aristocracy has become necessary to resist the terrible increase of Socialism which we must all so much deplore."

"You are not making a speech, dear," the Duchess remarked, looking coldly across the room at him. "We are all anxious to hear what the Prince has to say to us."

"Your anxiety," the Duke continued, "and the anxiety of our friends must be restrained for a few minutes, for there are certain things which I am determined to say, and to say them now. I must confess that it was at first a painful shock to me to realise that the time had come when it was

E. PHILLIPS OPPENHEIM

necessary for us to take any heed of the uneducated rabble who seem born into the world discontented with their station in life, and instead of making honest attempts to improve it waste their time railing against us who are more fortunately placed, and in endeavours to mislead in every possible way the electorate of the country."

The Prince sighed softly, and lit a cigarette. Lady Carey and Felix were already smoking.

"However," the Duke continued, "I was convinced. I have always believed in the principle of watching closely the various signs of the times, and I may say that I came to the conclusion that a combination of the thinking members of the aristocratic party throughout the world was an excellent idea. I therefore became what is, I believe, called a general member of the Order, of which I believe you, Prince, are the actual head."

"My dear James," the Duchess murmured, "the Prince has something to say to us."

"The Prince," her husband answered coldly, "can keep back his information for a few minutes. I am determined to place my position clearly before all of you who are present here now. It is only since I have joined this Society that I have been made aware that in addition to the general members, of which body I believe that the Duchess and I are the sole representatives here, there are special members, and members of the inner circle. And I understand that in connection with these there is a great machinery of intrigue going on all the time, with branches all over the world, spies everywhere with unlimited funds, and with huge opportunities of good or evil. In effect I have become an outside member of what is nothing more nor less than a very powerful and, it seems to me, daring secret society."

"So far as you are concerned, Duke," the Prince said, "your responsibility ceases with ordinary membership. You can take no count of anything beyond. The time may come when the inner circle may be opened to you."

The Duke coughed.

"You misapprehend me," he said. "I can assure you I am not anxious for promotion. On the contrary, I stand before you an aggrieved person. I have come to the conclusion that my house, and the shelter of my wife's name, have been used for a plot, the main points of which have been kept wholly secret from me."

The Prince flicked his cigarette ash into the grate.

"My dear Dorset," he said gently, "if you will allow me to explain—"

"I thank you, Saxe Leinitzer," the Duke said coldly, "but it is beginning to occur to me that I have had enough of your explanations. It seemed natural enough to me, and I must say well conceived, that some attempt should be made to modify the views of, if not wholly convert, Reginald Brott by means of the influence of a very charming woman. It was my duty as a member of the Order to assist in this, and the shelter of my house and name were freely accorded to the Countess. But it is news to me to find that she was brought here practically by force. That because she was an inner member and therefore bound to implicit obedience that she was dragged away from her husband, kept apart from him against her will, forced into endeavours to make a fool of Brott even at the cost of her good name. And now, worst of all, I am told that a very deeply laid plot on the part of some of you will compel her to leave England almost at once, and that her safety depends upon her inducing Reginald Brott to accompany her."

"She has appealed to you," the Prince muttered.

"She has done nothing so sensible," the Duke answered drily. "The facts which I have just stated are known to every one in this room. I perhaps know less than any one. But I know enough for this. I request, Saxe Leinitzer, that you withdraw the name of myself and my wife from your list of members, and that you understand clearly that my house is to be no more used for meetings of the Society, formal or informal. And, further, though I regret the apparent inhospitality of my action, my finger is now, as you see, upon the bell, and I venture to wish you all a very good-morning. Groves," he added to the servant who answered the door, "the Prince of Saxe Leinitzer's carriage is urgently required."

The Prince and Lady Carey descended the broad steps side by side. She was laughing softly but immoderately. The Prince was pale with fury.

"Pompous old ass," he muttered savagely. "He may have a worse scandal in his house now than he dreams of."

She wiped her eyes.

"Have I not always told you," she said, "that intrigue in this country was a sheer impossibility? You may lay your plans ever so carefully, but you cannot foresee such a contretemps as this."

"Idiot!" the Prince cried. "Oh, the dolt! Why, even his wife was amazed."

"He may be all those pleasant things," Lady Carey, said, "but he is a gentleman."

He stopped short. The footman was standing by the side of Lady Carey's victoria with a rug on his arm.

"Lucille," he said thoughtfully, "is locked in the morning-room. She is prostrate with fear. If the Duke sees her everything is over. Upon my word, I have a good mind to throw this all up and cross to Paris to-night. Let England breed her own revolutions. What do you say, Muriel? Will you come with me?"

She laughed scornfully.

"I'd as soon go with my coachman," she said.

His eyebrows narrowed. A dull, purple flush crept to his forehead.

"Your wit," he said, "is a little coarse. Listen! You wish our first plan to go through?"

"Of course!"

"Then you must get Lucille out of that house. If she is left there she is absolutely lost to us. Apart from that, she is herself not safe. Our plan worked out too well. She is really in danger from this Duson affair."

The laughter died away from Lady Carey's face. She hesitated with her foot upon the step of her carriage.

"You can go back easily enough," the Prince said. "You are the Duke's cousin, and you were not included in his tirade. Lucille is in the morning-room, and here is the key. I brought it away with me. You must tell her that all our plans are broken, that we have certain knowledge that the police are on the track of this Duson affair. Get her to your house in Pont Street, and I will be round this afternoon. Or better still, take her to mine."

Lady Carey stepped back on to the pavement. She was still, however, hesitating.

"Leave her with the Duke and Duchess," the Prince said, "and she will dine with her husband to-night."

Lady Carey took the key from his hand.

"I will try," she said. "How shall you know whether I succeed?"

"I will wait in the gardens," he answered. "I shall be out of sight, but I shall be able to see you come out. If you are alone I shall come to you. If she is with you I shall be at your house in an hour, and I promise you that she shall leave England to-night with me."

"Poor Brott!" she murmured ironically.

The Prince smiled.

"He will follow her. Every one will believe that they left London together. That is all that is required."

Lady Carey re-entered the house. The Prince made his way into the gardens. Ten minutes passed—a quarter of an hour. Then Lady Carey with Lucille reappeared, and stepping quickly into the victoria were driven away. The Prince drew a little sigh of relief. He looked at his watch, called a hansom, and drove to his club for lunch.

Another man, who had also been watching Dorset House from the gardens for several hours, also noted Lucille's advent with relief. He followed the Prince out and entered another hansom.

"Follow that victoria which has just driven off," he ordered. "Don't lose sight of it. Double fare."

The trap-door fell, and the man whipped up his horse.

XXXVI

M r. Sabin received an early visitor whilst still lingering over a slight but elegant breakfast. Passmore seated himself in an easy-chair and accepted the cigar which his host himself selected for him.

"I am glad to see you," Mr. Sabin said. "This affair of Duson's remains a complete mystery to me. I am looking to you to help me solve it."

The little man with the imperturbable face removed his cigar from his mouth and contemplated it steadfastly.

"It is mysterious," he said. "There are circumstances in connection with it which even now puzzle me very much, very much indeed. There are circumstances in connection with it also which I fear may be a shock to you, sir."

"My life," Mr. Sabin said, with a faint smile, "has been made up of shocks. A few more or less may not hurt me."

"Duson," the detective said, "was at heart a faithful servant!"

"I believe it," Mr. Sabin said.

"He was much attached to you!"

"I believe it."

"It is possible that unwittingly he died for you."

Mr. Sabin was silent. It was his way of avoiding a confession of surprise. And he was surprised. "You believe then," he said, after a moment's pause, "that the poison was intended for me?"

"Certainly I do," the detective answered. "Duson was, after all, a valet, a person of little importance. There is no one to whom his removal could have been of sufficient importance to justify such extreme measures. With you it is different."

Mr. Sabin knocked the ash from his cigarette.

"Why not be frank with me, Mr. Passmore?" he said. "There is no need to shelter yourself under professional reticence. Your connection with Scotland Yard ended, I believe, some time ago. You are free to speak or to keep silence. Do one or the other. Tell me what you think, and I will tell you what I know. That surely will be a fair exchange. You shall have my facts for your surmises."

Passmore's thin lips curled into a smile. "You know that I have left Scotland Yard then, sir?"

"Quite well! You are employed by them often, I believe, but you are not on the staff, not since the affair of Nerman and the code book."

If Passmore had been capable of reverence, his eyes looked it at that moment.

"You knew this last night, sir?"

"Certainly!"

"Five years ago, sir," he said, "I told my chief that in you the detective police of the world had lost one who must have been their king. More and more you convince me of it. I cannot believe that you are ignorant of the salient points concerning Duson's death."

"Treat me as being so, at any rate," Mr. Sabin said.

"I am pardoned," Passmore said, "for speaking plainly of family matters—my concern in which is of course purely professional?"

Mr. Sabin looked up for a moment, but he signified his assent.

"You left America," Passmore said, "in search of your wife, formerly Countess of Radantz, who had left you unexpectedly."

"It is true!" Mr. Sabin answered.

"Madame la Duchesse on reaching London became the guest of the Duchess of Dorset, where she has been staying since. Whilst there she has received many visits from Mr. Reginald Brott."

Mr. Sabin's face was as the face of a sphinx. He made no sign.

"You do not waste your time, sir, over the Society papers. Yet you have probably heard that Madame la Duchesse and Mr. Reginald Brott have been written about and spoken about as intimate friends. They have been seen together everywhere. Gossip has been busy with their names. Mr. Brott has followed the Countess into circles which before her coming he zealously eschewed. The Countess is everywhere regarded as a widow, and a marriage has been confidently spoken of."

Mr. Sabin bowed his head slightly. But of expression there was in his face no sign.

"These things," Passmore continued, "are common knowledge. I have spoken up to now of nothing which is not known to the world. I proceed differently."

"Good!" Mr. Sabin said.

"There is," Passmore continued, "in the foreign district of London a man named Emil Sachs, who keeps a curious sort of a wine-shop, and supplements his earnings by disposing at a high figure of certain rare and deadly poisons. A few days ago the Countess visited him and secured a small packet of the most deadly drug the man possesses."

Mr. Sabin sat quite still. He was unmoved.

"The Countess," Passmore continued, "shortly afterwards visited these rooms. An hour after her departure Duson was dead. He died from drinking out of your liqueur glass, into which a few specks of that powder, invisible almost to the naked eye, had been dropped. At Dorset House Reginald Brott was waiting for her. He left shortly afterwards in a state of agitation."

"And from these things," Mr. Sabin said, "you draw, I presume, the natural inference that Madame la Duchesse, desiring to marry her old admirer, Reginald Brott, first left me in America, and then, since I followed her here, attempted to poison me."

"There is," Passmore said, "a good deal of evidence to that effect."

"Here," Mr. Sabin said, handing him Duson's letter, "is some evidence to the contrary."

Passmore read the letter carefully.

"You believe this," he asked, "to be genuine?"

Mr. Sabin smiled.

"I am sure of it!" he answered.

"You recognise the handwriting?"

"Certainly!"

"And this came into your possession—how?"

"I found it on the table by Duson's side."

"You intend to produce it at the inquest?"

"I think not," Mr. Sabin answered.

There was a short silence. Passmore was revolving a certain matter in his mind—thinking hard. Mr. Sabin was apparently trying to make rings of the blue smoke from his cigarette.

"Has it occurred to you," Passmore asked, "to wonder for what reason your wife visited these rooms on the morning of Duson's death?"

Mr. Sabin shook his head.

"I cannot say that it has."

"She knew that you were not here," Passmore continued. "She left no message. She came closely veiled and departed unrecognised." Mr. Sabin nodded.

"There were reasons," he said, "for that. But when you say that she left no message you are mistaken."

Passmore nodded.

"Go on," he said.

Mr. Sabin nodded towards a great vase of La France roses upon a side table.

"I found these here on my return," he said, "and attached to them the card which I believe is still there. Go and look at it."

Passmore rose and bent over the fragrant blossoms. The card still remained, and on the back of it, in a delicate feminine handwriting:

> "For my husband,
> "with love from
> "Lucille."

Mr. Passmore shrugged his shoulders. He had not the vice of obstinacy, and he knew when to abandon a theory.

"I am corrected," he said. "In any case, a mystery remains as well worth solving. Who are these people at whose instigation Duson was to have murdered you—these people whom Duson feared so much that suicide was his only alternative to obeying their behests?"

Mr. Sabin smiled faintly.

"Ah, my dear Passmore," he said, "you must not ask me that question. I can only answer you in this way. If you wish to make the biggest sensation which has ever been created in the criminal world, to render yourself immortal, and your fame imperishable—find out! I may not help you, I doubt whether you will find any to help you. But if you want excitement, the excitement of a dangerous chase after a tremendous quarry, take your life in your hands, go in and win."

Passmore's withered little face lit up with a gleam of rare excitement.

"These are your enemies, sir," he said. "They have attempted your life once, they may do it again. Assume the offensive yourself. Give me a hint."

Mr. Sabin shook his head.

"That I cannot do," he said. "I have saved you from wasting your time on a false scent. I have given you something definite to work upon. Further than that I can do nothing."

Passmore looked his disappointment, but he knew Mr. Sabin better than to argue the matter.

"You will not even produce that letter at the inquest?" he asked.

"Not even that," Mr. Sabin answered.

Passmore rose to his feet.

"You must remember," he said, "that supposing any one else stumbles upon the same trail as I have been pursuing, and suspicion is afterwards directed towards madame, your not producing that letter at the inquest will make it useless as evidence in her favour."

"I have considered all these things," Mr. Sabin said. "I shall deposit the letter in a safe place. But its use will never be necessary. You are the only man who might have forced me to produce it, and you know the truth."

Passmore rose reluctantly.

"I want you," Mr. Sabin said, "to leave me not only your address, but the means of finding you at any moment during the next four-and-twenty hours. I may have some important work for you."

The man smiled as he tore leaf from his pocketbook and a made a few notes.

"I shall be glad to take any commission from you, sir," he said. "To tell you the truth, I scarcely thought that you would be content to sit down and wait."

Mr. Sabin smiled.

"I think," he said, "that very shortly I can find you plenty to do."

XXXVII

Mr. Sabin a few minutes afterwards ordered his carriage, and was driven to Dorset House. He asked for Lucille, but was shown at once into the library, where the Duke was awaiting him. Then Mr. Sabin knew that something had happened.

The Duke extended his hand solemnly.

"My dear Souspennier," he said, "I am glad to see you. I was in fact on the point of despatching a messenger to your hotel."

"I am glad," Mr. Sabin remarked, "that my visit is opportune. To tell you the truth, Duke, I am anxious to see my wife."

The Duke coughed.

"I trust," he said, "that you will not for a moment consider me guilty of any discourtesy to the Countess, for whom I have a great respect and liking. But it has come to my knowledge that the shelter of my roof and name were being given to proceedings of which I heartily disapproved. I therefore only a few hours ago formally broke off all connection with Saxe Leinitzer and his friends, and to put the matter plainly, I expelled them from the house."

"I congratulate you heartily, Duke, upon a most sensible proceeding," Mr. Sabin said. "But in the meantime where is my wife?"

"Your wife was not present at the time," the Duke answered, "and I had not the slightest intention of including her in the remarks I made. Whether she understood this or not I cannot say, but I have since been given to understand that she left with them."

"How long ago?" Mr. Sabin asked.

"Several hours, I fear," the Duke answered. "I should like, Souspennier, to express to you my regrets that I was ever induced to become connected in any way with proceedings which must have caused you a great deal of pain. I beg you to accept my apologies."

"I do not blame you, Duke," Mr. Sabin said. "My one desire now is to wrest my wife away from this gang. Can you tell me whether she left alone or with any of them?"

"I will endeavour to ascertain," the Duke said, ringing the bell.

But before the Duke's somewhat long-winded series of questions had gone very far Mr. Sabin grasped the fact that the servants had been tampered with. Without wasting any more time he took a somewhat

E. PHILLIPS OPPENHEIM

hurried leave and drove back to the hotel. One of the hall porters approached him, smiling.

"There is a lady waiting for you in your rooms, sir," he announced. "She arrived a few minutes ago."

Mr. Sabin rang for the elevator, got out at his floor and walked down the corridor, leaning a little more heavily than usual upon his stick. If indeed it were Lucille who had braved all and come to him the way before them might still be smooth sailing. He would never let her go again. He was sure of that. They would leave England— yes, there was time still to catch the five o'clock train. He turned the handle of his door and entered. A familiar figure rose from the depths of his easy-chair. Her hat lay on the table, her jacket was open, one of his cigarettes was between her lips. But it was not Lucille.

"Lady Carey!" he said slowly. "This is an unexpected pleasure. Have you brought Lucille with you?"

"I am afraid," she answered, "that I have no ropes strong enough."

"You insinuate," he remarked, "that Lucille would be unwilling to come."

"There is no longer any need," she declared, with a hard little laugh, "for insinuations. We have all been turned out from Dorset House neck and crop. Lucille has accepted the inevitable. She has gone to Reginald's Brott's rooms."

Mr. Sabin smiled.

"Indeed. I have just come from Dorset House myself. The Duke has supplied me with a highly entertaining account of his sudden awakening. The situation must have been humorous."

Her eyes twinkled.

"It was really screamingly funny. The Duke had on his house of Lords manner, and we all sat round like a lot of naughty children. If only you had been there."

Mr. Sabin smiled. Suddenly she laid her hand upon his arm.

"Victor," she said, "I have come to prove that I am your friend. You do not believe that Lucille is with Reginald Brott. It is true! Not only that, but she is leaving England with him to-night. The man's devotion is irresistible—he has been gaining on her slowly but surely all the time."

"I have noticed," Mr. Sabin remarked calmly, "that he has been wonderfully assiduous. I am sure I congratulate him upon his success, if he has succeeded."

"You doubt my word of course," she said. "But I have not come here to tell you things. I have come to prove them. I presume that what you see with your own eyes will be sufficient."

Mr. Sabin shook his head.

"Certainly not," he answered. "I make it a rule to believe nothing that I see, and never to trust my ears."

She stamped her foot lightly upon the floor.

"How impossible you are," she exclaimed. "I can tell you by what train Lucille and Reginald Brott will leave London to-night. I can tell you why Lucille is bound to go."

"Now," Mr. Sabin said, "you are beginning to get interesting."

"Lucille must go—or run the risk of arrest for complicity in the murder of Duson."

"Are you serious?" Mr. Sabin asked, with admirably assumed gravity.

"Is it a jesting matter?" she answered fiercely. "Lucille bought poison, the same poison which it will be proved that Duson died of. She came here, she was the last person to enter your room before Duson was found dead. The police are even now searching for her. Escape is her only chance."

"Dear me," Mr. Sabin said. "Then it is not only for Brott's sake that she is running away."

"What does that matter? She is going, and she is going with him."

"And why," he asked, "do you come to give me warning? I have plenty of time to interpose."

"You can try if you will. Lucille is in hiding. She will not see you if you go to her. She is determined. Indeed, she has no choice. Lucille is a brave woman in many ways, but you know that she fears death. She is in a corner. She is forced to go."

"Again," he said, "I feel that I must ask you why do you give me warning?"

She came and stood close to him.

"Perhaps," she said earnestly, "I am anxious to earn your gratitude. Perhaps, too, I know that no interposition of yours would be of any avail."

Mr. Sabin smiled.

"Still," he said, "I do not think that it is wise of you. I might appear at the station and forcibly prevent Lucille's departure. After all, she is my wife, you know."

She shrugged her shoulders.

E. PHILLIPS OPPENHEIM

"I am not afraid," she said. "You will make inquiries when I have gone, and you will find out that I have spoken the truth. If you keep Lucille in England you will expose her to a terrible risk. It is not like you to be selfish. You will yield to necessity."

"Will you tell me where Lucille is now?" he asked.

"For your own sake and hers, no," she answered. "You also are watched. Besides, it is too late. She was with Brott half an hour after the Duke turned us out of Dorset House. Don't you understand, Victor—won't you? It is too late."

He sat down heavily in his easy-chair. His whole appearance was one of absolute dejection.

"So I am to be left alone in my old age," he murmured. "You have your revenge now at last. You have come to take it."

She sank on her knees by the side of his chair, and her arms fell upon his shoulders.

"How can you think so cruelly of me, Victor," she murmured. "You were always a little mistaken in Lucille. She loved you, it is true, but all her life she has been fond of change and excitement. She came to Europe willingly—long before this Brott would have been her slave save for your reappearance. Can't you forget her—for a little while?"

Mr. Sabin sat quite still. Her hair brushed his cheeks, her arms were about his neck, her whole attitude was an invitation for his embrace. But he sat like a figure of stone, neither repulsing nor encouraging her.

"You need not be alone unless you like," she whispered.

"I am an old man," he said slowly, "and this is a hard blow for me to bear. I must be sure, absolutely sure that she has gone."

"By this time to-morrow," she murmured, "all the world will know it."

"Come to me then," he said. "I shall need consolation."

Her eyes were bright with triumph. She leaned over him and kissed him on the lips. Then she sprang lightly to her feet.

"Wait here for me," she said, "and I will come to you. You shall know, Victor, that Lucille is not the only woman in the world who has cared for you."

There was a tap at the door. Lady Carey was busy adjusting her hat. Passmore entered, and stood hesitating upon the threshold. Mr. Sabin had risen to his feet. He took one of her hands and raised it to his lips. She gave him a swift, wonderful look and passed out.

Mr. Sabin's manner changed as though by magic. He was at once alert and vigorous.

"My dear Passmore," he said, "come to the table. We shall want those Continental time-tables and the London A.B.C. You will have to take a journey to-night."

XXXVIII

T he two women were alone in the morning-room of Lady Carey's house in Pont Street. Lucille was walking restlessly up and down twisting her handkerchief between her fingers. Lady Carey was watching her, more composed, to all outward appearance, but with closely compressed lips, and boding gleam in her eyes.

"I think," Lady Carey said, "that you had better see him."   ·

Lucille turned almost fiercely upon her.

"And why?"

"Well, for one thing he will not understand your refusal. He may be suspicious."

"What does it matter? I have finished with him. I have done all that I pledged myself to. What more can be expected of me? I do not wish to see him again."

Lady Carey laughed.

"At least," she said, "I think that the poor man has a right to receive his congé from you. You cannot break with him without a word of explanation. Perhaps—you may not find it so easy as it seems."

Lucille swept around.

"What do you mean?"

Lady Carey shrugged her shoulders.

"You are in a curious mood, my dear Lucille. What I mean is obvious enough. Brott is a strong man and a determined man. I do not think that he will enjoy being made a fool of."

Lucille was indifferent.

"At any rate," she said, "I shall not see him. I have quite made up my mind about that."

"And why not, Countess?" a deep voice asked from the threshold. "What have I done? May I not at least know my fault?"

Lady Carey rose and moved towards the door.

"You shall have it out between yourselves," she declared, looking up, and nodding at Brott as she passed. "Don't fight!"

"Muriel!"

The cry was imperative, but Lady Carey had gone. Mr. Brott closed the door behind him and confronted Lucille. A brilliant spot of colour flared in her pale cheeks.

"But this is a trap!" she exclaimed. "Who sent for you? Why did you come?"

He looked at her in surprise.

"Lucille!"

His eyes were full of passionate remonstrance. She looked nervously from him towards the door. He intercepted her glance.

"What have I done?" he asked fiercely. "What have I failed to do? Why do you look as though I had forced myself upon you? Haven't I the right? Don't you wish to see me?"

In Brott's face and tone was all the passionate strenuousness of a great crisis. Lucille felt suddenly helpless before the directness of his gaze, his storm of questions. In all their former intercourse it had been she who by virtue of her sex and his blind love for her had kept the upper hand. And now the position was changed. All sorts of feeble explanations, of appeals to him, occurred to her dimly, only to be rejected by reason of their ridiculous inadequacy. She was silent-abjectly silent.

He came a little closer to her, and the strength of the man was manifest in his intense self-restraint. His words were measured, his tone quiet. Yet both somehow gave evidence of the smouldering fires beneath.

"Lucille," he said, "I find you hard to understand to-day. You have made me your slave, you came once more into my life at its most critical moment, and for your sake I have betrayed a great trust. My conscience, my faith, and although that counts for little, my political career, were in the balance against my love for you. You know which conquered. At your bidding I have made myself the jest of every man who buys the halfpenny paper and calls himself a politician. My friends heap abuse upon me, my enemies derision. I cannot hold my position in this new Cabinet. I had gone too far for compromise. I wonder if you quite understand what has happened?"

"Oh, I have heard too much," she cried. "Spare me the rest."

He continued as though he had not heard her.

"Men who have been my intimate associates for many years, and whose friendship was dear to me, cross the road to avoid: meeting me, day by day I am besieged with visitors and letters from the suffering people to whom my word had been pledged, imploring me for some explanation, for one word of denial. Life has become a hell for me, a pestilent, militant hell! Yet, Lucille, unless you break faith with me I make no complaint. I am content."

"I am very sorry," she said. "I do not think that you have properly understood me. I have never made you any promise."

For a moment he lost control of himself. She shrank back at the blaze of indignation, half scornful, half incredulous, which lit up his clear, grey eyes.

"It is a lie!" he answered. "Between you and me it can be no question of words. You were always very careful of your pledges, but there are limits even to your caution—as to my forbearance. A woman does not ask a man who is pleading to her for her love to give up everything else he cares for in life without hope of reward. It is monstrous! I never sought you under false pretenses. I never asked you for your friendship. I wanted you. I told you so plainly. You won't deny that you gave me hope—encouraged me? You can't even deny that I am within my rights if I claim now at this instant the reward for my apostasy."

Her hands were suddenly locked in his. She felt herself being drawn into his arms. With a desperate effort she avoided his embrace. He still held her left wrist, and his face was dark with passion.

"Let me go!" she pleaded.

"Not I!" he answered, with an odd, choked little laugh. "You belong to me. I have paid the price. I, too, am amongst the long list of those poor fools who have sold their gods and their honour for a woman's kiss. But I will not be left wholly destitute. You shall pay me for what I have lost."

"Oh, you are mad!" she answered. "How could you have deceived yourself so? Don't you know that my husband is in London?"

"The man who calls himself Mr. Sabin?" he answered roughly. "What has that to do with it? You are living apart. Saxe Leinitzer and the Duchess have both told me the history of your married life. Or is the whole thing a monstrous lie?" he cried, with a sudden dawning sense of the truth. "Nonsense! I won't believe it. Lucille! You're not afraid! I shall be good to you. You don't doubt that. Sabin will divorce you of course. You won't lose your friends. I—"

There was a sudden loud tapping at the door. Brott dropped her wrist and turned round with an exclamation of anger. To Lucille it was a Heaven-sent interposition. The Prince entered, pale, and with signs of hurry and disorder about his usually immaculate person.

"You are both here," he exclaimed. "Good! Lucille, I must speak with you urgently in five minutes. Brott, come this way with me."

Lucille sank into a chair with a little murmur of relief. The Prince led Brott into another room, and closed the door carefully behind him.

"Mr. Brott," he said, "can I speak to you as a friend of Lucille's?"

Brott, who distrusted the Prince, looked him steadily in the face. Saxe Leinitzer's agitation was too apparent to be wholly assumed. He had all the appearance of being a man desperately in earnest.

"I have always considered myself one," Brott answered. "I am beginning to doubt, however, whether the Countess holds me in the same estimation."

"You found her hysterical, unreasonable, overwrought!" the Prince exclaimed. "That is so, eh?"

The Prince drew a long breath.

"Brott," he said, "I am forced to confide in you. Lucille is in terrible danger. I am not sure that there is anybody who can effectually help her but you. Are you prepared to make a great sacrifice for her sake—to leave England at once, to take her to the uttermost part of the world?"

Brott's eyes were suddenly bright. The Prince quailed before the fierceness of his gaze.

"She would not go!" he exclaimed sharply.

"She will," the Prince answered. "She must! Not only that, but you will earn her eternal gratitude. Listen, I must tell you the predicament in which we find ourselves. It places Lucille's life in your hands."

"What?"

The exclamation came like a pistol shot. The Prince held up his hand.

"Do not interrupt. Let me speak. Every moment is very valuable. You heard without doubt of the sudden death at the Carlton Hotel. It took place in Mr. Sabin's sitting-room. The victim was Mr. Sabin's servant. The inquest was this afternoon. The verdict was death from the effect of poison. The police are hot upon the case. There was no evidence as to the person by whom the poison was administered, but by a hideous combination of circumstances one person before many hours have passed will be under the surveillance of the police."

"And that person?" Brott asked.

The Prince looked round and lowered his voice, although the room was empty.

"Lucille," he whispered hoarsely.

Brott stepped backwards as though he were shot.

"What damned folly!" he exclaimed.

"It is possible that you may not think so directly," Saxe Leinitzer continued. "The day it happened Lucille bought this same poison, and it is a rare one, from a man who has absconded. An hour before this man was found dead, she called at the hotel, left no name, but went upstairs to Mr. Sabin's room, and was alone there for five minutes, The man died from a single grain of poison which had been introduced into Mr. Sabin's special liqueur glass, out of which he was accustomed to drink three or four times a day. All these are absolute facts, which at any moment may be discovered by the police. Added to that she is living apart from her husband, and is known to be on bad terms with him."

Brott as gripping the back of a chair. He was white to the lips.

"You don't think," he cried hoarsely. "You can't believe—"

"No" the Prince answered quickly, "I don't believe anything of the sort. I will tell you as man to man that I believe she wished Mr. Sabin dead. You yourself should know why. But no, I don't believe she went so far as that. It was an accident. But what we have to do is to save her. Will you help?"

"Yes."

"She must cross to the Continent to-night before the police get on the scent. Afterwards she must double back to Havre and take the Bordlaise for New York on Saturday. Once there I can guarantee her protection."

"Well?"

"She cannot go alone."

"You mean that I should go with her?"

"Yes! Get her right away, and I will employ special detectives and have the matter cleared up, if ever it can be. But if she remains here I fear that nothing can save her from the horror of an arrest, even if afterwards we are able to save her. You yourself risk much, Brott. The only question that remains is, will you do it?"

"At her bidding—yes!" Brott declared.

"Wait here," the Prince answered.

XXXIX

S axe Leinitzer returned to the morning-room, and taking the key from his pocket unlocked the door. Inside Lucille was pale with fury.

"What! I am a prisoner, then!" she exclaimed. "How dare you lock me in? This is not your house. Let me pass! I am tired of all this stupid espionage."

The Prince stood with his back to the door.

"It is for your own sake, Lucille. The house is watched."

She sank into a low chair, trembling. The Prince had all the appearance of a man himself seriously disturbed.

"Lucille," he said, "we will do what we can for you. The whole thing is horribly unfortunate. You must leave England to-night. Muriel will go with you. Her presence will help to divert suspicion. Once you can reach Paris I can assure you of safety. But in this country I am almost powerless."

"I must see Victor," she said in a low tone. "I will not go without."

The Prince nodded.

"I have thought of that. There is no reason, Lucille, why he should not be the one to lead you into safety."

"You mean that?" she cried.

"I mean it," the Prince answered. "After what has happened you are of course of no further use to us. I am inclined to think, too, that we have been somewhat exacting. I will send a messenger to Souspennier to meet you at Charing Cross to-night."

She sprang up.

"Let me write it myself."

"Very well," he agreed, with a shrug of the shoulders. "But do not address or sign it. There is danger in any communication between you."

She took a sheet of note-paper and hastily wrote a few words.

"I have need of your help. Will you be at Charing Cross at twelve o'clock prepared for a journey.—Lucille."

The Prince took the letter from her and hastily folded it up.

"I will deliver it myself," he announced. "It will perhaps be safest. Until I return, Lucille, do not stir from the house or see any one. Muriel has given the servants orders to admit no one. All your life," he added, after a moment's pause, "you have been a little cruel to me, and this time also. I shall pray that you will relent before our next meeting."

E. PHILLIPS OPPENHEIM

She rose to her feet and looked him full in the face. She seemed to be following out her own train of thought rather than taking note of his words.

"Even now," she said thoughtfully, "I am not sure that I can trust you. I have a good mind to fight or scream my way out of this house, and go myself to see Victor."

He shrugged his shoulders.

"The fighting or the screaming will not be necessary, dear Countess," he said. "The doors are open to you. But it is as clear as day that if you go to the hotel or near it you will at once be recognised, and recognition means arrest. There is a limit beyond which one cannot help a wilful woman. Take your life in your hands and go your own way, or trust in us who are doing our best to save you."

"And what of Reginald Brott?" she asked.

"Brott?" the Prince repeated impatiently. "Who cares what becomes of him? You have made him seem a fool, but, Lucille, to tell you the truth, I am sorry that we did not leave this country altogether alone. There is not the soil for intrigue here, or the possibility. Then, too, the police service is too stolid, too inaccessible. And even our friends, for whose aid we are here—well, you heard the Duke. The cast-iron Saxon idiocy of the man. The aristocracy here are what they call bucolic. It is their own fault. They have intermarried with parvenus and Americans for generations. They are a race by themselves. We others may shake ourselves free from them. I would work in any country of the globe for the good of our cause, but never again in England."

Lucille shivered a little.

"I am not in the humour for argument," she declared. "If you would earn my gratitude take that note to my husband. He is the only man I feel sure of—whom I know can protect me."

The Prince bowed low.

"It is our farewell, Countess," he said.

"I cannot pretend," she answered, "to regret it."

Saxe Leinitzer left the room. There was a peculiar smile upon his lips as he crossed the hall. Brott was still awaiting for him.

"Mr. Brott," he said, "the Countess is, as I feared, too agitated to see you again for the present, or any one else. She sends you, however, this message."

He took the folded paper from his waistcoat pocket and handed it to the other man. Brott read it through eagerly. His eyes shone.

"She accepts the situation, then?" he exclaimed.

"Precisely! Will you pardon me, my friend, if I venture upon one other word. Lucille is not an ordinary woman. She is not in the least like the majority of her sex, especially, I might add, amongst us. The fact that her husband was living would seriously influence her consideration of any other man—as her lover. The present crisis, however, has changed everything. I do not think that you will have cause to complain of her lack of gratitude."

Brott walked out into the streets with the half sheet of note-paper twisted up between his fingers. For the first time for months he was conscious of a distinct and vivid sense of happiness. The terrible period of indecision was past. He knew now where he stood. Nor was his immediate departure from England altogether unpleasant to him. His political career was shattered—friends and enemies were alike cold to him. Such an act of cowardice as his, such pitiful shrinking back at the last fateful moment, was inexplicable and revolting. Even Letheringham was barely civil. It was certain that his place in the Cabinet would be intolerable. He yearned for escape from it all, and the means of escape were now at hand. In after years he knew very well that the shadow of his broken trust, the torture of his misused opportunities, would stand for ever between him and the light. But at that moment he was able to clear his mind of all such disquieting thoughts. He had won Lucille— never mind at what cost, at what peril! He had won Lucille!

He was deeply engrossed, and his name was spoken twice in his ear before he turned round. A small, somewhat shabby-looking man, with tired eyes and more than a day's growth of beard upon his chin, had accosted him.

"Mr. Brott, sir. A word with you, please."

Brott held out his hand. Nevertheless his tone when he spoke lacked heartiness.

"You, Hedley! Why, what brings you to London?"

The little man did not seem to see the hand. At any rate he made no motion to take it.

"A few minutes' chat with Mr. Brott. That's what I've come for."

Brott raised his eyebrows, and nodded in somewhat constrained fashion.

"Well," he said, "I am on my way to my rooms. We can talk as we go, if you like. I am afraid the good people up in your part of the world are not too well pleased with me."

The little man smiled rather queerly.

"That is quite true," he answered calmly. "They hate a liar and a turn-coat. So do I!"

Brott stopped short upon the pavement.

"If you are going to talk like that to me, Hedley," he said, "the less you have to say the better."

The man nodded.

"Very well," he said. "What I have to say won't take me very long. But as I've tramped most of the way up here to say it, you'll have to listen here or somewhere else. I thought you were always one who liked the truth."

"So I do!" Brott answered. "Go on!"

The man shuffled along by his side. They were an odd-looking pair, for Brott was rather a careful man as regards his toilet, and his companion looked little better than a tramp.

"All my life," he continued, "I've been called 'Mad Hedley,' or 'Hedley, the mad tailor.' Sometimes one and sometimes the other. It don't matter which. There's truth in, it. I am a bit mad. You, Mr. Brott, were one of those who understood me a little. I have brooded a good deal perhaps, and things have got muddled up in my brain. You know what has been at the bottom of it all.

"I began making speeches when I was a boy. People laughed at me, but I've set many a one a-thinking. I'm no anarchist, although people call me one. I'll admit that I admire the men who set the French Revolution going. If such a thing happened in this country I'd be one of the first to join in. But I've never had a taste for bloodshed. I'd rather the thing had been done without. From the first you seemed to be the man who might have brought it about. We listened to you, we watched your career, and we began to have hopes. Mr. Brott, the bodies and souls of millions of your fellow-creatures were in the hollow of your hand. It was you who might have set them free. It was you who might have made this the greatest, the freest, the happiest country in the world. Not so much for us perhaps as for our children, and our children's children. We didn't expect a huge social upheaval in a week, or even a decade of years. But we did expect to see the first blow struck. Oh, yes, we expected that."

"I have disappointed you, I know, you and many others," Brott said bitterly. "I wish I could explain. But I can't!"

"Oh, it doesn't matter," the man answered. "You have broken the hearts of thousands of suffering men and women—you who might have led them into the light, have forged another bolt in the bars which stand between them and liberty. So they must live on in the darkness, dull, dumb creatures with just spirit enough to spit and curse at the sound of your name. It was the greatest trust God ever placed in one man's hand—and you—you abused it. They were afraid of you—the aristocrats, and they bought you. Oh, we are not blind up there—there are newspapers in our public houses, and now and then one can afford a half-penny. We have read of you at their parties and their dances. Quite one of them you have become, haven't you? But, Mr. Brott, have you never been afraid? Have you never said to yourself, there is justice in the earth? Suppose it finds me out?"

"Hedley, you are talking rubbish," Brott said. "Up here you would see things with different eyes. Letheringham is pledged."

"If any man ever earned hell," Hedley continued, "it is you, Brott, you who came to us a deliverer, and turned out to be a lying prophet. 'Hell,'" he repeated fiercely, "and may you find it swiftly."

The man's right hand came out of his long pocket. They were in the thick of Piccadilly, but his action was too swift for any interference. Four reports rang suddenly out, and the muzzle of the revolver was held deliberately within an inch or so of Brett's heart. And before even the nearest of the bystanders could realise what had happened Brott lay across the pavement a dead man, and Hedley was calmly handing over the revolver to a policeman who had sprang across the street.

"Be careful, officer," he said, "there are still two chambers loaded. I will come with you quite quietly. That is Mr. Reginald Brott, the Cabinet Minister, and I have killed him."

XL

"For once," Lady Carey said, with a faint smile, "your 'admirable Crichton' has failed you."

Lucille opened her eyes. She had been leaning back amongst the railway cushions.

"I think not," she said. "Only I blame myself that I ever trusted the Prince even so far as to give him that message. For I know very well that if Victor had received it he would have been here."

Lady Carey took up a great pile of papers and looked them carelessly through.

"I am afraid," she said, "that I do not agree with you. I do not think that Saxe Leinitzer had any desire except to see you safely away. I believe that he will be quite as disappointed as you are that your husband is not here to aid you. Some one must see you safely on the steamer at Havre. Perhaps he will come himself."

"I shall wait in Paris," Lucille said quietly, "for my husband."

"You may wait," Lady Carey said, "for a very long time."

Lucille looked at her steadily. "What do you mean?"

"What a fool you are, Lucille. If to other people it seems almost certain on the face of it that you were responsible for that drop of poison in your husband's liqueur glass, why should it not seem so to himself?"

Lucille laughed, but there was a look of horror in her dark eyes.

"How absurd. I know Victor better than to believe him capable of such a suspicion. Just as he knows me better than to believe me capable of such an act."

"Really. But you were in his rooms secretly just before."

"I went to leave some roses for him," Lucille answered. "And if you would like to know it, I will tell you this. I left my card tied to them with a message for him."

Lady Carey yawned.

"A remarkably foolish thing to do," she said. "That may cause you trouble later on. Great heavens, what is this?"

She held the evening paper open in her hand. Lucille leaned over with blanched face.

"What has happened?" she cried. "Tell me, can't you!"

"Reginald Brott has been shot in Piccadilly," Lady Carey said.

"Is he hurt?" Lucille asked.

"He is dead!"

They read the brief announcement together. The deed had been committed by a man whose reputation for sanity had long been questioned, one of Brott's own constituents. He was in custody, and freely admitted his guilt. The two women looked at one another in horror. Even Lady Carey was affected.

"What a hateful thing," she said. "I am glad that we had no hand in it."

"Are you so sure that we hadn't?" Lucille asked bitterly. "You see what it says. The man killed him because of his political apostasy. We had something to do with that at least."

Lady Carey was recovering her sang froid.

"Oh, well," she said, "indirect influences scarcely count, or one might trace the causes of everything which happens back to an absurd extent. If this man was mad he might just as well have shot Brott for anything."

Lucille made no answer. She leaned back and closed her eyes. She did not speak again till they reached Dover.

They embarked in the drizzling rain. Lady Carey drew a little breath of relief as they reached their cabin, and felt the boat move beneath them.

"Thank goodness that we are really off. I have been horribly nervous all the time. If they let you leave England they can have no suspicion as yet."

Lucille was putting on an ulster and cap to go out on deck.

"I am not at all sure," she said, "that I shall not return to England. At any rate, if Victor does not come to me in Paris I shall go to him."

"What beautiful trust!" Lady Carey answered. "My dear Lucille, you are more like a school-girl than a woman of the world."

A STEWARD ENTERED WITH A telegram for Lucille. It was banded in at the Haymarket, an hour before their departure. Lucille read it, and her face blanched. "I thank you for your invitation, but I fear that it would not be good for my health.—S."

Lady Carey looked over her shoulder. She laughed hardly.

"How brutal!" she murmured. "But, then, Victor can be brutal sometimes, can't he?"

Lucille tore it into small pieces without a word. Lady Carey waited for a remark from her in vain.

E. PHILLIPS OPPENHEIM

"I, too," she said at last, "have had some telegrams. I have been hesitating whether to show them to you or not. Perhaps you had better see them."

She produced them and spread them out. The first was dated about the same time as the one Lucille had received.

"Have seen S. with message from Lucille. Fear quite useless, as he believes worst."

The second was a little longer.

"Have just heard S. has left for Liverpool, and has engaged berth in Campania, sailing to-morrow. Break news to Lucille if you think well. Have wired him begging return, and promising full explanation."

"If these," Lucille said calmly, "belonged to me I should treat them as I have my own."

"What do you mean?"

"I should tear them up."

Lady Carey shrugged her shoulders with the air of one who finds further argument hopeless.

"I shall have no more to say to you, Lucille, on this subject," she said. "You are impossible. In a few days you will be forced to come round to my point of view. I will wait till then. And in the meantime, if you think I am going to tramp up and down those sloppy decks and gaze at the sea you are very much mistaken. I am going to lie down like a civilized being, and try and get a nap. You had better do the same."

Lucille laughed.

"For my part," she said, "I find any part of the steamer except the deck intolerable. I am going now in search of some fresh air. Shall I send your woman along?"

Lady Carey nodded, for just then the steamer gave a violent lurch, and she was not feeling talkative. Lucille went outside and walked up and down until the lights of Calais were in sight. All the time she felt conscious of the observation of a small man clad in a huge mackintosh, whose peaked cap completely obscured his features. As they were entering the harbour she purposely stood by his side. He held on to the rail with one hand and turned towards her.

"It has been quite a rough passage, has it not?" he remarked.

She nodded.

"I have crossed," she said, "when it has been much worse. I do not mind so long as one may come on deck."

"Your friend," he remarked, "is perhaps not so good a sailor?"

"I believe," Lucille said, "that she suffers a great deal. I just looked in at her, and she was certainly uncomfortable."

The little man gripped the rail and held on to his cap with the other hand.

"You are going to Paris?" he asked.

Lucille nodded.

"Yes."

They were in smoother water now. He was able to relax his grip of the rail. He turned towards Lucille, and she saw him for the first time distinctly—a thin, wizened-up little man, with shrewd kindly eyes, and a long deeply cut mouth.

"I trust," he said, "that you will not think me impertinent, but it occurred to me that you have noticed some apparent interest of mine in your movements since you arrived on the boat."

Lucille nodded.

"It is true," she answered. "That is why I came and stood by your side. What do you want with me?"

"Nothing, madam," he answered. "I am here altogether in your interests. If you should want help I shall be somewhere near you for the next few hours. Do not hesitate to appeal to me. My mission here is to be your protector should you need one."

Lucille's eyes grew bright, and her heart beat quickly.

"Tell me," she said, "who sent you?"

He smiled.

"I think that you know," he answered. "One who I can assure you will never allow you to suffer any harm. I have exceeded my instructions in speaking to you, but I fancied that you were looking worried. You need not. I can assure you that you need have no cause."

Her eyes filled with tears.

"I knew," she said, "that those telegrams were forgeries."

He looked carefully around.

"I know nothing about any telegrams," he said, "but I am here to see that no harm comes to you, and I promise you that it shall not. Your friend is looking out of the cabin door. I think we may congratulate ourselves, madam, on an excellent passage."

Lady Carey disembarked, a complete wreck, leaning on the arm of her maid, and with a bottle of smelling salts clutched in her hand. She slept all the way in the train, and only woke up when they were nearing Paris. She looked at Lucille in astonishment.

"Why, what on earth have you been doing to yourself?" she exclaimed. "You look disgustingly fit and well."

Lucille laughed softly.

"Why not? I have had a nap, and we are almost at Paris. I only want a bath and a change of clothes to feel perfectly fresh."

But Lady Carey was suspicious.

"Have you seen any one you know upon the train?" she asked.

Lucille shook her head.

"Not a soul. A little man whom I spoke to on the steamer brought me some coffee. That is all."

Lady Carey yawned and shook out her skirts. "I suppose I'm getting old," she said. "I couldn't look as you do with as much on my mind as you must have, and after traveling all night too."

Lucille laughed.

"After all," she said, "you know that I am a professional optimist, and I have faith in my luck. I have been thinking matters over calmly, and, to tell you the truth, I am not in the least alarmed."

Lady Carey looked at her curiously.

"Has the optimism been imbibed," she asked, "or is it spontaneous?"

Lucille smiled.

"Unless the little man in the plaid mackintosh poured it into the coffee with the milk," she said, "I could not possibly have imbibed it, for I haven't spoken to another soul since we left."

"Paris! Here we are, thank goodness. Celeste can see the things through the customs. She is quite used to it. We are going to the Ritz, I suppose!"

XLI

At eight o'clock in the evening Lucille knocked at the door of Lady Carey's suite of rooms at the hotel. There was no answer. A chambermaid who was near came smiling up.

"Miladi has, I think, descended for dinner," she said.

Lucille looked at her watch. She saw that she was a few minutes late, so she descended to the restaurant. The small table which they had reserved was, however, still unoccupied. Lucille told the waiter that she would wait for a few moments, and sent for an English newspaper.

Lady Carey did not appear. A quarter of an hour passed. The head waiter came up with a benign smile.

"Madam will please to be served?" he suggested, with a bow.

"I am waiting for my friend Lady Carey," Lucille answered. "I understood that she had come down. Perhaps you will send and see if she is in the reading-room."

"With much pleasure, madam," the man answered.

In a few minutes he returned.

"Madam's friend was the Lady Carey?" he asked.

Lucille nodded.

The man was gently troubled.

"But, Miladi Carey," he said, "has left more than an hour ago."

Lucille looked up, astonished.

"Left the hotel?" she exclaimed.

"But yes, madam," he exclaimed. "Miladi Carey left to catch the boat train at Calais for England."

"It is impossible," Lucille answered. "We only arrived at midday."

"I will inquire again," the man declared. "But it was in the office that they told me so."

"They told you quite correctly," said a familiar voice. "I have come to take her place. Countess, I trust that in me you will recognise an efficient substitute."

It was the Prince of Saxe Leinitzer who was calmly seating himself opposite to her. The waiter, with the discretion of his class, withdrew for a few paces and stood awaiting orders. Lucille looked across at him in amazement.

"You here?" she exclaimed, "and Muriel gone? What does this mean?"

The Prince leaned forward.

"It means," he said, "that after you left I was in torment. I felt that you had no one with you who could be of assistance supposing the worst happened. Muriel is all very well, but she is a woman, and she has no diplomacy, no resource. I felt, Lucille, that I should not be happy unless I myself saw you into safety."

"So you followed us here," Lucille remarked quietly.

"Exactly! You do not blame me. It was for your sake—as well as my own."

"And Muriel—why has she left me without farewell—without warning of any sort?"

The Prince smiled and stroked his fair moustache.

"Well," he said, "it is rather an awkward thing for me to explain, but to tell you the truth, Muriel was a little—more than a little—annoyed at my coming. She has no right to be, but—well, you know, she is what you call a monopolist. She and I have been friends for many years."

"I understand perfectly what you have wished to convey," Lucille said. "But what I do not understand are the exact reasons which brought you here."

The Prince took up the carte de jour.

"As we dine," he said, "I will tell you. You will permit me to order?"

Lucille rose to her feet.

"For yourself, certainly," she answered. "As for me, I have accepted no invitation to dine with you, nor do I propose to do so."

The Prince frowned.

"Be reasonable, Lucille," he pleaded. "I must talk with you. There are important plans to be made. I have a great deal to say to you. Sit down."

Lucille looked across at him with a curious smile upon her lips.

"You have a good deal to say to me?" she remarked. "Yes, I will believe that. But of the truth how much, I wonder?"

"By and bye," he said, "you will judge me differently. For hors d'oeuvres what do you say to oeufs de pluvier? Then—"

"Pardon me," she interrupted, "I am not interested in your dinner!"

"In our dinner," he ventured gently.

"I am not dining with you," she declared firmly. "If you insist upon remaining here I shall have something served in my room. You know quite well that we are certain to be recognised. One would imagine that this was a deliberate attempt on your part to compromise me."

"Lucille," he said, "do not be foolish! Why do you persist in treating me as though I were your persecutor?"

"Because you are," she said coolly.

"It is ridiculous," he declared. "You are in the most serious danger, and I have come only to save you. I can do it, and I will. But listen—not unless you change your demeanour towards me."

She laughed scornfully. She had risen to her feet now, and he was perforce compelled to follow her example.

"Is that a challenge?" she asked.

"You may take it as such if you will," he answered, with a note of sullenness in his tone. "You know very well that I have but to lift my finger and the gendarmes will be here. Yes, we will call it a challenge. All my life I have wanted you. Now I think that my time has come. Even Souspennier has deserted you. You are alone, and let me tell you that danger is closer at your heels than you know of. I can save you, and I will. But I have a price, and it must be paid."

"If I refuse?" she asked.

"I send for the chief of the police."

She looked him up and down, a measured, merciless survey. He was a tall, big man, but he seemed to shrink into insignificance.

"You are a coward and a bully," she said slowly. "You know quite well that I am innocent of any knowledge even concerning Duson's death. But I would sooner meet my fate, whatever it might be, than suffer even the touch of your fingers upon my hand. Your presence is hateful to me. Send for your chief of the police. String your lies together as you will. I am satisfied."

She left him and swept from the room, a spot of colour burning in her cheeks, her eyes lit with fire. The pride of her race had asserted itself. She felt no longer any fear. She only desired to sever herself at once and completely from all association with this man. In the hall she sent for her maid.

"Fetch my cloak and jewel case, Celeste," she ordered. "I am going across to the Bristol. You can return for the other luggage."

"But, madam—"

"Do as I say at once," Lucille ordered.

The girl hesitated and then obeyed. Lucille found herself suddenly addressed in a quiet tone by a man who had been sitting in an easy-chair, half hidden by a palm tree.

"Will you favour me, madam, with a moment's conversation?"

Lucille turned round. She recognised at once the man with whom she had conversed upon the steamer. In the quietest form of evening dress, there was something noticeable in the man's very insignificance. He seemed a little out of his element. Lucille had a sudden inspiration, The man was a detective.

"What do you wish to say?" she asked, half doubtfully.

"I overheard," he remarked, "your order to your maid. She had something to say to you, but you gave her no opportunity."

"And you?" she asked, "what do you wish to say?"

"I wish to advise you," he said, "not to leave the hotel."

She looked at him doubtfully.

"You cannot understand," she said, "why I wish to leave it. I have no alternative."

"Nevertheless," he said, "I hope that you will change your mind."

"Are you a detective?" she asked abruptly.

"Madam is correct!"

The flush of colour faded from her cheeks.

"I presume, then," she said, "that I am under your surveillance?"

"In a sense," he admitted, "it is true."

"On the steamer," she remarked, "you spoke as though your interest in me was not inimical."

"Nor is it," he answered promptly. "You are in a difficult position, but you may find things not so bad as you imagine. At present my advice to you is this: Go upstairs to your room and stay there."

The little man had a compelling manner. Lucille made her way towards the elevator.

"As a matter of fact," she murmured bitterly, "I am not, I suppose, permitted to leave the hotel?"

"Madam puts the matter bluntly," he answered; "but certainly if you should insist upon leaving, it would be my duty to follow you."

She turned away from him and entered the elevator. The door of her room was slightly ajar, and she saw that a waiter was busy at a small round table. She looked at him in surprise. He was arranging places for two.

"Who gave you your orders?" she asked.

"But it was monsieur," the man answered, with a low bow. "Dinner for two."

"Monsieur?" she repeated. "What monsieur?"

"I am the culprit," a familiar voice answered from the depths of an easy-chair, whose back was to her. "I was very hungry, and it occurred to me that under the circumstances you would probably not have dined either. I hope that you will like what I have ordered. The plovers' eggs look delicious."

She gave a little cry of joy. It was Mr. Sabin.

XLII

The Prince dined carefully, but with less than his usual appetite. Afterwards he lit a cigarette and strolled for a moment into the lounge. Celeste, who was waiting for him, glided at once to his side.

"Monsieur!" she whispered. "I have been here for one hour."

He nodded.

"Well?"

"Monsieur le Duc has arrived."

The Prince turned sharply round.

"Who?"

"Monsieur le Duc de Souspennier. He calls himself no longer Mr. Sabin."

A dull flush of angry colour rose almost to his temples.

"Why did you not tell me before?" he exclaimed.

"Monsieur was in the restaurant," she answered. "It was impossible for me to do anything but wait."

"Where is he?"

"Alas! he is with madam," the girl answered.

The Prince was very profane. He started at once for the elevator. In a moment or two he presented himself at Lucille's sitting-room. They were still lingering over their dinner. Mr. Sabin welcomed him with grave courtesy.

"The Prince is in time to take his liqueur with us," he remarked, rising. "Will you take fin champagne, Prince, or Chartreuse? I recommend the fin champagne."

The Prince bowed his thanks. He was white to the lips with the effort for self-mastery.

"I congratulate you, Mr. Sabin," he said, "upon your opportune arrival. You will be able to help Lucille through the annoyance to which I deeply regret that she should be subjected."

Mr. Sabin gently raised his eyebrows.

"Annoyance!" he repeated. "I fear that I do not quite understand."

The Prince smiled.

"Surely Lucille has told you," he said, "of the perilous position in which she finds herself."

"My wife," Mr. Sabin said, "has told me nothing. You alarm me."

The Prince shrugged his shoulders.

"I deeply regret to tell you," he said, "that the law has proved too powerful for me. I can no longer stand between her and what I fear may prove a most unpleasant episode. Lucille will be arrested within the hour."

"Upon what charge?" Mr. Sabin asked.

"The murder of Duson."

Mr. Sabin laughed very softly, very gently, but with obvious genuineness.

"You are joking, Prince," he exclaimed.

"I regret to say," the Prince answered, "that you will find it very far from a joking matter."

Mr. Sabin was suddenly stern.

"Prince of Saxe Leinitzer," he said, "you are a coward and a bully."

The Prince started forward with clenched fist. Mr. Sabin had no weapon, but he did not flinch.

"You can frighten women," he said, "with a bogie such as this, but you have no longer a woman to deal with. You and I know that such a charge is absurd—but you little know the danger to which you expose yourself by trifling with this subject. Duson left a letter addressed to me in which he announced his reasons for committing suicide."

"Suicide?"

"Yes. He preferred suicide to murder, even at the bidding of the Prince of Saxe Leinitzer. He wrote and explained these things to me— and the letter is in safe hands. The arrest of Lucille, my dear Prince, would mean the ruin of your amiable society."

"This letter," the Prince said slowly, "why was it not produced at the inquest? Where is it now?"

"It is deposited in a sealed packet with the Earl of Deringham," Mr. Sabin answered. "As to producing it at the inquest—I thought it more discreet not to. I leave you to judge of my reasons. But I can assure you that your fears for my wife's safety have been wholly misplaced. There is not the slightest reason for her to hurry off to America. We may take a little trip there presently, but not just yet."

The Prince made a mistake. He lost his temper.

"You!" he cried, "you can go to America when you like, and stay there. Europe has had enough of you with your hare-brained schemes and foolish failures. But Lucille does not leave this country. We have need of her. I forbid her to leave. Do you hear? In the name of the Order I command her to remain here."

Mr. Sabin was quite calm, but his face was full of terrible things.

"Prince," he said, "if I by any chance numbered myself amongst your friends I would warn you that you yourself are a traitor to your Order. You prostitute a great cause when you stoop to use its machinery to assist your own private vengeance. I ask you for your own sake to consider your words. Lucille is mine—mine she will remain, even though you should descend to something more despicable, more cowardly than ordinary treason, to wrest her from me. You reproach me with the failures of my life. Great they may have been, but if you attempt this you will find that I am not yet an impotent person."

The Prince was white with rage. The sight of Lucille standing by Mr. Sabin's side, her hand lightly resting upon his, her dark eyes full of inscrutable tenderness, maddened him. He was flouted and ignored. He was carried away by a storm of passion. He tore a sheet of paper from his pocket book, and unlocking a small gold case at the end of his watch chain, shook from it a pencil with yellow crayon. Mr. Sabin leaned over towards him.

"You sign it at your peril, Prince," he said. "It will mean worse things than that for you."

For a second he hesitated. Lucille also leaned towards him.

"Prince," she said, "have I not kept my vows faithfully? Think! I came from America at a moment's notice; I left my husband without even a word of farewell; I entered upon a hateful task, and though to think of it now makes me loathe myself—I succeeded. I have kept my vows, I have done my duty. Be generous now, and let me go."

The sound of her voice maddened him. A passionate, arbitrary man, to whom nothing in life had been denied, to be baulked in this great desire of his latter days was intolerable. He made no answer to either of them. He wrote a few lines with the yellow crayon and passed them silently across to Lucille.

Her face blanched. She stretched out an unwilling hand. But Mr. Sabin intervened. He took the paper from the Prince's hand, and calmly tore it into fragments. There was a moment's breathless silence.

"Victor!" Lucille cried. "Oh, what have you done!"

The Prince's face lightened with an evil joy.

"We now, I think," he said, "understand one another. You will permit me to wish you a very pleasant evening, and a speedy leave-taking."

Mr. Sabin smiled.

"Many thanks, my dear Prince," he said lightly. "Make haste and complete your charming little arrangements. Let me beg of you to avoid bungling this time. Remember that there is not in the whole of Europe to-day a man more dangerous to you than I."

The Prince had departed. Mr. Sabin lit a cigarette and stood on the hearthrug. His eyes were bright with the joy of fighting.

"Lucille," he said, "I see that you have not touched your liqueur. Oblige me by drinking it. You will find it excellent."

She came over to him and hung upon his arm. He threw his cigarette away and kissed her upon the lips.

"Victor," she murmured, "I am afraid. You have been rash!"

"Dearest," he answered, "it is better to die fighting than to stand aside and watch evil things. But after all, there is no fear. Come! Your cloak and dressing case!"

"You have plans?" she exclaimed, springing up.

"Plans?" He laughed at her a little reproachfully. "My dear Lucille! A carriage awaits us outside, a special train with steam up at the Gard de L'ouest. This is precisely the contingency for which I have planned."

"Oh, you are wonderful, Victor," she murmured as she drew on her coat. "But what corner of the earth is there where we should be safe?"

"I am going," Mr. Sabin said, "to try and make every corner of the earth safe."

She was bewildered, but he only laughed and held open the door for her. Mr. Sabin made no secret of his departure. He lingered for a moment in the doorway to light a cigarette, he even stopped to whisper a few words to the little man in plain dinner clothes who was lounging in the doorway. But when they had once left the hotel they drove fast.

In less than half an hour Paris was behind them. They were traveling in a royal saloon and at a fabuulous cost, for in France they are not fond of special trains. But Mr. Sabin was very happy. At least he had escaped an ignominious defeat. It was left to him to play the great card.

"And now," Lucille said, coming out from her little bed-chamber which the femme de chambre was busy preparing, "suppose you tell me where we are going."

Mr. Sabin smiled.

"Do not be alarmed," he said, "even though it will sound to you the least likely place in the world. We are going to Berlin."

XLIII

The great room was dimly enough lit, for the windows looking out upon the street were high and heavily curtained, The man who sat at the desk was almost in the shadow. Yet every now and then a shaft of sunlight fell across his pale, worn face. A strange combination this of the worker, the idealist, the man of affairs. From outside came the hum of a great city. At times, too, there came to his ears as he sat here the roar of nations at strife, the fierce underneath battle of the great countries of the world struggling for supremacy. And here at this cabinet this man sat often, and listened, strenuous, romantic, with the heart of a lion and the lofty imagination of an eagle, he steered unswervingly on to her destiny a great people. Others might rest, but never he.

He looked up from the letter spread out before him. Lucille was seated at his command, a few yards away. Mr. Sabin stood respectfully before him.

"Monsieur le Duc," he said, "this letter, penned by my illustrious father to you, is sufficient to secure my good offices. In what manner can I serve you?"

"Your Majesty," Mr. Sabin answered, "in the first place by receiving me here. In the second by allowing me to lay before you certain grave and very serious charges against the Order of the Yellow Crayon, of which your Majesty is the titular head."

"The Order of the Yellow Crayon," the Emperor said thoughtfully, "is society composed of aristocrats pledged to resist the march of socialism. It is true that I am the titular head of this organisation. What have you to say about it?"

"Only that your Majesty has been wholly deceived," Mr. Sabin said respectfully, "concerning the methods and the working of this society. Its inception and inauguration were above reproach. I myself at once became a member. My wife, Countess of Radantz, and sole representative of that ancient family, has been one all her life."

The Emperor inclined his head towards Lucille.

"I see no reason," he said, "when our capitals are riddled with secret societies, all banded together against us, why the great families of Europe should not in their turn come together and display a united front against this common enemy. The Order of the Yellow Crayon has had more than my support. It has had the sanction of my name. Tell me what you have against it."

"I have grave things to say concerning it," Mr. Sahin answered, "and concerning those who have wilfully deceived your Majesty. The influences to be wielded by the society were mainly, I believe, wealth, education, and influence. There was no mention made of murder, of an underground alliance with the 'gamins' of Paris, the dregs of humanity, prisoners, men skilled in the art of secret death."

The Emperor's tone was stern, almost harsh.

"Duc de Souspennier, what are these things which you are saying?" he asked.

"Your Majesty, I speak the truth," Mr. Sabin answered firmly. "There are in the Order of the Yellow Crayon three degrees of membership. The first, which alone your Majesty knows of, simply corresponds with what in England is known as the Primrose League. The second knows that beneath is another organisation pledged to frustrate the advance of socialism, if necessary by the use of their own weapons. The third, whose meetings and signs and whose whole organisation is carried on secretly, is allied in every capital in Europe with criminals and murderers. With its great wealth it has influence in America as well as in every city of the world where there are police to be suborned, or desperate men to be bought for tools. At the direction of this third order Lavinski died suddenly in the Hungarian House of Parliament, Herr Krettingen was involved in a duel, the result of which was assured beforehand, and Reginald Brott, the great English statesman, was ruined and disgraced. I myself have just narrowly escaped death at his hands, and in my place my servant has been driven to death. Of all these things, your Majesty, I have brought proofs."

The Emperor's face was like a carven image, but his tone was cold and terrible.

"If these things have been sanctioned," he said, "by those who are responsible for my having become the head of the Order; they shall feel my vengeance."

"Your Majesty," Mr. Sabin said earnestly, "a chance disclosure, and all might come to light. I myself could blazon the story through Europe. Those who are responsible for the third degree of the Order of the Yellow Crayon, and for your Majesty's ignorance concerning its existence, have trifled with the destiny of the greatest sovereign of modern times."

"The Prince of Saxe Leinitzer," the Emperor said, "is the acting head of the Order."

"The Prince of Saxe Leinitzer," Mr. Sabin said firmly, "is responsible for the existence of the third degree. It is he who has connected the society with a system of corrupt police or desperate criminals in every great city. It is the Prince of Saxe Leinitzer, your Majesty, and his horde of murderers from whom I have come to seek your Majesty's protection. I have yet another charge to make against him. He has made, and is making still, use of the society to further his own private intrigues. In the name of the Order he brought my wife from America. She faithfully carried out the instructions of the Council. She brought about the ruin of Reginald Brott. By the rules of the society she was free then to return to her home. The Prince, who had been her suitor, declined to let her go. My life was attempted. The story of the Prince's treason is here, with the necessary proofs. I know that orders have been given to the hired murderers of the society for my assassination. My life even here is probably an uncertain thing. But I have told your Majesty the truth, and the papers which I have brought with me contain proof of my words."

The Emperor struck a bell and gave a few orders to the young officer who immediately answered it. Then he turned again to Mr. Sabin.

"I have summoned Saxe Leinitzer to Berlin," he said. "These matters shall be gone into most thoroughly. In the meantime what can I do for you?"

"We will await the coming of the Prince," Mr. Sabin answered grimly.

LADY CAREY PASSED FROM HER bath-room into a luxurious little dressing-room. Her letters and coffee were on a small table near the fire, an easy-chair was drawn up to the hearthrug. She fastened the girdle of her dressing-gown, and dismissed her maid.

"I will ring for you in half an hour, Annette," she said. "See that I am not disturbed."

On her way to the fireplace she paused for a moment in front of a tall looking-glass, and looked steadily at her own reflection.

"I suppose," she murmured to herself, "that I am looking at my best now. I slept well last night, and a bath gives one colour, and white is so becoming. Still, I don't know why I failed. She may be a little better looking, but my figure is as good. I can talk better, I have learnt how to keep a man from feeling dull, and there is my reputation. Because I played at war correspondence, wore a man's clothes, and didn't shriek when I was under fire, people have chosen to make a heroine of me. That should have counted for something with him—and it didn't. I could have taken my choice of any man in London—and I wanted him. And I have failed!"

She threw herself back in her easy-chair and laughed softly.

"Failed! What an ugly word! He is old, and he limps, and I—well, I was never a very bashful person. He was beautifully polite, but he wouldn't have anything to say to me."

She began to tear open her letters savagely.

"Well, it is over. If ever anybody speaks to me about it I think that I shall kill them. That fool Saxe Leinitzer will stroke his beastly moustache, and smile at me out of the corners of his eyes. The Dorset woman, too—bah, I shall go away. What is it, Annette?"

"His Highness the Prince of Saxe Leinitzer has called, milady."

"Called! Does he regard this as a call?" she exclaimed, glancing towards the clock. "Tell him, Annette, that your mistress does not receive at such an hour. Be quick, child. Of course I know that he gave you a sovereign to persuade me that it was important, but I won't see him, so be off."

"But yes, milady," Annette answered, and disappeared.

Lady Carey sipped her coffee.

"I think," she said reflectively, "that it must be Melton."

Annette reappeared.

"Milady," she exclaimed, "His Highness insisted upon my bringing you this card. He was so strange in his manner, milady, that I thought it best to obey."

Lady Carey stretched out her hand. A few words were scribbled on the back of his visiting card in yellow crayon. She glanced at it, tore the card up, and threw the pieces into the fire.

"My shoes and stockings, Annette," she said, "and just a morning wrap—anything will do."

The Prince was walking restlessly up and down the room, when Lady Carey entered. He welcomed her with a little cry of relief.

"Heavens!" he exclaimed. "I thought that you were never coming."

"I was in no hurry," she answered calmly. "I could guess your news, so I had not even the spur of curiosity."

He stopped short.

"You have heard nothing! It is not possible?"

She shrugged her shoulders.

E. PHILLIPS OPPENHEIM

"No, but I know you, and I know him. I am quite prepared to hear that you are outwitted. Indeed, to judge from your appearance there can be no doubt about it. Remember I warned you."

The Prince was pale with fury.

"No one could foresee this," he exclaimed. "He has walked into the lion's den."

"Then," Lady Carey said, "I am quite prepared to hear that he tamed the lion."

"If there was one person living whom I could have sworn that this man dared not visit, it was our Emperor," the Prince said. "It is only a few years since, through this man's intrigues, Germany was shamed before the world."

"And yet," Lady Carey said sweetly, "the Emperor has received him."

"I have private intelligence from Berlin," Saxe Leinitzer answered. "Mr. Sabin was in possession of a letter written to him by the Emperor Frederick, thanking him for some service or other; and the letter was a talisman."

"How like him," Lady Carey murmured, "to have the letter."

"What a pity," the Prince sneered, "that such devotion should remain unrewarded."

Lady Carey sighed.

"He has broken my heart," she replied.

The Prince threw out his hands.

"You and I," he cried, "why do we behave like children! Let us start afresh. Listen! The Emperor has summoned me to Berlin."

"Dear me," Lady Carey murmured. "I am afraid you will have a most unpleasant visit."

"I dare not go," the Prince said slowly. "It was I who induced the Emperor to become the titular head of this cursed Order. Of course he knew nothing about the second or third degree members and our methods. Without doubt he is fully informed now. I dare not face him."

"What shall you do?" Lady Carey asked curiously.

"I am off to South America," he said. "It is a great undeveloped country, and there is room for us to move there. Muriel, you know what I want of you."

"My good man," she answered, "I haven't the faintest idea."

"You will come with me," he begged. "You will not send me into exile so lonely, a wanderer! Together there may be a great future before us.

You have ambition, you love intrigue, excitement, danger. None of these can you find here. You shall come with me. You shall not say no. Have I not been your devoted slave? Have—"

She stopped him. Her lips were parted in a smile of good-natured scorn.

"Don't be absurd, Saxe Leinitzer. It is true that I love intrigue, excitement and danger. That is what made me join your Order, and really I have had quite a little excitement out of it, for which I suppose I ought to thank you. But as for the rest, why, you are talking rubbish. I would go to South America to-morrow with the right man, but with you, why, it won't bear talking about. It makes me angry to think that you should believe me capable of such shocking taste as to dream of going away with you."

He flung himself from the room. Lady Carey went back to her coffee and letters. She sent for Annette.

"Annette," she directed, "we shall go to Melton to-morrow. Wire Haggis to have the Lodge in order, and carriages to meet the midday train. I daresay I shall take a few people down with me. Let George go around to Tattersalls at once and make an appointment for me there at three o'clock this afternoon. Look out my habits and boots, too, Annette."

Lady Carey leaned back in her chair for a moment with half-closed eyes.

"I think," she murmured, "that some of us in our youth must have drunk from some poisoned cup, something which turned our blood into quicksilver. I must live, or I must die. I must have excitement every hour, every second, or break down. There are others too—many others. No wonder that that idiot of a man in Harley Street talked to me gravely about my heart. No excitement. A quiet life! Bah! Such wishy-washy coffee and only one cigarette."

She lit it and stood up on the hearthrug. Her eyes were half closed, every vestige of colour had left her cheeks, her hand was pressed hard to her side. For a few minutes she seemed to struggle for breath. Then with a little lurch as though still giddy, she stooped, and picking up her fallen cigarette, thrust it defiantly between her teeth.

"Not this way," she muttered. "From a horse's back if I can with the air rushing by, and the hot joy of it in one's heart. . . Only I hope it won't hurt the poor old gee. . . Come in, Annette. What a time you've been, child."

E. PHILLIPS OPPENHEIM

THE EMPEROR SENT FOR MR. SABIN. He declined to recognise his incognito.

"Monsieur le Duc," he said, "if proof of your story were needed it is here. The Prince of Saxe Leinitzer has ignored my summons. He has fled to South America."

Mr. Sabin bowed.

"A most interesting country," he murmured, "for the Prince."

"You yourself are free to go when and where you will. You need no longer have any fears. The Order does not exist. I have crushed it."

Mr. Sabin bowed.

"Your Majesty," he said, "has shown exemplary wisdom."

"From its inception," the Emperor said, "I believe that the idea was a mistaken one. I must confess that its originality pleased me; my calmer reflections, however, show me that I was wrong. It is not for the nobles of the earth to copy the methods of socialists and anarchists. These men are a pest upon humanity, but they may have their good uses. They may help us to govern alertly, vigorously, always with our eyes and ears strained to catch the signs of the changing times. Monsieur le Duc, should you decide to take up your residence in this country I shall at all times be glad to receive you. But your future is entirely your own."

Mr. Sabin accepted his dismissal from audience, and went back to Lucille.

"The Prince," he told her, "has gone—to South America. The Order does not exist any longer. Will you dine in Vienna, or in Frankfort?"

She held out her arms.

"You wonderful man!" she cried.

A Note About the Author

E. Phillips Oppenheim (1866–1946) was a British writer who rose to prominence in the late nineteenth century. He was born in London to a leather merchant and began working at an early age. Oppenheim spent nearly 20 years in the family business, while juggling a freelance writing career. He composed short stories and eventually novels with more than 100 titles to his credit. His first novel, *Expiation* was published in 1886 followed by *The Mystery of Mr. Bernard Brown* (1896) and *The Long Arm of Mannister* (1910). Oppenheim is best known for his signature tales full of action and espionage.

A Note from the Publisher

Spanning many genres, from non-fiction essays to literature classics to children's books and lyric poetry, Mint Edition books showcase the master works of our time in a modern new package. The text is freshly typeset, is clean and easy to read, and features a new note about the author in each volume. Many books also include exclusive new introductory material. Every book boasts a striking new cover, which makes it as appropriate for collecting as it is for gift giving. Mint Edition books are only printed when a reader orders them, so natural resources are not wasted. We're proud that our books are never manufactured in excess and exist only in the exact quantity they need to be read and enjoyed.

Discover more of your favorite classics with Bookfinity™.

- Track your reading with custom book lists.
- Get great book recommendations for your personalized Reader Type.
- Add reviews for your favorite books.
- AND MUCH MORE!

Visit **bookfinity.com** and take the fun Reader Type quiz to get started.

Enjoy our classic and modern companion pairings!